THE ARR

THE
ARROW GARDEN

矢
の
庭

Andrew J King

Aderyn

First published in Great Britain in 2023 by Aderyn Press
Gweledfa, Felindre, Swansea, Wales, SA5 7NA

www.aderynpress.com

A CIP catalogue record for this book is available from the British
Library

ISBN 978-1-9163986-4-1
eISBN 978-1-9163986-5-8

Cover design: Kari Brownlie
Text design: Elaine Sharples
Printed in Great Britain by 4edge Ltd

In memory of Anne
1933 – 2022
Mother, teacher, supporter and astute critic

The Void

There is a moment when the arrow stands in the target. And there is a moment, just before that, when it does not. No matter how I stare, I can never catch the instant of its arrival.

If I look towards the archer, I can just see the brief flash of movement as it leaves the bow. The eye can track its flight, but often arrives at the target to find the arrow already planted, as if it had grown there.

A camera, perhaps, could resolve the uncertainty between the note of the bowstring and the percussion of the target. The image might reveal a flying stick, naked and exposed, quivering with all the chances of its flight. Even a bursting of the paper as it pierced the target. But would that satisfy? After all, if it was a fair shot, then it already stands in the target. And no camera can ever capture the moment between there and not there.

But there must be something in the void, in the moment between moments. For everything else, forwards and backwards, grows out of that.

1 Ashibumi

The archer takes up position at the shooting line, feet braced well apart, establishing the foundations of the shot.

'Of course, you've never met my aunt.'

Hiroshi's English was impeccable. Probably because it was patched together from textbook phrases like 'Hiroshi's English was impeccable' or 'Of course, you've never met my aunt'. Of course I'd never met his aunt. Weeks squashed together in an attic office and this was the first time he'd admitted to having any sort of personal life, never mind an actual living relative.

'Quite a character. A very nice person…'

'Eh?'

'… although, as a matter of fact, she had some odd ways.'

He didn't seem to register my puzzled silence.

'We felt it might be because of her experiences in the Pacific War. She lost all her family, except for my father.'

I admit, I was struggling. Thirty seconds before, we had been deep in the minutiae of translation, wrestling the maintenance schedule for a medical waste incinerator out of Japanese and into English.

'She was almost killed herself. A real survivor. She never spoke about it, certainly not to us children.'

In the middle of a section entitled 'Schedule of Monthly Inspections', he'd pushed back his chair, put his glasses down on the desk and come out with this … stuff.

'To my sister and I she was just Auntie Mie. She bought us little treats: shaved ice with syrup in the summer, cakes in the winter, presents on our birthdays. She never married, but

3

apart from that she lived a perfectly normal life, most of the time.'

The yellow stained fingertips strayed upward toward his mouth, but finding no cigarette, settled on his tie instead and unnecessarily re-arranged it.

'She could be very ... determined.'

He paused, as if waiting for something.

'But quite humorous also, more ... uninhibited than most people.'

Again, a pause, during which it dawned on me that what he was waiting for, was me.

'Sounds fun!' I said and immediately regretted it.

'Yes! My sister and I adored her! But the presents were a little odd.'

His tone became confidential.

'At first she would just buy us the usual little toys. But as we got older, she started giving us things that were rather... strange.'

Our desks stood side by side, facing the low wall under the slope of the attic roof, his to the right of mine. I sensed he was looking at me. Waiting for me to say something like: *'Oh? What sort of strange things?'* I cleared my throat and pointed out, as tactfully as I could, that we had a minor deadline to meet. He gave a grunt, snapped his glasses back on and twenty seconds later we were once more tussling over the correct usage of *'air filter retention ring'* and *'flexible drive-belt tensioner'*.

At first, I congratulated myself on having steered our relationship back onto professional ground. As the morning wore on, I began to suspect my satisfaction had been premature. There was an atmosphere. By lunchtime, I was desperate to get out of the office.

*   *   *

From where she stands, some of the houses look almost untouched. Here, in the suburbs nearer the edge of the city, it had not been one single, terrible firestorm, but many smaller blazes caused by embers flying on the hot wind. The still leafless ginkgo on the corner seems unhurt, though many other trees are dreadfully scorched. The neighbourhood is still recognisable. But it is not the same place changed, as after a snowfall. It is the corpse of the place she once knew. Wherever its angry and tormented spirit roams, it is not here.

A sheet of paper, tied to the ginkgo's trunk, is rattling softly in the fitful wind. A list of the dead. The local fire-watch have already taken what remained of the bodies to the temple, where they will be laid in the courtyard with hundreds of others. She ought to follow them. There are rites she should attend. They never set much store by such things in life. And she cannot face more burning.

At the end of the street, a thin boy in a police uniform that is too big for him clutches a bamboo stave. His face looks as if it has never smiled and never could. He sees her and fidgets, but does nothing as she enters the charred gate.

In the ruined garden a stand of arrow bamboo droops under the weight of fine grey ash that stirs and fumes like smoke as she brushes by. An unfamiliar silence. No trickle of water falling into the little stone cistern. She reaches out for the bamboo dipper, also grey with ash, laid across its cracked and blackened edge. Her hand closes on nothing but a soft, crunching texture, a grey powder that sifts away between her fingers. She looks at her hand, bewildered, as if it were unaccountably covered in blood. It had not been the dipper at all, but only its charred ghost. She reaches down into the darkness of the once brimming cistern. Groping desperately for something real, something that is not a phantom of fire. Somewhere near the bottom, she feels water, but so tepid it might be blood. Something bumps against her hand. She snatches it back and peers nervously in. A small green frog, its nose just breaking the surface. 'Just a little please!' she whispers and, cupping her hand, dips it carefully in.

*   *   *

Descending into the hushed corporate regions of the lower floors, I could hear Hiroshi starting to follow me down. His tread on the uncarpeted wooden attic stairs was slower, probably because he was rolling a cigarette. Going for a smoke I guessed, in the dank, derelict little pit of a garden behind the eighteenth-century townhouse in which we worked. I crossed reception, slipped out of the nineteenth-century glass shop front with its recessed door and turned left.

I needed to walk and to think. Bristol is good for that. Always a sense of something going on, rarely crowded enough to overwhelm and if you need peace and quiet, it's usually just around the next corner. In the relaxed bustle of the suburban street, my thoughts began to flow.

'*Of course, you've never met my aunt*' is a conventional opening, the redundant statement of a fact known to both parties. It isn't meant to sound like an exclamation. All too easy, I knew, to be fluent, but still get things like that wrong. And yet, his statement about the presents had been finely calibrated in both content and tone, to pique curiosity.

Grabbing my usual sandwich and juice in the corner shop, I turned left again, up a street between the old houses, so steep I had to concentrate to keep my balance on the worn, uneven flagstones.

Was it cultural? My kind of work usually needed a team of two: a native speaker who would hash out a rough English draft and me. My job was to put the 'technical' into 'technical translation' and something resembling actual English into 'English Language Version'. The native speakers came and went, depending on the contract. I'd got on pretty well with most of them. There hadn't been *that* many arguments and none of them had tried to talk about their aunts.

I crossed the back-road at the top of the street, climbed the short flight of stone steps sunk into the steep, walled bank on the opposite side and stepped out onto the broad green flanks of Brandon Hill. A city park for nearly four hundred years, the lower slopes seemed to hold memories of open fields: thick meadow-grass, old lone trees, an overgrown wildlife reserve with a pond and, running part way up the hill, what I took to be the remnant of an ancient hedgerow. A lunchtime escape from mental overload and a handy evening short cut home. After a few lunch-hours spent exploring the place, I had settled on a habitual route: a more or less direct line from the little flight of stone steps, to just below the tower on the summit of the hill. It was also a habit to do it barefoot, so I stuffed my footwear into my backpack and began to walk slowly up through the lush spring grass.

I had always tried to get in early on the first day of a new contract. Clear the decks and prepare. The morning of Hiroshi's arrival, the smell of stale tobacco and citrus after-shave drifting down from the open office door told me I'd been beaten to the draw. Entering the small attic room braced for a greeting, I had been confronted instead with the back of a blue business suit. The hand I had been expecting to shake was resting on what would be his chair, the one nearest the door. The calendar tacked to the wall behind the desk was getting all his attention, as if he wasn't sure he had the right day. His turn caught me off-guard. Hastily dropping my gaze, I took a breath, carefully looked up again and did that artificial smile that means my eyes are closed as we shake.

'Hiroshi... Hiroshi Tanaka?'

The tone. As if he were not announcing, but confirming his name.

'Gareth,' I said.

'Yes! Gareth! Pleased to meet you at last!' Tone again: as if we were already, somehow, acquainted. A little formal too. Most people call me Gary, even when they know I hate it. The pronunciation wasn't bad either. He must have been practising.

'It feels like greeting a member of the family!'

Maybe he missed my confused expression, because he was already glancing round the little room.

'I'm glad you transferred here. It seems much more interesting than that other place.'

I came to a stop in the middle of the slope, staring thoughtfully at my own feet. Had my CV been passed around at some meeting I hadn't been invited to? It had been just like the peculiar 'aunt' conversation. Undue familiarity, combined with disarming deference. Maybe he just wanted to practise his English conversation. Medical waste disposal machinery has its fascinations, but the vocabulary isn't much for everyday social interaction.

Glancing up at the summit tower to check my bearings, I went back to keeping my head down and putting one foot in front of the other.

* * *

She stands at last, alone, in the empty ruin of her parents' house. In a corner, some collapsed remains of her father's library. Wiping her wet hand on her skirt, she stoops to pick up a small, slim book. Soft, dark blue paper covers, embossed with a faint pattern of chrysanthemums. It is smudged with ash. The white threads that bind it have broken and begun to unravel. Holding it carefully, she turns the pages, feeling the movement, seeing the thinly inked, ash-grey characters spin past her fingers. But then she stops. Turns back a few pages, a few more, carefully separates two.

A hot wine burns in her empty throat. She is the bright-faced child, who once knelt here, not as now, under the open sky, but when this was a dark, old space, boxed in by plaster and polished wood. Watching his steady hand hold the smooth, muscular, brown bamboo stem of the brush elegantly vertical. Watching as its tip lightly, laughingly, tickles over the paper, creating the little boy, his cane and the recalcitrant, grumpy ox throwing a resentful glance over his shoulder as he gallops heavily away.

All for her delighted eyes and hers alone. She can hear the soft click as he puts the brush down on its porcelain rest in the shape of five tiny mountains. The whistle of his brown silk haori jacket as he pulls his sleeves back down. His voice, deep and warm, like the brown handle of the brush, as he begins to tell her, very softly and precisely, the story of the Boy and his Ox.

Tears that sting like smoke. Choking down a pain in her throat.

That time in the evening when Father would stretch and yawn and say: 'That's enough! No more politics!' When the last of the loud grown-up talk had gone out of the door and down the street. When the family had eaten. When the house was quiet. Sometimes she would hear, from under her coverlet, low adult voices and the closing of the door of Father's study.

She had learned that if she got out of bed at those times, to ask for a drink of water, or to complain that she could not sleep, or was frightened of the thunder, she would sometimes, just occasionally, be allowed in to sit next to that after-supper-Father, leaning against his warmth as he sipped from a tiny square wooden measure of sake and read poetry. Sometimes he would read fragments aloud for her and sometimes she would ask questions, very softly, so as not to disturb the moths sitting near the lamp. And sometimes he would answer and sometimes his answers became stories. And as he talked, his words were not grey like the adults' daytime, politics-and-business talk, but colourful, like old prints. And like the prints, his talk was full of incomprehensible but fascinating things and among them, every now and then, something she could recognise, like a frog peeping out from under a leaf in the green, wet garden.

Had he read to her from this book? She could only remember the little drawing, the warmth of his body and the glow of the bronze-brown silk in the lamplight. How did it begin, the story that went with this picture? Only the drawing, the room, the lamp, the silk, his presence, remain in memory. The words had come and gone, like music. Or like smoke.

*　*　*

The small wood that hems the skirt of the hill was dropping behind me as I steadily climbed, as was the grandly titled 'Wildlife Reserve' – in reality a small thicket of bushes and brambles with a dank pond lurking in the middle. Having once studied its colourful but mossy information board, I had never gone that way again.

'I'll not have you turning into a nature freak. You're a freak of nature as it is.'

My father is standing over me. In front of us is a low shelf. On it are arranged a few pinecones, the skull of a small bird, some magazine clippings and a book about nature. I am holding a waste bin. His big red hand sweeps steadily along and everything cascades into the bin.

He escorts me outside, where I have to tip the contents into the household rubbish. Back in my room I stare at the empty shelf, trying to understand what it means. He had seemed so pleased with his play on words.

After Nature is thrown away, I learn to be interested in things small and easily hidden in pockets. When those are discovered, I turn to things that can be hoarded entirely in the mind, like the names of colours on paint charts, or the different patterns of car tyres. I live a life no one else sees.

It had been the office military historian who had burst my pastoral bubble about the 'ancient hedgerow', explaining in exhaustive detail, its origin and role as part of the English Civil War defences of Bristol. That was the problem with open-plan offices: no proper defences.

From the height I had now reached, the roof-line of a modern business block begins to be visible. It's just a few doors up from the agency on the opposite side of the street. In there, as a faceless drone in an airless open-plan hive, I had helped churn out product manuals, sales literature and training materials for a big engineering multinational. The work was repetitive and the 90s economic situation hadn't been doing much for office morale either. New projects were fought over like meat thrown into a tiger cage. My last memories of the place were of a Christmas-decorated snake-pit of seething resentments. I let myself get caught up in petty office wars. I said things I should not have said.

On a particularly damp and depressing Friday evening just after New Year, I was standing in my flat, staring glumly down into the street, when I realised a man on the opposite pavement was staring back at me. In a long-practised reflex, I squeezed my eyes shut, then scrabbled in panic for the curtain cords. Even so, after-images remained in memory: a cigarette, a beige raincoat, a dark blue cap, and a small notebook in his hand. A few days later, I saw in the distance what I thought was the same man, standing in the park with his notebook, turning it this way and that and looking about him, as if orienting a map.

On this admittedly rather slender evidence I decided that management had set a private investigator onto me. I got rather angry. I always turned my work in complete, accurate and on time. What if I did sometimes linger in the park at lunchtimes, or knock off a few minutes early for the weekend?

I had sat down at my keyboard ready to rip out some heavy-duty sarcasm, when it suddenly washed over me that, even if it wasn't paranoia, I'd had enough of the place and its toxic attitudes. I cleared my desk, wrote a terse resignation letter and dropped it on the floor outside the 'Executive Suite' on my way out.

Passing the top end of the old defensive line, my reminiscences were interrupted by a narrow path that runs horizontally across the slope. Stepping on to it, I turned to look back. The trees on the edge of the park were not yet in full leaf and I could just glimpse through their branches the slates of the attic roof under which Hiroshi and I had spent our morning. An empty landscape of grey peaks and valleys, home territory only to pigeons.

* * *

She slips the book into her blouse. Pats it softly into place. Begins to move about the remnants of the house, finding small things, here and there. A tortoise-shell comb that was Mother's. An old, cracked netsuke in the form of a rabbit suckling its young. Effortfully, she recalls the world they were once part of. Now, they seem to have different souls.

On the floor, near the charred remnant of Father's desk, a commercial calendar. Has time really continued, from date to date, from square to square, of this flimsy paper grid? How long has it been, since real life ended? How many squares filled by nightmares and shadows?

A date is ringed. *March 11. Founding Day.*

Twenty years ago, Mother had invited the priest of the shrine in her family's home village, to come down to the city and consecrate the new dojo, the shooting-hall, at its opening ceremony. Sponsorship of the dojo had been a project of Mother's. Every year since then, the students and their teachers had made a pilgrimage to the village shrine to perform a housha, a shooting ceremony for the god.

March 11. The day that is supposed to begin with the arrival, in the early morning, of a hired car to collect the family. She has passed many cars on her way out of the city. Most were barely recognisable as things made by human beings.

March 11 1925. In the event, Mother had not been able to attend the opening. For that had been the day Mie was born. She and the dojo had grown up together, its senior teacher, known to her only as 'Sensei', a constant presence in her life.

March 11 1945. Her birthday. Twenty years of existence. It makes no sense to Mie that she continues to live. But that is how things seem to be.

March 11 1945. Tomorrow.

It will not be a poet's road to the north, although it will be narrow and hard enough. How to proceed? There will be no vehicle, great or small. She is not unused to walking, but never as far as this, in one journey. It is like old stories from a time when distance was measured in worn out and discarded rice-straw sandals. How many pairs of waraji? How long before her tread unravels each set of rope soles? But she has only her low-heeled western shoes.

She does not want to spend another night in the city, but in the old tales, faceless things haunt the roads by night. Deliberately, she pushes away further thought and gathers up the few things she has brought with her from the dojo. Her glove and practice uniform in a cloth furoshiki bundle, her case of arrows and her bow, its blue and white wrapping-cloth, grey with ash.

March. The hills will be cool. It seems impossible in this strange hell-world. In the remains of an outhouse, she finds the old padded jacket and blue cotton hat her mother used to wear when gardening and slips them on.

Pushing back out into the street, she glances left and right. It is empty. Stunned by her own decision, she sets off, face towards the hills. As she turns the corner, she hears shouts from the direction of the house: men's voices, commanding sharply.

She sets her feet to the road and begins beating time to her own desire to move, to act, to choose and not to listen.

*　*　*

The ad in the window of the old-fashioned shop-front had been calling to me for a while. Just a few doors down on the opposite side of the street, they wanted a freelance technical writer to work on 'a variety of accounts'. The 'freelance' part was fake of course, just a scam to get round employment law. What really seduced me was that siren word 'variety'. I like routine, but only up to a point.

The interview was a bit of a formality, which was good because, naturally, I don't present particularly well in interviews. I had the qualifications and experience, they were in a hurry to hire and either overlooked or failed to notice my discomfort with eye-contact. For my part, I was only too glad to exchange a noisy, low-ceilinged, open-plan office for a quiet attic in a raffish eighteenth-century townhouse.

I had wondered at first, what sort of an outfit would occupy such ramshackle premises. The building started out quite grand and spacious on the lower storeys, but the higher you climbed the more you encountered crooked wooden staircases and poky little rooms with drunkenly sloping floors. Still, the outfit seemed reassuringly sober: part PR consultancy, part copywriting services and translation and now with a developing line in high-end technical documentation. There must have been about fifteen people in the building at any one time, with others coming and going, but I rarely saw them.

My reflections were cut short by hunger and the desire to reach my usual alfresco lunch venue. Turning right, I followed the path westward a short way, to where it ends alongside the foot of a flight of concrete steps that climb the last steep bank to the summit.

Father had eventually given up patrolling my shelves, cupboards, drawers and pockets. Books on technical subjects were, it seemed, respectable. Validated at last, I had begun a new collection: homework marks, exam scores and, long after he had lost interest in me and wandered away, an engineering degree at Cardiff University. From there I climbed step by step via an internship on a technical journal, part-time and temporary copywriting contracts to arrive at a steady job, a girlfriend, a shared flat on the English side of the estuary and a lunchtime routine of strolling up a grassy hill to get away from the office.

For several years it had been the peak effort of my daily exercise regime to climb the steps to the broad semi-circular promenade with its panoramic views from the summit. There I would hope to find an unoccupied bench on which to sit and eat lunch, while letting the focus of my eyes roll out to infinity after hours of close screen work.

The view to the north is blocked by Brandon Hill itself. A promontory of a much larger hill that the city had once climbed up and sat down on, at some time the summit of this remaining green space had been laid out with walks, beautified with trees and adorned with artfully wild shrubberies, rockeries, cascades and ponds. Planted in the middle of this arrangement was the tall, square tower of red-brown sandstone, its upper storeys decorated with alarming balconies. Four large, old-fashioned electric lanterns hung from iron brackets near the top. Walking home through the park on windy nights, I would see them swinging restlessly about, giving the place a wild and haunted air.

To the east, the lower lying suburbs straggle away to a horizon cut off by the green hills of the river valley. Westward, the higher parts of the city block the view of its most iconic feature, just as the high ground of The Downs beyond blocks the Atlantic westerlies that bring much of its weather. There the tidal river has sawn down through a thousand feet of rock, the resulting gorge spanned by a suspension bridge. The bridge goes nowhere in particular, but has found its vocation as Bristol's alternative civic badge, borrowed for dozens of local business logos that criss-cross the city on the sides of a thousand vans. I still notice things like that.

South was my favourite direction. There, I could let my gaze fly out over tree-tops and house-roofs, across the docks and the river, beyond the edge of the city, and on to the distant hills, to rest on the blue grey line where clouds and fields meet.

*   *   *

Hours pass, counted out by the steps of increasingly sore feet. Her shoes are beginning to raise blisters, so she takes them off and carries them. Added to her other burdens, they begin to seem an impossible weight. Her arm aches. She thinks of putting them into her bundle, then sees they are nearly destroyed. Placing them neatly side by side on a stone at the edge of the road, she walks on, barefoot.

That degree of hunger, when the thought of food makes one feel nauseous. That was a point on the road she had passed – when? She begins to think she must be lost. But then, a cluster of little houses she recognises, tucked in between the freshly-tilled rice-fields and the tall bamboo of the hillside. She is dully astonished at their unburnt state.

Why are the village children squealing and pointing at her? An old man with a box of picture-story cards has been entertaining them. The children are repeating something over and over again, almost hysterically delighted: '*The Ash-Covered Princess! The Ash-Covered Princess!*'

The storyteller peers shortsightedly across the street, following the pointing fingers and button-eyed stares of his little audience. He says something to the children, the tone of his voice decent and kind, calling on them to show respect. He offers round tiny candies to regain their attention. She slips by with a brief bow of thanks. He is old and kind. His face shows where all the young men go – if only they are allowed to live.

Alone on the road again, she looks at her grey, ash-stained hands. Why is she alive? Is this life? A kind of panic seizes her. She can no longer feel any awareness of being present in the moment through which she is, apparently, living.

Under the shade of some old trees, a little shrine at the entrance to a graveyard. She stops. A trickle of silver falls into a moss-covered stone basin. She picks up the battered old copper ladle. Rinses her mouth with icy mountain water, drinks, pours a little over her hands in a feeble attempt to clean them. Still wet, she claps them together and bows, surrounded by a brief nimbus of diamonds she cannot see. It is hardly a prayer, more an act of surrender.

* * *

I think it was in the last year of the old job that my route changed. Reaching the foot of the concrete steps I had glanced up to see that early spring sunshine and a school half-term had filled the summit promenade with sitters and strollers. To cover my hesitation, I pretended I had always been intending to go straight ahead and strolled through a gap in the shrubbery into a hidden space I had never explored before.

A broad, level square had been at some time cut into the side of the hill. Ahead and to my right, high stone walls, tall trees and dark, overhanging laurels shaded the ground. To the left of the entrance was a low concrete platform, the stumps of iron bolts evoking the ghost of a wooden building. Combine this with the proportions of the level square and it became easy to see in imagination, the lost bowling green. Like the club house, the carefully tended square of grass was long gone, replaced by crumbling asphalt. Faded pitch-markings suggested that more active ball games had also failed to flourish in this spot.

I became a regular visitor. Few others ventured in, even on sunny days. I would sit on the concrete slab, eating my sandwiches in peace and passing the time by imagining other uses for this empty space. A swimming pool, shimmering in sunlight, the stone walls echoing shouts and splashes, the margins splattered with bare footprints fading in the sun, until over-stamped with more. Or maybe an open air cafe, with a colourful pavilion and tables with umbrellas set out across the square, sprinkled with elegant people and their lattes, frappés and cappuccinos.

At home in the evenings I would sometimes catch myself half-wondering where I had put my wet swimming things, or feeling for the little biscotti wrapped in paper that for some reason I always slip into my pocket for later.

Today however, daydreams were replaced with reflection. Odd conversations aside, I told myself, I'd had worse colleagues than Hiroshi. The working relationship itself was pretty efficient. I couldn't really complain. And if things did get a bit odd, well, there was always this place to escape to.

Just as I reached this happy conclusion, I noticed that I was no longer alone. With a surge of irritation, I threw a not very friendly glance in the direction of the intruder's legs. It was Hiroshi. The damn fellow had tracked me to my lair. Sticking his hands in his pockets he surveyed the bowling green, nodding in approval.

'So, this is where you appear!'

'It's peaceful.' I growled, hoping he might take the hint.

Instead, pulling his hands out of his pockets, he spread his legs out, as if rooting himself to the ground. Then he made a strange, expansive gesture with his arms, apparently express-ing in dumbshow his appreciation of its spaciousness. This was too much. I crumpled my sandwich wrapper fiercely and got up to leave. He made no attempt to follow, but stood there, legs akimbo, arms thrust out, nodding in complacent approval as if he owned the place. Just as I reached the exit he called out.

'You do not do archery?'

I stopped dead. Again, an incongruous tone. As if there could be some genuine doubt about the matter. When I eventually turned to mutter a puzzled and embarrassed 'No!' he merely said, 'Ah! Oh!' – in a way that managed to convey both surprise and disappointment.

About a week later, as we were packing up at the end of the day, Hiroshi shoved a business card at me, tapping it with his finger.

'Visit me at this address at eight o'clock this evening. I will teach you archery.' Then he picked up his case and hurried off, not even pausing to say goodnight.

After getting home and having something to eat, I took out the card, fully intending to call the number and make my apologies. It was rather nicely printed in both Japanese and English, naming Hiroshi as a company director. The business name, in the English version at any rate, was of the kind that gives nothing much away. It didn't look like my idea of a sports club, but what did I know? I reached confidently for the phone, but then hesitated.

'This is a gift,' I thought, turning Hiroshi's card round and round in my fingers, 'Odd, but potentially, quite generous.' I put the card down on the table and stared at it. The one serious adult relationship in my life had ended six years before. We had come together more or less accidentally, driven more by a shared need to rent a flat in Bristol than romance. When Jo left, my social life, such as it was, left with her. I had retreated into work and solitude. Talking about feelings had seemed unnecessary, we both knew the score. But I had mistaken her silence for agreement. For a few blistering minutes, now that the years were past mending, she had found the strength to tell me how wrong I was.

'It's not like you're a bad person, you just make me feel invisible. So now I really am going to disappear. For good.'

I didn't have the heart to argue. She so obviously had a point.

I turned the card one more time. 'What happens if I say no?' Hiroshi might be occasionally annoying, but if he were to become more than just a work colleague, it would represent the first time since the split with Jo that my social circle had increased, even by one. And, while new faces would always be a challenge, something like a sports club would widen my horizons even more. A sport that wouldn't involve too much physical effort. I could handle that. I had got into habits of evasion and refusal. It was time to change course.

I looked at the clock. I didn't have a car and it was getting a bit late for buses, so I ordered a cab. When I showed the address to the driver, he had to look it up. I didn't have much clue either, so it was with some misgivings that I watched the city morph around me from polite suburbs to the sketchier wilds of free enterprise.

*　*　*

The road is climbing now, through soft and hilly country. She can smell pinewoods on the wind, or the bare earth of ploughed fields, as the breeze shifts or the road turns. But these scents are all masked, like friends waving and mouthing to her from a distance. Mile after mile she drags herself, hill after hill and yet the stench of the city's burning is still wrapped around her. How far can it reach?

Every so often, a little valley opens out to one side, floored with dark mats of tiny rice-fields, a cluster of houses squeezed in where the land becomes too steep to grow rice, but not steep enough to abandon to the bamboo groves. Wedged even more tightly into a spare corner between field, road, river and hill, a small family graveyard, the long Buddhist name-stelae sticking up, a bleak flower-arrangement of black stems.

For a long time, the river has kept company with the road, leaping and chuckling in the distance. Now, glimpses of the water are getting fewer: chopped off curls of a blue-green thread, seen far below through gaps in the trees. The skein is increasingly tangled with rapids and tumbled rocks, the broad, pale stone-gardens of the lower banks, swallowed up as the mountain forest hugs it closer.

As evening approaches, the valleys below begin to fill with cold pools of white mist that creep among the tree-tops. Soon, a white blanket covers both river and valley and only the ghostly whisper of the rapids escapes from the underworld. The trees have gathered close to the mountain road too, as it curves left into the night.

A figure is emerging from the darkness. An uncouth, shaggy-pelted outline, walking forward on thick ungainly legs, carrying a long weapon.

*　　*　　*

By the time the car halted in a deserted industrial estate, my misgivings had become serious doubts. I gave the driver a generous tip and asked him to wait for a minute while I checked I had got the right place. A few of the units had signboards and looked occupied, but Hiroshi's seemed to be one of the anonymous, deserted-looking ones. Finding, to my relief, a crisply lettered name-card on the entry phone I waved the driver off and pressed the button. After a brief, shouty exchange the metal door was unbolted, releasing a familiar waft of rough roll-ups.

My relief was short-lived. As he ushered me into the narrow, dimly lit passageway, it became apparent that Hiroshi was wearing an ankle-length, pleated black skirt with deep cutaways at the sides and what looked like a choirboy's white surplice tucked into it. I followed him into a small, rather spartan office.

'Please, sit down.'

I perched gingerly on the rather seedy looking office chair. Busying himself with a kettle, he produced, without asking, two mugs of rather rough black coffee.

'I hope it was not too difficult to find this place.'

'No. Fine,' I said.

Parking his own coffee on a filing cabinet, he turned with a dramatic swirl of skirts, yanked open a drawer of the very battered old desk and handed me a document.

'This is called Hassetsu.'

At first glance it looked rather like the kind of thing Hiroshi and I dealt with at work on a daily basis. Sucking a burnt tongue, I put down my coffee and ran a professional eye over it. Twelve photocopied pages, with the tell-tale shadow of an unfamiliar paper size in the margins. Title page in both Japanese and roman characters, table of contents, some short paragraphs of text. Eight full-page diagrams, with various labels and headings in Japanese, but written in roman characters.

So far, so normal. The diagrams were a bit outside our line

of work though. Instead of flowcharts, circuits or exploded drawings, a series of eight human figures in stiff postures, reminiscent of a Chinese Medicine chart, or Leonardo's *Vitruvian Man*, but with the addition of bows and arrows. Someone had written terse English translations underneath the main captions. From the neat, round hand and some characteristically stiff-collared idioms, I suspected Hiroshi's work.

'You can study this later,' he said firmly. 'Tonight I will demonstrate. This way please.'

Leaving the document with my jacket on the chair, I followed Hiroshi's swishing black skirts out of the office. We turned right along a plywood-walled passage and crossed what was evidently a loading bay, a big roller-shutter door to our right. Turning left, we pushed through one of those transparent plastic-strip curtains you can drive a fork-lift truck through. Shaking the last heavy strip off my shoulder, I looked anxiously around.

* * *

The woman wears a wide straw hat, a sedge-grass rain-cape and faded, baggy blue trousers, patched many times, no doubt by evening lamplight. A long hoe slants above her shoulder. She speaks harshly, jabbing an accusatory finger, brown and earth-stained, at Mie's face. Too tired and desperate to speak, Mie can only shake her head and bow in apology. The woman clucks disapproval. She wants Mie to turn around. Head down, sullen, Mie steps sideways, trying to pass the obstacle. The woman steps in front of her, blocking the way with the basket of vegetables she carries. Mie stands in the road, stubborn, silent, immovable.

The woman's tone softens. She touches Mie gently on the arm, gestures down the hill in apparent invitation. But Mie cannot bear to lose even a little hard-won ground. Feeling herself to be not quite human, she recoils too, from the thought of human kindness, human company, hearth-fire – and smoke.

The woman is silent for a moment. Then, not to be completely rebuffed, she pulls out of her basket a small bundle of mountain asparagus, neatly tied with a strip of rice-straw. She puts the bundle gently into Mie's hand, closing the unresisting fingers over it. It has begun to rain. The woman puts down her basket, slips off the sedge-grass cloak and sweeps it gently around Mie's shoulders. An embrace without touching.

Mie knows she should protest, should utter thanks, but is too tired, confused and grateful. She bows and her unkempt hair slips forward over her face, sweeping the night across her eyes.

The woman picks up her basket and continues on her way, calling words of advice or encouragement as she goes. Mie can no more understand them, or reply, than if it were a foreign language. She has become a speechless child again.

Red eaves and walls glow dimly among the deepening shadows of the trees. A familiar waymark on those former journeys to the village shrine, the hired car bumping slowly past, tyres slithering uneasily on the damp stones. Now, the road is as empty and deserted as the temple. The rain sifts down, fine and soaking. It begins to drip from branches and seep in dark, trickling threads down dry trunks.

The temple is tightly shuttered and padlocked. She drinks awkwardly from a thread of water pouring from the eaves, then takes shelter under the overhanging roof of the verandah, huddled against the wooden wall.

Peeling the asparagus shoots with her teeth, she chews listlessly on the bittersweet flesh. Eating them makes her feel a little sick. Painfully, she lies down, drawing the rustling grass cloak around her and somehow falls asleep, too tired to remember to be frightened by the lonely shriek of a deer, or of the ghosts that must cluster thickly in this deserted spot.

The sun, having climbed just high enough to peer through the treetops, shouts in her face and the pain in her limbs greets her like an unwelcome acquaintance from yesterday. For a moment, she cannot remember where she is or why. She slips off the grass cloak, shivering in the morning cold. Shaking it loose, she lays it carefully in front of the temple doors, bows deeply, then gathers up her belongings. Stiffly, wincing with pain, she descends the steps and limps toward the road.

It cannot be far now surely, this last and steepest part of the journey, where the car used to labour and whine, jolting over the rough road. It seems an unlikely fantasy, that car. Somehow, she has woken up to find herself living in another, older age. A time that was always there, waiting patiently beneath the present.

*   *   *

A square of thick rush matting is laid in the middle of the concrete floor. Two utility lamps, suspended on long chains from the high corrugated metal roof, bathe this improvised stage-set in soft light. In the darkness beyond, pallet-loads of cardboard boxes line two sides of the space, stacked high on metal shelving. A dusty silence reigns, broken only by the occasional ticking of the cooling metal building.

Hiroshi beckons me forward, only to stop me with a raised hand as I am about to step onto the mat.

'Please remove your shoes.'

Squatting to undo my laces, I see that beneath his long skirts, Hiroshi's own feet are clad in white cloth socks, with a divided toe to accommodate the sandals he is already stepping out of.

Leaving them neatly side by side on the concrete floor, he indicates, with a white-clad toe, a spot on the mat.

'Stand here,' he orders. 'Watch carefully, remain silent.'

Padding over to a rack on the far side, Hiroshi picks up something that does not look quite like my layman's idea of a bow. It is rather long and there seems to be a lot more of it above the handgrip than below.

Holding it at arm's length, Hiroshi squints at it, then gives the string an experimental pluck. A soft, unfamiliar sound jitters around the room.

Returning the bow to the rack, he kneels gracefully on the floor, to tie what looks like half a suede leather glove onto his right hand. Rising again with equal grace, he visits a tall cardboard box, much mended with gaffer tape, that stands near the bow rack. The feathers of a dozen or so arrows or so stick up from inside. He picks out a pair, gripping them in his gloved hand just behind the heads, as if they were dangerous snakes. Finally, retrieving the bow, he returns to centre stage.

The target I see is not to be some distant mark, but a thing resembling a small blackboard set up at the left hand side of the matting. Strips of thick, stiff black foam have been clamped together between two bars of wood to make an arrow catcher.

It is fixed to an old step-ladder, itself ballasted against the shock of impact by a couple of breeze-blocks. Behind it, swags of fine, dark green netting have been slung.

Hiroshi bows, bending from the waist, as if the 'blackboard' is some kind of holy image. The bow is held by his left side, upper tip angled down to a point just an inch or two above the floor in front of him. The tails of the arrows stick out from the far side of his body, echoing the angle of the bow.

And then he begins to dance.

His feet return in a couple of sweeping steps to their former wide stance, his back once more toward me, his left shoulder presented towards the target. One arrow is fitted to the bow, while the second hangs from his right hand. Arms, hands, bow and arrows, rise, then slowly fall, the exquisite curves of the bow swelling, until the first arrow rests steady and level at the height of Hiroshi's cheek. Those stiff diagrams on the photocopied sheets, I realise, are moments in this slow, stately pavane.

'Tuesday and Thursday?' We were back in the warehouse office. Hiroshi had changed and was rolling a cigarette in preparation for the open air. I looked at the few straggly brown threads showing at the end of the thin, crumpled paper tube in his fingers. He seemed to be putting less and less tobacco in them these days. 'Is that OK for you?' 'Um…' I said, mentally totting up taxi fares with rising alarm. Perhaps, I thought, a bus might bring me at least close enough to walk the rest of the way.

'Yes,' I said.

Hiroshi grunted. Then, carefully licking and sealing the cigarette paper, he stood up and headed for the door.

'Good. We need to get a move on.'

If I didn't then understand the need for haste, I certainly agreed with it. Back there in the warehouse, I had glimpsed a different reality: Hiroshi standing with right arm thrown back, level with his extended forearm. The sound of the bowstring reverberating in the high dark roof. An arrow standing in the target. As if it had always been there.

* * *

A group of flowers made of bright silks, the girls stand chatting in the shade of the shrine's courtyard. They do not talk about The War, but smile a lot – little, tight smiles, hidden behind modest fingertips. Sometimes, they cast down their eyes and breathe: 'How sad it is!' about this person or that who cannot be present. But not often, it is too unhappy a thought and today must be happy. But again, it cannot be helped, the lightest conversational topic somehow twists and betrays one into depths. How much a certain relative would have liked to be here. And of course, Sensei and 'our poor friends'. They cannot bring themselves to say the names, however softly, as if afraid of raising ghosts. 'Such a pity, such a fine old house, always such interesting company!' That last, perhaps, a little too daring. Everyone is silent for a moment, embarrassed. Then the sparrows begin again.

The chatter is even, yet varied, a tree full of birds, or a stream dancing downhill. Until one of them notices that the shy girl in glasses at the back of the group has stopped flicking her eyes back and forth with the conversation and is staring through them all, towards the road. Some catch the expression on her face, some see their neighbours turning to look. All fall suddenly silent again, glancing around, confused. The girl in the glasses stares, white beneath her white make-up.

One by one, the others follow her gaze, peering through the dappled shadows of the tree-shaded courtyard, through the torii archway at the entrance to the shrine and out into the bright rectangle of sunlight framed by the red timbers. The old priest, who is just coming to invite everyone to enter and begin the ceremony, stops; his tall, narrow, black hat like the crest of some odd bird that turns to peer at danger.

In the sunlit dust of the road, framed by the heavy wooden pillars of the torii, stands a shape from an old tale. A shadow, snipped out of the bright surface of the day. In one hand, the rough, wavering brushstroke of an unstrung bow, wrapped in its long strip of patterned cloth. In the other, a furoshiki-bundle. Slung across its back, the lacquered rattan arrow-case protrudes above one shoulder.

The shadow moves slowly forwards, limping a little. The group stands rigid and still, bristling at the impropriety of this intrusion.

Tanaka Mie has the indecency to be alive.

It is the one who first saw, who shyly steps forward through the still rigid group, clutching a closed fan tightly to her silk-wrapped chest.

'Mie? Is it you?'

It is the shy girl's mother who dives in, taut in a pale green western suit and hat, firmly interposing a paler green glove between pristine kimono silk and dusty, travel-stained cotton.

A cool, dark, side-hall, full of bags and changes of clothes hanging up. In the shielding gloom, there is fussing and tutting, questions asked and answers never waited for. There is water and scrubbing, there is shaking and slapping as dust and ash are scolded out of clothes. There is a fierce assault with a hairbrush that jerks her head back and forth as if she is a small child being made ready for school. There is a kindness in these brutalities that makes Mie wish she were able to cry.

Six of the girls, who have just danced a kagura for the god in front of the shrine, enter the hall to change out of formal kimono ready for the shooting ceremony. As she is returned slowly to human shape, Mie braces herself against their horrified curiosity.

A clean pair of white tabi are pulled over her blisters and her battered feet wedged into a painfully tight pair of borrowed geta. Finally, she is ejected, tottering, back into the glaring light. The bright birds shift uneasily, opening their ranks to admit this disturbing, dark creature, still a little dusty, pale enough without the aid of make-up, but with its long, black plumage, loosely tied, gleaming darkly in the sun. Mie slips in among the group who are to shoot, grateful for the anonymity of the black and white uniform.

Tanaka Mie, clinging to the familiar ritual as to a rope on a mountain path. Nothing else seems bearable, graspable. She unwraps the bow slowly and carefully, cruelly conscious of the smell still lingering, fearful that puffs of ash will fly out from the cloth. Someone helps her to string it, she does not remember who. She is concerned that it might have taken some harm, but too exhausted to worry. She can only trust to fate, assuming that it will do what it has always done. All she can do is play her part, with absolute intensity, for that is all she has left to play it with. Nothing less is possible.

The dipping, bowing, kneeling and rising dance of shooting in a line begins. The old priest presides smilingly over the scene from the seat of honour. The parents, mostly represented by mothers, admire, faces stony with pride. They shoot across an inner courtyard, to targets arranged on makeshift stands before a backcloth.

Afterwards, Mie will remember almost nothing of this scene, not even the moment when, at full Kai, the old photographer's shutter presaged the release of her bowstring by half a heartbeat. She does not remember her two perfect shots that place two arrows in the centre spot. And she does not remember fainting, or striking her head on the wooden floor, or being carried, unconscious, into a side room.

The flock disperses, chattering and fluttering with farewells and promises, a flickering of hands, eyelids, lips and fans. The untoward is not mentioned, except for a few polite hints of concern, assurances rapidly accepted, responsibility, gladly left lying.

*　　*　　*

When I take an interest in something, I want to know everything. I swept my shelves of past obsessions and began to fill them instead with books and articles on Kyudo, 'The Way of the Bow'.

As a practical aid to my studies, Hiroshi had, on our second meeting, presented me with a gomu-yumi – a short stick, approximating to the shape and thickness of a real bow's handgrip. Attached to the top is a loop of bicycle tyre inner-tube. If you hook your right thumb through the loop of rubber and grip the stick correctly with your left, it does enable you to practise the movements of shooting, against a real resistance not unlike that of bow and bowstring. Just how much resistance came as rather a shock. I had naively thought of archery as a gentle form of exercise.

Letting go was even more of a problem. The Hassetsu calls for the right hand to fly back in an elegant reaction 'as if rapping on a drum'. Unfortunately, it was often not an imaginary drum my knuckles rapped, but the very solid door frames and cupboards of my flat.

Of course, it had not taken me long to remember Hiroshi's odd gestures in the derelict bowling green. Again, that assumption of familiarity. Why would I have any idea what he was at? It was like a lot of things about Hiroshi. I could tie myself in knots wondering what went on in his head. Easier just to go along with his enthusiasm.

As I could not see myself joining the student slack-liners, jugglers and poi-poi whirlers that sometimes manifested on summer evenings in the open park, the bowling green with its relative privacy was an obvious solution. Surrounded by the green spaces of the park, yet secluded by walls and trees, it did indeed look a bit like the setting of some of the more splendid dojos pictured in my newly acquired books and articles. I could readily imagine a calm hall floored in polished wood, looking out onto a square of moss or raked gravel. Of course, I couldn't actually shoot there, but my goal for the moment was only to embed the movements of the Hassetsu into muscle-memory.

The park was less than thirty minutes walk from my flat. I wandered over one dull Sunday evening, just to take a look. Standing on the base of the old clubhouse, eyeing the dark, laurel-shaded wall opposite, I thought 'I should really do this' – and immediately realised it was going to be nearly as embarrassing as taking all my clothes off. I took a deep breath and began.

By the end of the following week, my self-consciousness had almost evaporated. Even so, I stuck to evenings and the cover of dusk. Following the pattern of Hiroshi's lessons, I would do some warm-up exercises, then try my strength with three or four slow pulls and releases of the gomu-yumi. Finally I would go through the Hassetsu sequence again in more detail, this time using only an imaginary bow and equally unsubstantial arrows.

Of course, imaginary shots can be as good as you like. On this particular evening, the last one had seemed especially good, as my idea of an arrow flew, unerringly, towards my notion of a target. In the semi-darkness it was easier to visualise the tall, asymmetric bow. I had not yet been allowed even to handle a real weapon, let alone shoot one and yet I could almost feel the shock of the reaction, followed by the gentle tap of the string on the outside of the wrist as the bow spins on its axis in the elegant movement of *yugaere.* The only thing missing was the note of the bowstring, and the sound of the arrow piercing the paper target-drum, to be stopped and held in a bank of soft river sand. It was time to leave on a high note. I made the concluding bow and turned to pick up my bag.

As I straighten up, something on the edge of vision catches my attention. Something, that in the first instant of awareness, I take for a low-flying night bird. But nocturnal birds do not as a rule, hover as rock-steady as hawks, just three or four feet off the ground. Without any wind.

It teases my vision. If I look directly, I can see nothing. But as soon as my gaze slides away, there it is, at the edge of sight. My eyes stretch wide in the dark as I try to resolve it into something that would make daylight sense. Softly, I put down my bag and take a sidelong step towards it, the blood whispering in my ears. For a few seconds I cannot work out how near or far the thing is, but as I move it seems to lengthen in perspective, a dull gleam briefly reflecting from some invisible source. I edge closer. Close enough to pass my hand above and below. No invisible threads. Neither my nervous movements, nor a little breath of evening breeze, disturb its perfect stillness in any way.

I sweep my gaze around the shadows of the bowling green, half-hoping to catch the smirking perpetrator of the illusion, but the darkness is empty and silent. I blink hard several times, screwing my eyes up tight and opening them again. Nothing. But then, as I look away, there it is, hanging resolutely still and level in the dusk. Cautiously, disbelievingly, I reach out to touch it – but at the last second snatch back my hand, suddenly convinced that it might be as fatal as touching a bare electric cable.

Impossible.

Intractable.

Floating perfectly still,

a foot or two above the ground…

A single arrow.

* * *

2 Dozukuri

*Complete the posture, adjust the balance. Align oneself
to the target and to the universe, vertically, horizontally,
forwards and backwards.*

A few faces loom in her vision, mouthing kind wishes for
recovery, apologies for departing so soon, but…

She is barely conscious of their presence, except as beings
she is drifting away from, as if the spinning earth itself were
rushing them away from her. Like petals in a high wind, they
disperse and are gone.

They leave the shrine in family groups, squeezing into shared
cars and elderly taxis that roll and bump slowly down the hill,
headed for distant villages, small towns, or suburbs in the
unburnt margins of the city. The dust raised by their wheels is
swept away into the trees by a southerly wind that smells of
Spring.

The old priest changes out of his robes into a faded indigo
cotton jacket and loose trousers. He exchanges his black eboshi
for an old, straw field-worker's hat. He fetches a broom and a
wooden bucket and with the same slow care with which he had
presided over the ceremonies, sweeps and waters the ground
inside the gate. An old woman fetches more water in a wooden
pitcher, carrying it into one of the cool, dark rooms that open
off the inner courtyard.

The shrine has many of these rooms. Years ago, when the
priest's grandfather was a young man, Buddhism and The Way
of the Gods had lived together like an old married couple, cheek
by jowl in the same house. This back-country shrine, once quite
large and busy in the days when so many more people lived on

the land, had been full of miscellaneous curiosities and local heroes of the spiritual. A jumble of beliefs and memories and their outward symbols and images.

But, one day, word had come down from 'above the clouds': the path of the Buddha must be disentangled from the National Faith, from Shinto. The local officials, keen to show enthusiasm and full of the national importance of their task, had come bustling through the gate, giving directions and bossing people around. A long, wavering procession of worm-eaten wooden images, large and small, had left through the torii gate, faded colours and a patchy psoriasis of crumbling gilt exposed, for the first time in generations, to sunlight. That evening, there had been a solemn bonfire on the river-bank. There followed some days of sweeping and chasing and chivvying of spiders, rats and mice out of their ancestral homes.

And so, the shrine had settled down to its new, barer life, as the pure receptacle of the ceremonies of the local mountain deity, relieved of its crowds of Buddhas, bodhis, arhats and boddhisatvas and burdened with an embarrassment of empty halls and rooms, from which the rats, mice and spiders, pious and persistent observants, had to be constantly chased.

Tanaka Mie does not remember the others leaving. She remembers only waking up in the dark, in a silent room, lying on a clean-smelling futon on the floor. The faces of the old priest and the old woman hovering above her, in the light of a smoky kerosene lamp.

For a whole day and a night, she only sleeps. On the second day, she accepts some of the old woman's proffered rice and vegetables and drinks very cold water from the garden well.

In the evening she gets up and takes her meal with the old priest and his housekeeper. Afterwards, they sit together, listening to the talk of the trees outside.

'Your shooting showed a good heart.'

She bows, not knowing how to reply.

'I was concerned at first, when you arrived like a wild

creature, or an uncanny spirit. But the sound of your string was bright.'

They are smiling at her in the dusk, the kerosene lamp as yet unlit. The old woman is holding some dark-red garment, offering it. Mie, puzzled, does not understand. The old woman smiles more broadly and holds it out to her, draped across her forearms as she bobs her head low. Red hakama.

'We would be glad, if you would...'

There is a white gi also, a kimono blouse, that the old woman has laid, neatly folded, on the low table. Now she stoops quickly, picks it up, places it on top of the hakama and holds out both garments, bowing once more. Mie takes them, slowly and carefully. They watch, a little curious, as she lifts them to her face, closes her eyes and breathes deeply. She holds her breath for a long time. The clothes smell of pine-resin, cedar and rain-washed mountain air. They are the first things she has handled that do not smell of smoke.

The old woman nods and smiles happily.

'Miko! Miko!' she repeats softly.

The priest turns and shuffles on his knees to the alcove in the corner. Reverently and gently, he withdraws a long bundle from the shadows and returns. Slowly, carefully, he unwraps it. It is a bow. A fine, black-lacquered bow, with rattan bindings down its whole length.

'This was given to the god, by the family of a young man who lived nearby, at the beginning of the War. There has been no one here who can use it...'

Miko. They want her to be a miko. A shrine-maiden.

This old priest and his housekeeper, who used to make a fuss of her when she was a small child. Her attendance always marking her birthday. A little taller each year. Until it was no longer fitting for her to be patted or to have sweets slipped into her hand when no one was looking. Always, she had been a spectator. To the ceremonies of the shrine, to the commem-oration of the dojo's foundation, to Sensei, making a dignified offering before the god. She had stood outside all this, outside adult life. Never dreamed of having anything more to do with this strange, rambling old place, its half-deserted buildings dreaming among the cedars, camphor trees and walnuts. Her childhood is a burned-out ruin: her parents dead, the dojo gone, friends and fellow students scattered who knows where after this final gathering. But the old people are calling her out of the fire, calling her across the boundary into adulthood.

She is to be an officiant, a shaman. A warder-off of evil spirits, an auspicious attendant at ceremonies. They are offering her a place, a life, a being. She bows deeply. The old woman gives a little, happy, girlish laugh and claps her hands twice.

That night, they heat the water. Mie carefully washes her hair and body, then takes a long bath, as hot as she can bear it. When she finally emerges, she gathers up her old clothes and on a sudden, fierce impulse, shoves them into the furnace, slamming the iron door shut, trying not to hear the rumble of the flames.

Afterwards, she sits on the worn tatami-mat floor in her little corner room, the paper screens pulled back on the night forest. She combs and combs her hair, letting the resin-scented air into it, then crawls beneath the padded coverlet. For a few moments the moon looks at her through the tops of the pines, an eye behind heavy lashes.

*　　*　　*

All the next morning, I kept catching myself nervously glancing left and right, trying to catch some defect in my vision that might explain my curious experience. Everything remained stubbornly normal. Had I dreamed the arrow? Where but in a dream does one see such a thing? But the memory of the previous evening was vivid and detailed in a way dreams are not. Some of the writings I had collected did speak of curious visual phenomena. But those were all about focusing on the target. None of them mentioned floating arrows. Had my obsession triggered something in my brain? Would it be wise, safe even, to carry on?

And yet. The night I had hesitated over accepting Hiroshi's invitation, I had seen rather clearly that my life was going nowhere healthy. He had shown me, given me, an enchanting and beautiful alternative. It was hardly his fault if I muddled dreams and real life or got myself into some fugue state compounded of over-work and over-excitement.

I had been intellectually drawn to Kyudo by its calming repetition, its framework of rules and gracious etiquette. But I had soon begun to feel the physical promise those moments in the dance of the Hassetsu seemed to contain.

Having shown my proficiency with the gomu yumi, Hiroshi had put into my hands a simple 'stick bow' made of an ordinary bamboo garden cane, the handgrip position marked by a wrapping of tape. Instead of an arrow, he produced a plain length of dowel, blunt at one end and with a notch for the string at the other.

I wasn't allowed to release any shots. The stick bow is only for practising the movements prior to release. But even with that simple stick I could feel the force of that great expansive gesture, reaching up, opening the universe, drawing down power that fills the moment with tension. Something seemed to flow into me, something huge, thrilling and for all my beginner's clumsiness, full of an unnameable potential. Perhaps for the first time ever, I felt truly centred and grounded in the space around me. I had already crossed a boundary. It was too late now, to go back.

Ashibumi, the 'first position', is a simple enough stance, but even that is achieved by a sequence of precise, flowing movements. Shaking his head and muttering: 'Try to relax, try to relax!', Hiroshi kicks my feet further apart, pulls and pushes at my head, hands and arms, prodding and poking, bending and moulding me into the shape he wants. Actually, I know perfectly well the shape he wants. I can remember the bloody diagram – I just didn't realise that *being* the diagram would feel like this.

When everything is set to Hiroshi's grudging satisfaction and I feel completely awkward and off-balance, he makes me reach both hands, clutching bow and arrow, high into the air.

'Higher, higher! Elbows out. Like you are reaching round the trunk of a great tree.'

I strain upwards, struggling to breathe normally while trying to keep the arrow horizontal above my head. My neck aches with the effort of looking sideways. 'Now, slowly, *push* to the target. *Pull* from the elbow.' As my hands move apart, the bow begins to belly forward, the arrow head draws back and the shaft, remaining horizontal all the time, sinks down and down. 'Line of the mouth! Line of the mouth!' he mutters warningly as I approach full draw. Still unsatisfied, he prods and pokes some more, before standing back to admire his human diagram of forces. The 'arrow' slips off the top of my left hand and clatters to the floor.

'Clumsy'. A word that had followed me through childhood like a malign imaginary friend. Even now, every time something like that happens, my father comes back. Even though he never did come back. Even though I waited. Even after Mother died, I waited. When I had almost given up, a letter came. 'Next of kin'. I had to go north, dispose of remains. I kept only his small photograph of the three of us, huddled on a windswept beach.

Hiroshi picks up the arrow and hands it back to me. At work,

Hiroshi never mentions archery, but defers readily to me on the thing where I have authority: the English text we are forging together. Here on the other hand, I am firmly his pupil, to be told and shown what to do. It is not my father who has authority in this place.

'Begin again. This time, less pressure in the right hand.'

*　*　*

Heart beating loud and fast, she sits up quickly in the grey light of dawn, already tensing to run. But it is only the lingering smell of the old housekeeper's paraffin lamp. A neatly folded square of clothing has been left by the side of her futon. In the dimness of the room she runs her fingers over a plain, strong weave. Not the miko's vestments. A samue, a monk's suit of working clothes.

Looking backwards, there is only darkness, fire and dreams. Looking forwards, there is only shadow. Only now, this moment and this and this. Only in this instant is there light. The grey light of dawn filtered to green by the mountain forest. The silver-grey timbers of the honden, the house of the god, its tall, forked gable catching the first ruddy light of the rising sun on its grey horns.

The housekeeper shows her how to fetch water from the well, how to wash down and sweep the porch of the haiden, the open-fronted hall where people come to stand and pray. After that, the courtyard must be swept and after that … a settled routine into which Mie slowly relaxes.

An odd flash of summer lightning, on a day of sunny skies. Nightmarish rumours. A new kind of burning that is also a plague. What took a whole night in her own city, repeated in a single instant. A few days after, a young boy is sent running from the village, arriving red in the face with effort and self-importance. The housekeeper hurries to fetch the priest. The Emperor has spoken. The voice of a kami. On the radio. Everyone must accept the unacceptable.

Later in the day, a delegation of elders arrives from the village. They go into conclave with the priest. The housekeeper anxiously hurries Mie into the miko's vestments. Mie assumes this is simply to maintain appearances, but then she finds herself called in to the meeting.

In the shadowy hall it is hard at first to see the old men, kneeling in dark kimonos on the worn matting. They are all looking at her. She makes a deep bow. She is asked to join them. She kneels. A formal request is put, relayed through the priest.

Will she consult the shrine's god, the village's tutelary kami and seek guidance?

Her parents had taken her to the usual seasonal festivities at shrine and temple. Her mother especially, had loved the forms of ritual, even if she disowned belief. It was she who had arranged the annual ceremony, here at the shrine in her ancestral village, to celebrate the founding of the city dojo. But in all other ways her parents had been thoroughgoing rationalists. Some of their friends might have been shocked to discover just how thorough.

In the same spirit, Mie has accepted gratefully this new place, this new way to be. Scrubbing and rinsing and sweeping away the terrors of the past, stilling her mind with daily work. *If the old woman keeps house for the priest, is it now my duty,* Mie had wondered, *to keep house for the kami?*

Standing alone now, on the bare wooden boards in front of the haiden. Boards scrubbed and rinsed by her own hands, just a few hours before. Her mind both filled and stilled by a kind of cold panic.

In the courtyard, some way behind her, the old men stand in two formal rows on the path of sharp, black volcanic gravel that imposes a slow and respectful approach to the sanctuary. They are waiting. Waiting for her to see into the future.

When she had been deemed old enough at twelve, to be given her first bow, Sensei had suggested a handgrip with a pattern of dragonflies on a dark purple ground. 'The tombo is a warrior,' he had said, 'always darting forward. When you are hesitant, think of the tombo and go forward.'

The thick white rope, so thick that two hands will barely circle it, hangs perpendicular before her. At its top, in the centre of the eaves of the haiden, a golden pellet bell, as big as a water-melon. The rope is mottled with mould and grey where years of supplicants have gripped it. She reaches up high, in a movement like that of uchiokoshi, raising the bow. Grasping it firmly, she gives a vigorous shake and the tarnished sanctuary bell shrills out its call. She lowers her arms and steps back. The two loud claps of her hands echo drily inside the haiden, where a few meagre offerings stand in front of the altar. The altar itself is almost bare but for the branches of ever-green sakaki tree, small offerings of salt and rice and the mirror, wrapped in its brocade.

She bows her head. As Sensei had taught, during that childhood that now seems so distant, she has emptied her mind. 'Like a mirror, not waiting, but ready'. Like an archer. 'Neither holding on, nor letting go'. It is all she knows how to do. Silence.

Things will get smaller. They will glitter. They will multiply. Ten thousand. Eight million. Uncountable myriads.

Another handclap. Like dew falling from the tip of the leaf. Action, without intention. A dragonfly, darting forward.

She turns to face the old men.

She closes her eyes.

The images, the dream, she cannot give them.

Only the hope.

'In time, there will be prosperity. In greater abundance than before.'

The first words she has spoken, since arriving here. The old men bow deeply in unison. She stands for a moment, looking at the tops of their heads in bewilderment, before hastily returning the gesture. Is it Mie, or the god, who has spoken?

Although, who exactly the kami is, is not altogether clear. Sometimes it seems to be the distant mountain behind the village fields. Sometimes, a person, resident in the shrine itself, who goes by several different names. In the worship hall, there is only the mirror on the altar, that might reflect the question back at her, if it were not, most of the time, wrapped in a brocade cloth so tarnished with age it is almost black.

When the old men have gone, she plucks up the courage to ask the priest about it. He seems to listen attentively, but only smiles. Is it that he pities her profound ignorance? Or has he simply not heard?

The first Autumn festival is a miserable affair. The harvest is bad. Everyone is depressed, exhausted and hungry. In the almost empty house at the far end of the village, a woman who lost her husband and all four sons to the war, is found dead. The pool of blood on the floor, smeared and diluted by rain dripping through the unrepaired roof.

That the gods are angry, seems the only possible conclusion. The elders take to meeting regularly at the shrine, although, to Mie's great relief, they make no further calls for divination. If times are bad, yet prosperity is to come, then it simply means, they reason, that there is work to be done.

* * *

I did once start driving lessons. At the end of the first one, the instructor said I needed to develop 'spatial awareness'. During the third one, he remarked that in some traffic situations, it could be helpful to establish eye contact with other road users. I pulled carefully to the side of the road, got out of the car, thanked him and walked away.

As a confirmed city dweller, I much preferred public transport anyway. Buses however, have their limits, and I was finding it quite tight to get home from work, change, eat and get all the way over to Hiroshi's warehouse on the other side of town in good time. He made no complaint about my frequent late arrivals, either overtly or in his manner, but I was sure it must be irritating him. He was always so damn professional at work.

It didn't come as a surprise therefore, when he obliquely raised the subject. We were having an after-lesson coffee in the warehouse office; Hiroshi had produced one of his small roll-ups and was enlivening the stale air with fresh fumes. I was asking him about one of the moves in the Hassetsu.

'How do you travel here?' Hiroshi enquired, ignoring my question. I told him. I looked at the time. I was alarmed to see that it was surprisingly late – already approaching last bus territory.

'I can give you a lift.'

I sensed a tilt of the head – amusement.

'Thanks,' I said, a little embarrassed, but relieved.

'I could pick you up on my way here also. It would be more… punctual.'

I blushed inwardly. This was definitely embarrassing.

Briskly sucking the last out of his roll-up, Hiroshi started to pull on an old waxed jacket – one that to my eyes looked rather heavy for the weather. I stepped outside to wait while he locked up and set the alarm. Looking around, I wondered what sort of a car someone like Hiroshi might drive. The only vehicle in sight was an old van with a flat tyre parked outside the opposite unit. I guessed he must have left his wheels out on the main road, under a streetlamp maybe, for better security. Satisfied that the alarm was set, he jingled his keys and beckoned me to follow him. I had already started to turn toward the road, when I realised he was gesturing the other way. I turned and peered into the shadows. I had seen the rusty old Italian scooter lurking in the corner of the loading dock before. I just hadn't connected it with Hiroshi.

Never before having entrusted myself to any form of transport having less than four good wheels, I felt a sudden twinge of apprehension. As a child I had been anxiously lectured by Mother on the appalling dangerousness of riding bicycles, while Father, with his usual lack of confidence in my physical abilities, had wanted to know what the hell had made her think I would be *able* to? As with most of my parents' rows, I had been confused by this. I hadn't even asked for a bike.

Trying to play it cool, I couldn't help reading a certain teasing amusement in Hiroshi's body language as he handed me a large white helmet.

'You have quite a big head,' he announced, factually. 'I brought this just in case.'

I pulled it onto my cranium. It felt like being swallowed by something. Something cold with breath that smelt of vinyl and someone else's aftershave. I fumbled for the strap and tried to buckle it. Seeing my difficulty, Hiroshi batted my fingers away and took over. It felt like having Mummy spit on a hankie and rub your face. Released, I looked apprehensively at the scooter. Hiroshi had already climbed on and was pushing it back off its stand. He fired up the engine and conversation immediately became unfeasible. There had to be a hole in the silencer, surely? The snarling, crackling thing was manoeuvred out onto the road. Hiroshi slapped the pillion seat invitingly. Awkwardly cocking my leg, I collapsed onto the throbbing tin beast. My head swung disconcertingly about with the extra weight of the helmet as I looked for something to hold onto. Next second,

Hiroshi had reached back, grabbed my wrists and firmly pulled my hands around the stiff, cool, waxed cotton that enclosed his torso. As we lurched off, I tried not to squeeze too hard. There didn't seem to be much of him.

The suddenly unruly mass of my being, swinging this way and that in the night, disconcerted me. I hung uncertainly on to Hiroshi's insubstantial waist, my thighs clamped in an aching death-grip on the seat, convinced at every bend in the road that I was going to fall off, dragging Hiroshi with me. By the time he finally brought his tinny contraption to a halt, I was feeling in danger of losing my grip on quite a lot of things. Quivering with relief, I clambered stiffly off and after a brief struggle, handed back the helmet. 'Thanks for the ride.' I said, without much real conviction. Hiroshi stowed the helmet away and rocketed off into the night. I stood for a moment, enjoying the unfamiliar sensation of sweat cooling on my scalp. My ears were burning from the friction of the helmet and ringing with Hiroshi's parting shout, yelled above the crackle of the exhaust:

'You should relax more!'

*   *   *

During the hard years of war, the liturgy of the shrine had become threadbare in its observances. Now, like a resuscitated heart, the pulse of ritual shudders back into life and begins to beat more steadily. The number and variety of rites is bewildering. Purifications, blessings small and large. The scattering of salt, the offering of fruits and of grains. The presentation of newborns and of children who have survived to the notable ages of three, five or seven.

One ceremony is absent from the March calendar: the housha, the annual thanksgiving for the city dojo Mother had so cherished. No-one had said anything on that final occasion, at least, not directly. The absence of Sensei, of her parents and her own dishevelled arrival had all made it painfully evident to everyone present that they were gathered for the last time and for what had become a remembrance of the dead. Curiously, it is Sensei she remembers and mourns most intensely, along with Mother. Father seems already a little distant, content to take his place among the ancestors.

The old men may not be asking her to consult the god, but the ordinary villagers, having heard of her performance, seek her out with a bewildering variety of questions and requests. She has taken to talking nightly to Sensei, at a little improvised shrine in her room. It is his teaching, she feels, that alone enables her to be, in this odd role, something just a little better than a fraud. When the questions come she empties her mind, as if preparing to shoot. Usually, a few ambiguous words of comfort and reassurance come to fill the space.

There are two or three local families that regularly attend the shrine and who form the core of support for its activities. Most of those who, with Mie's parents and their friends, used to drive out from the city every so often, no longer come. Instead, strangers begin to arrive. People whose great-grandfathers or grandmothers had once lived in the district, who come looking for some connection to the past that evades the dark shadows of war.

Some have no family connection with the place but had discovered it when travelling. Now they return in memory of a romantic moment of long ago, or simply to see if it was still as quiet and out of the way as they remembered it. Really, they all want to see if it has survived, but nobody says that.

And sometimes women come alone, or with children, to pray to a god who seems remote and safely distant from the city's taint of war. And sometimes couples, reunited after long years of separation, looking for somewhere peaceful to rest a moment and get to know one another once more. Often the men have injuries. Mostly, they are silent.

As the war fades and the Occupation becomes established, there are even occasional parties of Americans and a few other Westerners, coming up to take the air of the mountains in summer and to savour the atmosphere of past times.

But past times are gone, as the sparsely inhabited halls silently remind the old priest every day. As the shrine re-awakens, it is as if he is slowly falling asleep. Mie takes to shadowing him closely during ceremonies, ready to prompt when he forgets some word or action. One day, while blessing a new field-plot near the village, he stalls altogether, and Mie herself is forced to diffidently complete the rite. He is carried home on an improvised litter.

He recovers somewhat, but his movements become less, his daily walks across the courtyard slower. Sometimes she sees him stop and stand for minutes on end, staring at a branch in the sunshine, or some invisible insect on a post or fence-top. The housekeeper tuts and frets about him, but he is tranquil in his erratic wanderings. Occasionally, he disappears, but is usually to be found kneeling, reciting sutra in a deserted hall.

Mie speaks to the village council. It seems no replacement or assistant for him can be found. At least, not this year and perhaps not in the next. He will be cared for and the village will not let the central hall or the torii collapse from neglect, but, until better times come... All agree, the situation is serious.

That night, she finds herself walking back from the village, her path lit by the stars, the glow of the fireflies and the flicker of summer lightning dancing among the mountains. For the first time since… For the first time in a long while, she feels awake, fully present in the world. She is someone again. Someone even, with a certain importance. But nothing remains forever. If she stays here, catching the old man as he falls, the future will close around her like a shell.

She lies awake the most part of that short summer night, shocked by the return of an unfamiliar feeling – the will to act. As soon as it is light, she seeks out paper, brush, ink-stone and ink and, after several attempts, completes a polite, formal, old-fashioned letter.

She has the odd feeling, as she writes, of stepping into the life her parents have vacated. It is addressed to the high priest of a city shrine. An incongruous but regular fixture in her parents' intellectual and political salons. Always willing to pay close and intelligent attention to secular thought. Always immovably grounded in his own beliefs. He is someone who will perhaps understand her curious situation.

She posts it quickly, before she can regret her boldness. In the sag of fatigue that catches her in the middle of afternoon chores, she is convinced nothing will come of it.

Some days later, she meets the council chairman in the street. His manner towards her has changed markedly, hesitant respect now replaced by an insinuating condescension. But the news he delivers with such self-importance has already rendered him insignificant in Mie's life. She looks at her still faintly ink-stained fingers, disbelieving. With a few words, it seems, she has made the world move. A new assistant priest is coming from the capital. It has been, she thinks, almost three years since she turned twenty and was called into adulthood. Three years since that desperate flight from the city to the calm of this mountain sanctuary. There are young women here in the village already old enough to take her place. She is free to leave.

One day, in late summer, she squeezes into the back of a bulbous old black car. A family of visitors are returning to the city. She has negotiated a lift in return for a blessing, petrol money and a small gift of fresh vegetables. Tucked in with the family's children and some of the luggage, she feels like a child herself, being taken on a trip. The fine rattan-bound bow the priest put into her hands has been used only occasionally to send a demon-scaring arrow squealing aloft over the gable horns of the old sanctuary. More often it has merely been carried in formal procession, or plucked to evoke the evil-banishing sound of the bowstring. When she had announced her departure, in a rare moment of clarity the old priest had urged her to take it with her, assuming no doubt, that she was simply leaving to take up her duties at another shrine. 'A gift, from our god to theirs.' The thought had startled her, but she had also seen the sense in it. It could be a foothold, for starting a new life in the city.

Carefully wrapped in a long strip of oilcloth, the bow is tied to the roof with a lot of other baggage. She hopes it will not be bent out of shape by the journey. She hopes that like her, it will be able to stretch and expand and breathe again, once they reach their destination.

Her old bow is left in a corner of the shrine hall, together with five persimmons piled on a little red lacquer stand and a lock of her hair in a fold of paper, a gift of exchange with the kami, a plea that she might not be forgotten.

The car rolls off, slipping away into the high grasses and wild weeds that have invaded the field margins of late summer. The heavy sleep of afternoon rises out of the earth, flooding the sunlit spaces of the shrine and its grounds.

When she has gone, when the dust has settled back onto the road, when the sound of the engine is finally dissolved into the dense buzzing of the cicadas, the old priest turns away from the gate and walks slowly back across the courtyard. Later, he enters one of the cool, dark, empty halls and softly kneels on the patch of beaten earth where the gentle gaze of the Kannon once fell. Word perfect, yet almost inaudible, he begins to recite the Lotus Sutra. The night darkens around him.

The old woman goes into the village. Everyone wants to talk about the new young man coming from the city. In the evening she returns with rice and vegetables and draws water.

* * *

Once he had kicked and prodded me into and through the eight basic shapes, Hiroshi's teaching took on a gentler quality. Even so, if my concentration ever wavered, he was quick to notice and to deliver his usual dry rebuke:

'It is of no use only to come here. You must also *be* here.'

But the shapes are not mere poses, they are moments in a dance. Watching someone else dance is easy. One move flows from another and the eye follows. It all seems, to the optimistic beginner, if not exactly simple, at least somewhat obvious, logical even. But as soon as Hiroshi put me at the centre of the action, nothing seemed obvious or logical any more.

I don't remember precisely on which evening Hiroshi judged I was ready to be trusted with a real weapon. I do remember it was chilly as well as dark and full of wet leaves blown about by an increasingly gusty wind. The metal roof of the warehouse shivered and drummed and creaked, as if some irritable monster wanted to pull the lid off our little cave and see what business we were at inside. The two suspended lights swayed a little, making the shadows swim disconcertingly. Hiroshi picked out a bow from the rack and placed it into my hand.

While a bicycle inner tube can be a tough adversary, as my joints and muscles had discovered, it had not prepared me for the shock of my first encounter with a real bow.

My hand closes cautiously around the grip. More than seven feet long, its unfamiliar heft feels unwieldy after the stick bow. And then I touch the string. My fingers recoil. Implacable rigidity. The idea of disturbing, increasing, its already singing tension seems like dangerous folly. But already Hiroshi is making me reach up and up, following the Hassetsu drill. Legs in the 'A' shape, feet angled outward, arms reaching up around the invisible tree. How can I possibly pull bow and string apart at such an awkward angle? The first feeling of resistance almost makes me despair. How much force will it take to separate bow and string by the length of an arrow? These are serious, lethal powers.

Once more, I am regressing to childish distress, my father's scowling face, his eternal angry dissatisfaction with my physical inadequacies, haunt me as if he is in the room, watching. And yet, as a child, I had never seen him so much as attempt to lift a piece of furniture, or unscrew a stuck lid. He broke things more often than he mended them and not always through anger.

But my father is not here. It is Hiroshi who is standing in the shadows. Without judgement. Patiently holding a door open for me. If I don't go through, I am forever trapped in the past.

Sweat is prickling down my backbone. I can neither breathe in or out, my diaphragm paralysed. I have to do this. Hiroshi, with his slight frame can do this. I have to make the impossible thing happen too. I feel like my toes are on the edge of a precipice.

I resettle the grip of my left hand, flex and settle my thumb, hooked over the string. Softly, Hiroshi warns me not to release at any point. It begins. Bow and string move steadily apart, the burning tension increasing with equal steadiness in my up-stretched arms. I am so excited by this that I lose concentration and am forced to let bow and string push my hands back to the starting point. I lower the bow to ease my aching arms. I give an embarrassed little half grimace, half smile, trying to hold it together. Hiroshi says nothing.

I breathe, then start again. This time, I am reaching up to catch something fleeting. Something I had just begun to sense even in the moment of collapse. A point in the movement where the solid, dragging strain changes subtly. I am no longer drawing the bow by main strength. There is a leverage in the position of my arms. I can feel myself becoming part of this machine, part of the structure of forces in the moment I am creating. The charged moment of stillness at full draw. The moment before everything changes.

Following Hiroshi's instruction, I do not release the string, but gently raise my slightly shaky arms up again, returning the bow respectfully to its undrawn state, then lowering it. Under my clothes I am damp with sweat.

Afterwards, Hiroshi gives his verdict:

'You should do push-ups.'

*   *   *

One morning, not long after her arrival in the city, Mie is woken at dawn by the cries of a baby. In the silence that follows, she knows the meaning of this dream. Having salvaged herself from the wreckage of the past, it is time to go and see what else has survived. The child sent to stay with elderly relatives in the country, as the threats of war increased. It is time to go and find Younger Brother.

She writes. Apologies are offered for not having visited at an earlier date. She wonders privately if perhaps her mind has been affected somehow. Or was she always like this? Disconnected. At one remove from life. She remembers the baby brother teasing her for being 'stupid'. Suddenly, she longs to see him.

Leave is arranged. Tickets are bought. Travelling alone is still risky. A neighbour couple have a stall in one of the black market concessions that have sprung up around the station. Getting up several hours before dawn, she accompanies them on their early morning walk to work. Still far too early for the train, she spends an anxious hour hovering near the ticket office, trying to be invisible. On the train, she stays near the guard's compartment, even though it means she has to stand. She shuffles close to older couples, hoping to be seen as part of a family group. She does not look at the gangs of sullen, shabby looking men, even though she can feel their eyes on her.

The train threads south, missing fields and houses and bridges and trees by little more than an arrow's length, arriving almost empty at her chosen target, as dusk is falling. She steps carefully down onto the country platform and listens anxiously, as the clatter of the train fades away, to be swallowed by the rage of the cicadas.

A glow-worm light flickers and hovers under the trees behind the deserted station building. Someone walking towards her, wheeling a bicycle. She is shocked to hear a man's voice. The younger brother is much older than she remembers. His breath smells of tobacco.

Her first memory of him is the baby that cried in her dream.

She must have been quite young herself. Her last, is of a child, bundled in a padded kimono, crying on a station platform. It is a shock to meet this rising adolescent. After embarrassed greetings, they walk together in silence. Only the bicycle talks, ticking softly to itself, but its timid speech is defeated by the shouting insects.

The old people, distant country relatives, make a resentful kind of fuss of their city guest. Her small gifts are received with reluctant approval: 'Too generous!', 'Extravagant!' Mie is puzzled. Choosing them, she had followed her parents' sober tastes. They press food and drink on her while complaining at length of post-war shortages. She is made to feel thoroughly uncomfortable.

During her time at the village shrine, she had contrived to continue her mother's practice of sending small parcels of food and even sometimes, a little money. But then a stiffly worded letter of thanks had come, insisting that such generosity, though appreciated at the time, was really no longer necessary. She had felt a prickly, wounded pride emanating from the page and had closed the correspondence with a conciliatory note of apology. Now it seems, she confronts the same obscure resentment, no longer on the page, but in the flesh.

Younger Brother too, is openly sulky and unwelcoming. The old folks seem to think she has come to take him away to the big city. She would be alarmed at such responsibility, but Younger Brother angrily rejects any suggestion that he might be escorted to town by Big Sister. He has his own plans, he announces. A job, pre-arranged by Father, with a city merchant house. A girl he writes to in the suburbs. A month or so later and she would not have found him here, would not have had to make the journey south. Already it seems, this train has left. There is no way back.

In the morning, Younger Brother walks her back to the station. He seems more relaxed. 'Don't mind the old people', he says, 'they are upset because I'm leaving'. She wants to ask him how much he remembers of the old days, but she is afraid to intrude too far into a life that is his and no longer part of hers. Will she even see him again? The city is big, people become lost in it. But he hands her an address and a little map on a scrap of paper and solemnly writes down hers in his pocketbook. 'When the time comes, I will send you an invitation to the wedding. We would be honoured if you would attend.' Mie feels momentarily as if she is already on the train, the ground speeding away beneath her. So fast this life, so fast.

*　　*　　*

The night I was introduced to the glove, I remember as silent, still and deathly cold. Side by side, our breath fogging the chill air, we knelt on the matting Hiroshi had laid on the concrete warehouse floor. Practising the movements of shooting would have at least been some exercise, but instead I had to keep still and pay attention, as he inducted me into the essential mysteries of the yugake, the shooting glove.

Untying two bundles of silk cloth Hiroshi lays them flat in front of us, displaying the contents.

'Your hands are not too big. This will probably fit well enough.'

I examine mine. It looks rather worn. It makes me think of a surgical appliance designed for someone who has recently hit their thumb very hard with a big hammer. I surmise that repeatedly drawing and releasing the string without it, might have a similar effect.

'The thumb does not bend. It is made stiff, with leather or wood,' Hiroshi explains, picking up the glove in front of me. 'You see this groove on the inside of the thumb part? That is where the string is pulled.'

The light casts awkward shadows. I lean close to see, startled for a moment by the warmth of his cheek close to mine in the freezing air. He hands me the glove so I can get a proper look. It covers only the thumb and the first two fingers. It has a deep gauntlet with a long, inch-broad ribbon of leather trailing from it. Round the joint of the thumb, the suede leather seems grubby and stained. I start to gingerly slip my hand in, but Hiroshi stops me abruptly. Relieving me of the precious object, he lays it reverently back on the mat.

'No. First, you put on this. It is called shita-gake.'

Beside each glove, he spreads a scrap of delicate white cotton. Another three fingered glove, like a thin, ghostly version of the leather one. Following Hiroshi's lead, I slip my fingers and thumb in, laying the broad flap of cloth on the left over the palm.

'It protects the leather from the sweat of your hand.'

Only then do I get to put on the glove itself, Hiroshi showing me how to wind its long, soft leather strap around the wrist-gauntlet, before tucking the end up under itself in a tight loop to secure it. Are we now ready to shoot? Having learned my lesson, I wait patiently for the next instruction.

From a small, patterned cloth bag Hiroshi produces a thing like a tiny salt-shaker, from which he dispenses a little whitish powder onto the thumb of each glove. A faint scent appears and vanishes, as if the ghost of a pine tree has briefly appeared in the room. Copying Hiroshi's movements, I rub the thumb across the inside of the middle finger. As we work the rosin powder into the leather, the stillness is filled with odd little creaking noises: a pair of rheumatic crickets, chilled by the winter cold. Finally, my teacher produces another little salt shaker from which he dispenses a small amount of soft, fine grey powder into his left palm and mine. 'Ash' he explains, 'to stop the grip on the bow from becoming sweaty.'

Hiroshi stands up lightly, gracefully. I struggle to follow. If my knees are not already like the crickets', I feel sure a few more evenings like this will soon see to it. I didn't think it was possible to be any more chilled. Until Hiroshi spoke:

'Now we try with an arrow.'

'A single arrow.'

* * *

Time in the city seems to waver uncertainly. In places, a fresh spirit bustles amid new glass and paint. But walk only a little way, turn a corner and one is back in the city of grimed and shattered concrete, desperate makeshifts of tattered shacks and derelict plots worked as vegetable gardens. Hats tied down with scarves, bent-backed women chivvy the dark and sandy urban soil with hoes, the produce guarded by men who do not want to be seen.

The growing islands of bustle and glitter, are however, beginning to merge, wiping out old memories. But these little aftershocks recur, just as one begins to relax. As if time itself has become unstable, prone to tremors, each hour, each month, each year, a little uncertain of its place in the march.

For Mie, the bustle, the shine, although different in character from the old days, is reminiscent. A memory of a lost memory. A dream that recurs, even in waking hours, so that it seems like a memory. Tormenting, indistinct, unreasonable, ghostly.

The sense of awakening she had experienced in the mountains, that sense of being once more in the present, proves hard to retain. She tries to recapture it, immersing herself in the growing glitter of things. In the shopping streets, she finds herself drawn to displays of clocks and watches, seeking reassurance in their unanimity. On days off, she walks in the park, watching the families enjoying the cooler weather of autumn. *I am like a drifting leaf,* she thinks, *no longer connected to past, present or future.*

The city shrine is not large, but it has pleasant grounds, a refuge from the busy street. It is not old-established, two hundred years at most. Newly rebuilding after the war, it begins to look almost as brash and shiny as a department store. It even has a gift shop on the street frontage. The High Priest who had known her parents, the man she had written to from the village, had been glad to take her on as a miko. 'At last, someone who knows at least half the rituals and has some practical experience!' Youngsters, he had grumbled, were not interested these days and those few who were did not have a family history of such service and the knowledge that comes with it.

Mie continues to find her situation a little ironic. Although lovers of history and ritual, her parents had been thorough-going atheists. Now here she is, a professional religious figure of sorts. But at least she is no longer unique, being only the most senior miko among several. Most are students at the nearby university, supplementing their incomes. She is the reverse of them and goes seeking work in addition to her shrine duties. She finds a part-time job in a department store. It involves wearing smart but sober clothes and smiling gently but firmly all the time. It is rather like being a miko. After a few months, she is promoted from door-greeter to the ladies lingerie counter, where, as the male manager rather bluntly puts it, she will not be so young-looking as to frighten off the older ladies seeking advice.

Instead of going to the park on her days off, she walks the busiest streets, staring at new things, new images, new words, new symbols. And none of these things smell of ash or smoke. Even the truck exhaust has a different perfume. The fire and smoke has also begun to fade from the railway line by the river.

War seems like a half-forgotten nightmare. On the street, everyone is busy now in the light of day. No one wants to admit or remember how they so recently cried in the dark. No one wants to relate the bad dreams they had. No one wants to admit that they even had any. Everyone wants to wake up smiling and shiny-faced.

'O-genkidesuka?'

'Hai! Genkidesu!'

Everyone is OK. But in the bookshops are the memoirs of the living and the dead, to be read in darkness.

*   *   *

The arrow is laid across Hiroshi's upturned palms at chest height, like an offering. It is made of dark bamboo, the fletchings worn and bristly.

Trying to remain, outwardly, as calm as possible, I take it in my gloved hand and move to the beginning position. Hiroshi, I note, is being careful to stand well behind me. Steadying my misty breath, I try to relax my chilled muscles to stop the shivering and begin the slow dance of the Hassetsu.

Lay the foundation with the Ashibumi stance. Raise the bow slowly to the vertical. Reach around to place the arrow on the far side of the bow. I am still slow and clumsy, but the sequence is already familiar. With the arrow held in place by the left hand, bring the bow down to the resting position, lower tip just touching the inside of the left knee, upper tip, angled outwards away from the archer, the arrow horizontal across the body. More and more I am beginning to feel how these mechanical alignments build a new awareness of the space around me and my relationship to it. A space where I am no longer a hunted intruder, constantly wary of surprise.

Adjust the left-hand grip. Turn the head to look toward the target. Raise bow and arrow high into the air, pause for a heartbeat, then begin the draw, keeping the arrow level as it sinks down and down, until the moment of maximum tension is reached.

Something must have gone very wrong, because the next second the air is full of whirring, followed by a dull thump, a clatter and silence. The bow shudders angrily in my hand. One third of the arrow is stuck at a very oblique angle into the wood at the upper edge of the target board. The splintered remainder is embedded in one of Hiroshi's boxes of stock. With a thoughtful air, he produces a thick marker pen and carefully writes 'Damaged' on the carton. The inky felt rasps on the cardboard like a cat's tongue. I bring my arms and the bow, back to the starting position and wait for the axe of criticism to fall.

Hiroshi silently hands me a second arrow then resumes his

former position. With some effort at self control, I begin the steps again, settling finally into full draw, every sinew quivering with the tension of the powerful bow.

'Stop! Hold.'

He steps forward.

'Hold the shot. Do not release.'

I wonder how long I can hang on.

'Observe.' He is lightly grasping my now trembling left wrist between finger and thumb. 'You see how the wrist is angled?'

The touch of his fingers seems to make the tremor worse.

'That means it is not stable. To hold that position, you are having to fight against the bow. Straighten your wrist – so. Now, relax your hand a little. Keep your arm straight, let the weight of the bow settle onto it.'

My left arm slowly ceases to shake. The resistance of the bow is as hard as before, but now it is a stable pressure.

'The bones of the arm and wrist are like a pile of stones. If the pile is straight and well built, it will support the weight easily. If it tilts even a little to one side, it is likely to collapse.'

Hiroshi steps back.

'Do not release this shot. Relax and begin again.'

I do not remember the eventual release. I remember only 'before' and 'after'. Standing in that 'after', the arrow embedded square and deep in the target board, the bow still singing in my hand, I knew that Hiroshi had led me through another gateway. A gateway that from now on, I would be forever passing through, but through which I could never go back.

*   *   *

Sometimes, an old acquaintance of her father's, a rare survivor of his circle, emerges from the background and takes her to drink tea.

He is talking about a time that seems to her like a place on the other side of the sky. Heard of, but unimaginably far away. To think she once lived there is disorientating.

The city seems increasingly to deny that such a world ever existed. The glittering shopfronts are like a wall, a dam of clean white concrete and shiny glass, behind which the weight of dark water presses and presses invisibly. The ever-increasing bustle of the shops and the gleam of their merchandise, like the height and curve of that dam, mute testimony to the pressure it is holding back in the darkness behind.

He makes it seem like a tea-ceremony, though it is not. He has taken her once more to the little tea-shop in a quiet street not far from the shrine. It has a feeling of the old days about it, although whether it escaped the burning, or has simply been artfully created to seem that way, she cannot tell. Whatever the case, it feels old. It feels even more that way when the kimono-wrapped waitress, seeing the old man, makes a deep bow and ushers them into a cool, six-mat room, the wood and mulberry paper shoji screen slid back in one corner, to reveal a tiny garden.

He is a square man in an autumn-coloured kimono, embroidered in the correct places with five tiny mon of a very ancient family. She scarcely remembers his visits to her father's house, but has a strong memory of a mood, an impression of a child's sympathetic emotion – her father's dislike of this person. Once, his formal kimono would have seemed old-fashioned, but unremarkable. Now it seems, for all its sobriety, a little flamboyant, as if he were on his way to a festival, or as if an actor had wandered out of the theatre into everyday life, still in character.

'A very interesting person. I hope it does not distress you to talk of him? One of the few comforts of an old man, to remember the past. Forgive me.'

He shows no sign of being likely to give way to any objection she might make. He offers her no opening, no glimpse of sky through the wall of his talk. But there is a special atmosphere this time, it is less casual, more formal. She even wonders, with a sudden shiver, if he is going to propose marriage.

'Yes, we all enjoyed those afternoons at your father's house. So many interesting people. So sad to think how few of us are left. But we must carry on, of course.'

He blesses her with a smile of such self-satisfaction that her guts shrivel within her. For a wild moment she considers rising and leaving the room without a word. As he talks, the thought lengthens in her mind, and she wonders in some astonishment why she does not act on it. She does not belong to his world any more. Holds no claims on it, feels no obligations to it. She is not even sure that he and she exist in the same space. It is quite possible, she feels, that if they were to extend hands to touch, they would pass through one another like spectres.

'… shall we say, injudicious. But of course when one moves in political and diplomatic circles, one cannot always be overly strict about whom one admits into one's confidence, otherwise there would be no way to…' he hesitates a half-breath, '… gain a sense of what others are thinking.'

She stares blankly at him, expressing interest only through the slight angle of her upper body. The tea-bowl smokes by her hand, unheeded.

'Those of us – a few still remain and we are joined daily by younger men and women who agree with us, that things have taken an… unfortunate, direction, yes, that's it, an unfortunate, an inauspicious direction. Those of us who feel that way, would like to know, if you feel, as we do, that…'

Suddenly she is concentrating like a cat on a mouse. She did not understand the code-words at the time, but she remembers clearly this timbre, this cadence, the tune of this talk and of how her mild-mannered father would stride out of the room when the last of such guests had gone, closing the door with a quietness that spoke eloquently of deep anger.

'… I know your father never expressed any open support for our way of thinking, that was not his style, no, but I feel that, removed from some of the more, unfortunate, shall we say, influences he was … obliged … to ah, admit to his circle, he would have found sympathy with our views, as an expression of his very profound feelings for his country, which I know were always uppermost in his mind and so, I dared to think that his daughter might feel it appropriate to, in some way, represent her father's memory − as a friend to some of those who once gathered under his roof?'

She cannot answer. She can only ask herself repeatedly, as if it might somehow make things clear: *Which of the two of us is dead?*

She is aware that the silence has elongated uncomfortably − beyond all limits of rudeness in fact. He purses his lips and grunts. A hard little smile of indulgence settles on his face.

'Well, I am sure it is difficult even now. Such sad experiences. It does not matter. Perhaps when you feel more ready, more, able to speak of these things.'

He claps his hands twice. The waitress, who has been kneeling, waiting in the corridor, slides aside the shoji. Shuffling forward into the room with a bow, she places a small cloth-wrapped package next to the old man. He waves her away with a grunt and she withdraws. The shoji snicks shut, sealing Mie once more into his impossible box of obligations. He places the gift − she knows with a sinking heart that it is a gift − graciously between them, a little to one side. And sits back, smiling.

The smile stiffens on his face, as she slowly rises without touching the wrapping. She does not even bow. It is insupportable. She looks steadily down at the man, whose face has become confused. Her own voice startles her with its strength and conviction.

'I am afraid you no longer exist!'

Quickly, before her legs can give way, she strides to the screen and opens it herself. The waitress starts up anxiously, glancing past her to where the old man kneels immobile, next to his unopened gift.

Mie never sees him again. She knows that what she has done is irrevocable. For him, she no longer exists.

* * *

When we finally emerged into the night, a nimbus of freezing fog was glowing around the streetlights, and there was a sinister glitter of frost on the ground. Looking at Hiroshi's scooter I was seized with anxiety, although not for myself. The night of my first pillion ride, I had vowed would also be my last. That same evening I had made arrangements with a cab company for a regular two-way pick-up. I wanted no more shuddering, lurching intimacy with that rowdy clockwork toy. I had worried that Hiroshi might be offended, but he seemed to accept it without comment.

He must have shared my anxiety that night, because he readily accepted my invitation to share the taxi. We slumped into the back of the overheated car, condensation forming on our chilly clothes. Inside, I was still glowing with the excitement of my first real shots. Now I had really begun to understand what this thing was about, I was feeling more grateful than ever to Hiroshi.

As the driver eased the car cautiously out onto the main road, I decided to broach a delicate subject.

'Something I've been meaning to ask…'

If Hiroshi grunted in response, it was lost in the background rumble of the car. For a few sweaty seconds, I marinaded in my own embarrassment.

'I mean, even without the tuition, you probably had to spend quite a bit of money on equipment and stuff. Shouldn't I be paying you something for these lessons?'

This time his response was more eloquent. I could tell he had grunted because he shrugged as well.

'Actually, it is not considered appropriate for a teacher to ask for payment. But it is traditional that the pupil should give the teacher a small weekly fee, as a sign of their relationship, their agreement. Say, one pound for each lesson.'

'That's not much!'

'It is only a symbolic amount. And I do not need you to do that. But, pupils are expected to help with expenses when they arise. I will ask if I need help.'

'Oh. OK. Sure. Yes, do. I'll be happy to contribute.'

He nodded solemnly. The city lights were thickening and brightening around us as we approached the centre. Time was short.

'I hope you don't mind me asking another question, but... am I your only pupil? It's not about the money, I mean...'

Damn. I hadn't meant to say that.

'What I mean is, do you teach other people on other nights?'

'No.'

'Oh! ... Just me?'

'Yes.'

'Are you thinking of ... expanding?'

'No.'

'Oh. Right.'

After I got out of the taxi, leaving him to continue to his destination, I added a long misty breath to the already foggy air. *I should relax more.* I told myself. And perhaps not be so shy about asking questions. About the aunt, even.

'Damn.' I said, louder than I meant to. It was embarrassing. Hiroshi had evidently gone to some lengths to create a set-up where he could teach me, but only me, archery and for no particular reward. It was a really nice gesture and one I was coming to appreciate more and more, but...

'Why?'

We had been taking a break between shots one evening, kneeling side by side on the matting. He was silent for a moment, considering my question. At least that is what I hoped he was doing. Just as I had decided he was choosing to ignore me, he extended a hand toward the arcane paraphernalia arranged beneath his improvised lights.

'You need this.'

He spoke with the flat finality of a doctor whose prescription has been challenged by an uppity patient. I was, I confess, a little shocked at the truth, the insight of it.

'*I* need this!'

There was an edge of emotion in his voice that startled me. Then he let out a long breath that was not quite a sigh, as if deliberately relaxing.

'We all ... *need* ... this.'

* * *

Mr Yanaga is a very dry young lawyer, anxiously standing on his dignity, but prone to occasional outbursts of enthusiasm that entirely undermine it.

'The house of course, is a mere ruin. But the site! A most desirable location! The house is nothing, an expense in fact, for whoever pays to have it pulled down, but the site! The area! Most desirable! I imagine a considerable sum is realisable if placed in the right quarters!'

She looks at the reflection of the office lightbulbs in his glasses. They give him crazy alternative eyeballs. She cannot quite suppress a smile.

'Most beautiful!' he says, before trailing off into embarrassed silence as, for a moment, his eyes seem to accidentally become locked on hers. He flushes, conscious that he has somehow strayed from the path. He clears his throat and smooths down the front of his suit jacket.

'Let me explain', he says, in a soberer tone, sitting down at the desk and reaching for a pencil and paper. She relaxes and leans forward a little. It is pleasant to have things explained. Or rather, the process is pleasant. Usually, when people explain things carefully, she remembers little, so pleased is she by the act of listening. Already she is conscious of nothing but his energetic, attentive voice. It is good to be talked to in this way. Whatever he is explaining, she will have to come to her own effortful understanding of it later. For now, she relaxes into his attention like a hot bath. In the middle of this pleasure, it occurs to her how lonely she must be, to feel like this.

Going home, she sits down with the papers and, putting Mr Yanaga firmly out of her mind, studies the facts. There could indeed it seems, be a good sum of money. Enough perhaps, even to live on if invested wisely. Or she could borrow and rebuild the house herself. As the oldest of the family, it has come to her. She consults Younger Brother. His career is developing rapidly, he says and he has no desire to add another weighty responsibility to his existing portfolio. Older Sister, he is sure, will handle things wisely. Something in his tone makes her wonder if she herself is the responsibility he is glad to lose.

Before she left, Mr Yanaga had apologetically detained her at the entrance to the lift. 'As you know, this firm has been your family's legal advisors since your grandfather's time.'

He seems to swallow after every other word.

'Old Mr Shimoura, the late senior principal, was ... before the war ... a regular guest at your father's house ... at his ... ah ... political gatherings.'

Is this young man another of that group of people Father used to so detest? He continues, eagerly, confidentially, but with a certain shyness that is making his high forehead glisten.

'I, ah, am afraid I took the unpardonable liberty of studying Mr Shimoura's correspondence with your father, when we were organising his affairs – Mr Shimoura's affairs that is – after he departed. You see, I was, am, rather an admirer of your father's work. A progressive social reformer who held to his principles in a most difficult time. In fact is it not true that, as a student, he had been acquainted with no less a person than...'

This is not the comfortable warm bath kind of attention. It is more like standing in a cold shower of gusty rain. For one thing, people keep coming in and out of the lift, forcing them to shuffle to one side in the narrow corridor. Mr Yanaga stands too close, clutching a manila folder of papers to his chest. His knuckles are white with tension.

'... no less a person than Fukuzawa Yukichi, the great social philosopher? In fact, it was Old Mr Shimoura who quietly encouraged many of us younger ones to read Fukuzawa and I was most interested to discover, in Mr Shimoura's letters, how your father had carried forward many of those ideas, in spite of the climate of opinion at the time...'

'Mr Yanaga!'

She interrupts him.

'I am very sorry!'

'Please forgive me Mr Yanaga, but this is obviously a complicated matter and the business of the property is already going to take a good deal of thinking about. I am sorry to cut you short and please don't think that I am not interested. In fact, would you please write to me about it? Then I can study what you say carefully and at leisure.'

'Oh. Oh. Ah! Certainly, erm … to your home address?'

'No. Forgive me, but if you would be so kind, keep the envelope here for me. You can give it to me when I come next time. Or the time after.'

He bows. 'Certainly, certainly.'

She returns his politeness and just then, to her immense relief, the lift bell sounds. A second or two later, the doors open, she slips inside with another small bow and escapes.

The lift sinks down, carried on her long sigh. Why does this past, this world on the other side of the sky, keep trying to connect with her? She is nothing, no one, a leaf swept down the raging river of time. The tree she once belonged to, long fallen.

The doors open onto the busy foyer. She hurries out into the light of street-level day. Does she perhaps still have a right, she wonders, to lift her head, to feel the sun's warmth on her face? To be seen, recognised, reflected, in another person's eyes? Does she have the right to dare?

* * *

Hiroshi's talk of needs, whatever he meant by it, soon took a rather more practical – and expensive – turn.

'You need to think about getting your own equipment.'

I was momentarily proud. Evidently, I had passed some kind of threshold, making it worth investing in my future as an archer. Just how big an investment quickly became apparent.

'Put your hand on the paper, please. Flat. Spread fingers. Keep still.'

Hiroshi has spread a blank piece of paper on the warehouse office desk. A ballpoint pen tickles its way round my palm, fingers and thumb, as he draws a careful outline on the paper.

'Good. How much money do you have?'

'Eh?'

'This is going to cost maybe seven hundred, maybe eight hundred pounds. It depends a little on the exchange rate. Is that going to be a problem?'

I was somewhat staggered, but had to admit that, no, happily, it would not be an actual problem. Other than that of wincing when looking at the next bank statement.

'Good. This way!'

I follow him out into the warehouse. Instead of walking into the centre where the archery equipment is set up, he beckons me over into the shadows.

'Stand, please. Here.'

With a hand in the middle of my chest he pushes me firmly back against a section of plywood wall.

'OK, please hold your left arm horizontal. Stretch fingers out.'

I obediently do as I am told. Suddenly there is the dry catch in my throat of his tobacco breath and lemon scented cologne, the warmth of his cheek, inches from mine. I turn my head leftward as if looking at a target. The tape measure whistles out and I feel the firm pressure of his thumb holding it against my breastbone. Seconds later its cold steel edges brush my fingertips, before it slithers to the floor. Muttering to himself, he scribbles in his pocketbook.

'Stand straight, please.'

The thought that he might want an inside leg measurement makes me oddly flustered, but instead Hiroshi feels for my hipbone. The tape-measure hisses down to the floor, then, after a few seconds of muttering, snaps back. A quick embrace for a waist measurement comes next, before I am firmly pushed back again and told to 'Stand up straight, heels against the wall.'

It feels like I am back at school, having a medical inspection. The pencil presses briefly on the top of my head, before he ducks down to take the length of my foot from heel to toe. Standing, he motions me aside and measures off my height against the mark on the wall.

I glance down at the scribbled dimensions in his notebook. The vital statistics of an archer. Me. Hiroshi is studying the numbers, tapping his lips thoughtfully with the pencil.

'You have quite big feet, even for a westerner.'

* * *

Mr Yanaga's letter, when it comes, is very long and very dry. He admires her father. He admires Fukuzawa the reformer. He admires, she senses, with growing embarrassment, Mie. It can only be, she is sure, because of her connection with her admired parent, beside whom she feels such an empty vessel. Mr Yanaga believes in social reform, in democratic values, in the need for independent, rational, critical thinking. He believes in the rights of women, in education and in plenty of other things too.

In fact, three meetings go by with profuse and embarrassed apologies, until one day, solicitously escorting her from the office, he reverently and shyly places the large, thick, legal envelope in her hands, as they pause outside the lift. She bows, receiving it with simple thanks. He is, she notes with distaste, quivering with excitement.

It proves to be more an academic paper than any normal kind of letter. It is well-drafted, the writing driven forward by Mr Yanaga's enthusiasms, but restrained by his lawyer's concern for clarity of expression. Reading it has been salutary. It is astonishing to think that she lived and grew up in the same house as the man he writes about.

She winces sometimes, at the theories Mr Yanaga crisply summarises. As war beat and hammered its way closer and closer to home, they would have been hot irons to handle. As an adolescent, she had found both her parents hard to read. Somehow they had become, as time went by, colder and more distant. Only natural perhaps, but, she thinks guiltily, if she had paid more attention, might she have understood them better?

Perhaps they had done well, to keep her out of the forge. Things had evidently been dangerous enough without giving hostages to fortune, and children do tend to echo the opinions of their parents. Even as a single woman, spending too much time watching families in the park, she has noticed that.

Uneasy, those last years of war. After some unpleasant incidents, Father had taken the drastic step of removing her from high school and arranging a private tutor. Rejected by her peers, she had been grateful for the more relaxed community of the dojo where all sorts were welcomed, united in the discipline of practice. Archery practice for Mie had been Mother's idea. As a daughter of an old samurai family, she had received training as a girl and still liked to boast of her skill. 'Nothing more embarrassing than daughters who can't shoot straight,' Father had quipped. Mother had given him a shrewd look.

Only a short tram ride from a stop near her suburban home, the dojo, although in a relatively humble area of the city, had been an island of happy calm throughout her childhood. Among her friends and in familiar surroundings, it remained a refuge, where she could forget a little, the anxieties and privations of war. To excuse her increasingly frequent presence, Mie had found ways to be useful, keeping the place clean, learning to mend equipment, even helping a little with the accounts. The pages of the old ledger revealed that the dojo's assets had never been large. Apart from premises and equipment, the greatest current holding appeared to be a few bags of rice.

The dojo she knows, is family. Her mother's name appears on the founder's roll, the date of the inaugural ceremony, Mie's own birthday. In the early years, it had been surprisingly busy, considering how unfashionable archery had become. Latterly, running her ruler down the membership list, only the old and the young appear marked as active.

Quite a lot of the young seem barely of an age to handle even the smallest bow. One afternoon she had entered the dojo to find the little ones all sitting at Sensei's feet, listening to him tell the Story of the Ox. Arrested by the familiar words, the timbre of his voice, she had felt something inside her stir, like a child turning over in sleep.

After Older Brother was declared missing in action, there had been a change in atmosphere, both at home and in the dojo. The loss, so sudden, so unexplained, was hard to understand. He had been an admired guide, an example to follow. Always a little formal with her, but never unkind. It felt like a corner of the house of her being had been knocked away. Suddenly, everything else felt less secure. She became reluctant to linger at the dojo, where he also used to attend. There were rumours of things heard and seen there. Unpleasant images had taken root in her mind. Her brother, lost in some wilderness. Angry and unconsoled.

She pulls herself back into the present. Folds Mr Yanaga's letter and pushes it back into the brown legal envelope. Folding memory away, out of sight.

* * *

Continuing lessons after the arrow incident had been a relatively easy decision. Going back to the bowling green was more difficult. Hiroshi noticed my progress had slowed and asked me if I was keeping up practice. I made some excuse about the weather. His response made me blink.

'You will never hit the target if you allow yourself to be so easily discouraged.'

He was right of course. I needed somewhere to practise, optical illusions or no, so I headed back there the following weekend. Nothing strange happened, but just in case, I avoided late evenings. Daylight was less private, but on the odd occasion when someone did wander in, I would make it a test of my ability to stay focused and concentrate. Eventually, I became fairly relaxed about such intrusions. Most of the time, long before I had finished, I would find myself once more alone, barely aware that anyone had been present.

After a while however, I began to wonder if this was altogether reassuring. Daytime practice had restored my confidence so, as the days got shorter, I didn't worry at first about the failing light. But one gloomy evening, just as I was reaching full draw, the moment of most intense concentration, someone dressed in dark clothing entered the bowling green, crossed over behind me and stood, just on the edge of sight to my left, apparently watching.

I remained focused, 'released' the imaginary shot and made the concluding bow. Then I turned to see who was watching me with such still and silent intensity. Only bushes and the low boundary wall returned my gaze. I turned round to look behind me. Walked to the entrance and peered out. Looked up the steps to my left. Stared hard at a few suspicious trees and shrubs. Nothing.

I picked up my things and went home, annoyed, disturbed and somewhat embarrassed. Over the weekend, I sat at home, brooding. I had convinced myself that the arrow thing had been a minor aberration caused by overwork, stress and the excitement of finding, at last, a new path in life. But did concentrating on an imaginary target, with such focused attention, trigger a state of mind in which my subconscious over-interpreted things on the edge of vision? And yet I had been sure that someone had entered and stood in the shadows, watching.

I found myself thinking again of Hiroshi's 'pile of stones'. Was the little tower of my sanity not built quite straight?

*　　*　　*

The western-style dining room has dark, high-backed chairs. A group of older men and some of their wives are being entertained by Mother and Father. In the absence of Older Brother, she has been asked to join them, as the eldest child. She has spent the evening squirming under the gaze and the arch compliments, of the senior member of the group, a politician, whose flabby cheeks echo the width of his suit jacket breasts. Almost the only reason she remains in the room is her sense of obligation to her parents. In the fixed expression on Mother's face and the silent disapproval radiated by Father, she is beginning for the first time to sense the existence of the bubble that has surrounded her – and its fragility.

It is a new experience to join one of her parent's dinner parties. Indeed, they have become increasingly rare events. The meal is quite frugal and plain, enlivened only by a few fresh delicacies from the garden and other things bartered for in out of the way corners of the city. A few anxiously hoarded bottles of sake have emerged from their hiding place. Everyone is making a great effort at normality. Mie has been made to scrape up her hair and tie on a kimono with a brocade obi of Mother's.

This finery is in honour of the presence of someone very different from the politician. Quiet, in his late fifties, with short, iron-grey hair, the man Mother had sought out to be her archery teacher dominates the table by the force of a kind of modest dignity. He has come here, as he comes every year, to plan the annual ceremony of commemoration for the founding of the dojo. It will take place in the Shinto shrine in Mother's home village, and the travel arrangements are difficult enough in peacetime.

Mie is always intrigued to see him outside the dojo, outside his professional role. She is, as always in his presence, calmed and somehow encouraged by his ability to be unreadable without ever seeming unfriendly, but at the same time she is always a little curious about him.

Her covert study of Sensei from beneath lowered eyelashes

is rudely interrupted by the politician. He is gesturing with blunt fingers at Father.

'You sail damn close to the wind you know. Damn close! Man like you with sons and a young daughter, hm, ought to be more careful, ne?'

There is a silence so unpleasant, it is like swallowing stones. The other guests examine their plates. The politician does not appear to notice. Instead he is, rather unsteadily, but determinedly, warming to his theme:

'And as for this rogue here...'

He turns ponderously to Sensei, who is seated next to him across a corner of the table and prods him with dirty chopsticks that leave a grease mark on the silk of Sensei's kimono.

'... He's another of you sly foxes! Another of your weasilly crowd! I don't doubt he harbours the same kind of poisonous notions as the rest of your set!'

Father breaks in coldly.

'Sensei concerns himself, as a good teacher should, with his art.'

'Hah! That's a good one!' The politician roars, motioning blurrily for a refill of his sake-cup.

'Fat lot of good you'd be on the front line with a bow and arrow, you old fraud!'

Another prod of the chopsticks, which Sensei receives as indifferently as if he had been a bronze figure.

'And he does so,' Father continues, coldly and quietly, 'under the constant gaze of our Emperor...'

'Eh?'

'... whose photographic portrait holds the most honoured position in his shooting hall.'

'Whaat? Well, just as it should be! I should think so!'

The politician finally returns his chopsticks to their intended use and rummages around on his plate, muttering.

'Sly lot of foxes!'

Mie is a little surprised at Father's cold but emphatic defence of her teacher. Father has rarely spoken of him before and when he did, Mie had always sensed something sardonic in his tone. Sensei himself remains dignified, silent. And then catching her gaze upon him, suddenly gives Mie a little nod of solidarity.

Everyone relaxes, just a fraction, as the politician devotes himself to his food. But then he erupts again. Vaguely threatening both the grease-spotted kimono and his own suit with a piece of eggplant dipped in sauce, he roars:

'In fact, you would do better to turn that place of yours into a range for training machine gunners! You could actually do that since my chaps rebuilt your target shelter in solid brick for you!'

The meal concluded, the politician is getting seriously drunk. People begin to slip quietly away, embarrassed, or perhaps afraid, whispering apologetic sympathies to Mother as they depart.

'Hah! Running away are you?' He shouts at the departing guests, 'Just as things are warming up!'

He turns back to Sensei. 'At least you're enough of a soldier to stand your ground!'

'I am indeed Sir, most grateful for the assistance you were able to help us get from the Ministry for reinforcing the river bank. It has enabled us to continue upholding the spirit of the bow.'

Sensei's voice is level, his tone properly respectful, but firm.

'It was of course, inspected by the Butokukai, as a possible venue for military training. They told me it was too small for their needs.

'Hm. All very well. So-called martial training you were giving out to our young men for years. Well, they're all lying dead in trenches and jungles, aren't they?'

For a long moment, no one breathes. Father is pale and rigid. Mother's face, set hard. News of Older Brother had not been heard for many weeks, before the long-feared letter arrived. Since then, they have all tried not to dwell on what those weeks might have contained.

'So what are you doing now? Teaching little girls to shoot?'

Mie flinches as the chopsticks momentarily flick in her direction.

'What patriotic woman has time for that any more? Planning to send them into the front line are you? Machine gunners is what we need just now! Artillerymen! Not pretty archers!'

Father turns to Sensei, bows and says, very crisply and deliberately: 'I am sorry Sir, that you should be subjected to such remarks at my table.'

It is a grave insult to the politician. A dangerous man, as Mie even then, senses. His eyebrows shoot up. There is a sharp intake of breath from one of the remaining guests. The politician sweeps a gaze full of storm-clouds around the table. It is met by faces closed, tense, obdurately impassive.

'Heeeeei! Now then!'

He sways in his seat, reaching out a heavy, imprecise hand, that ruffles the neat silver-grey hair of the archery teacher. His own hair is glossy with oil and artificially black.

'Let's not fall out with each other!'

His thick arm slides round the unfortunate teacher's shoulders and he leans back towards Father, dragging Sensei with him.

'You're decent enough, you lot! I know you mean no real harm! You've done some excellent work for the widows and orphans ... But ... You ... Should ... Just ... Be ...More ... *Careful*. Don't let your, your, *mouths* run away with you!'

He releases the near neck-lock he has on Sensei at last and slumps in his chair, head drooping.

'Marvellous meal, Mrs...'

He begins to slide from his chair. Sensei gently arrests his fall and guides him softly to the floor. Mother, Father and Sensei all stand and briefly nod at one another. They gather round the politician, lift his considerable carcass and gently deposit him on a mat at the far side of the room. Mother looks down at him and wrinkles her nose.

*   *   *

The industrial unit was dark, except for the pool of light in front of the target board. The high metal roof sang with the soft roar of spring rain. We shot almost in silence, Hiroshi communicating only with a touch on the elbow here, or a gesture of the arm there. Afterwards, we sat in the office drinking black coffee out of mugs with medical company logos on them. The small and dirty window was rapidly dimming as the evening dusk gathered. The only other light came from a tiny lamp on Hiroshi's desk and the glowing end of a cheroot which he had lit up. I was surprised. I had never seen him smoke one of those before. There was a long silence while the rain came down outside and the steam and smoke rose up to the shadows.

'What's wrong?'

'How do you mean?'

Hiroshi took out his cheroot and stared appraisingly at the smouldering end.

'You are shooting more strongly now, but you have become more tense. Is something distracting you?'

Was it really that obvious? I had not been conscious of it, but he was right. I laughed sourly.

'I've been having a few problems.'

'Anything … in particular?'

It seemed an oddly personal inquiry, for Hiroshi.

'Well, with practice in the bowling green.'

'Ah!' he said.

I had taken the easy way out, all those months ago, keeping quiet about the arrow. I could not forget it, but I had pushed it to the back of my mind. Now, the phantom observers had brought it all back. I wanted to confide, to confess. To receive reassurance. Absolution even. But if I told him about the one, would I not have to confess my concealment of the other? As usual I tried to wriggle out by making light of things.

'Well, I suppose I get self-conscious in there sometimes. I start to think I'm being watched. I get nervous. Maybe it's affecting my shooting.'

Hiroshi drew on his cheroot and blew a smoke-ring at the ceiling.

'If you do something entertaining,' he said slowly, 'a performance, in fact … is it surprising to you that an audience gathers?'

'Erm…'

'Kyudo is not really a sport. Ceremonial archery was traditionally done to please the gods, or the ancestors. That is why we study hard. If you have an audience like that, you naturally try to do the best you can.'

His tone was teasing, ironic. I might have said more, but I was finding the joke, if joke it was, an uncomfortable one. As I stewed in my own silence, Hiroshi seemed to come to a decision.

'I am thinking of shutting up shop.'

'Oh, sorry – I'll help you put the stuff away.'

'I don't mean that. I mean, I am thinking of closing the business.'

'Oh!'

'It is doing well, but nothing special. And I think it's time that…' He stopped, wagging his hand, scattering smoke.

'I don't want to spend the rest of my days on it.' It shocked me to realise that I had never thought of Hiroshi as a man with a plan for the future. He rarely showed any sign of looking much further ahead than the next shot, the next deadline. He blew a last smoke ring and watched it rise.

'When this contract is finished, I am also going to resign from the agency.'

That was another shock.

'What will you do?'

'I will go home again. There are things I must do, things connected with my family.'

I nodded, stunned with an odd kind of shame that I had no such network of responsibilities and by the realisation that it was me that didn't have a plan. I took a risk.

'Your aunt?'

'You could say that.'

He was leaning against the edge of the desk, staring at the floor in front of him, frowning. Then he drew a long breath and slowly released it.

'Continue shooting.'

His tone was firm. Half-way between encouragement and command.

'Continue to practise. You are someone for whom it is necessary to follow the Way. Do not allow yourself to be distracted. Do not run away if others come to watch. You have a responsibility to them.'

'Responsibility?'

'To show them. To show them something good!'

This time, his tone was deeply serious.

'To continue doing that, you will need to find another teacher. I am very sorry. But I think that this is the right time. I am confident now, that you will continue to improve – *and* continue to practise.'

For a second I was sure he was looking directly into my eyes. But his were in deep shadow, so it did not matter. He took a last pull on his cheroot and ground it out in one of the mugs. The ash tray I noticed, had already gone.

*　*　*

Throughout the morning, the door to the western dining room has been kept firmly shut, but Mie has seen the family doctor coming out, his face grey as ash. Everybody looks pale and tight-lipped.

Mother bustles up to her with a sealed letter. It must be delivered immediately, in person. A neighbour will escort her. It is addressed, in Father's hand, to her archery teacher. Mother looks as if she wishes to say something more, but only encourages Mie to make haste and get ready to go.

She finds Sensei in the shooting hall, overseeing some of his younger pupils as they polish the floor. The children scamper rapidly up and down the width of the hall, buttocks in the air, pushing bags filled with rice bran with their hands.

She enters, bows and readies herself to wait, but the teacher steps briskly forward and takes the letter from her, almost before she has held it out to him. He reads carefully, his mouth set tight. The only sound in the hall is the thumping of bare feet as the youngsters run up and down the softly gleaming floor. Their bare legs seem spider-thin.

Finishing, he slips the letter into his kimono, claps his hands loudly and tells the children there is hot rice gruel in the changing room. Without a word to Mie, he disappears into a back office. As the children file out of the hall, bowing at the exit, it occurs to her that the food must have come from his own meagre supply.

A minute later Sensei comes back, carrying a small, unlit brazier. He settles it carefully in a gravelled patch just beyond the edge of the shooting hall floor. Pulling the letter and a silver cigarette-lighter from the breast of his kimono, he hitches back his sleeves, carefully sweeps the skirts of his hakama out of the way and kneels on the edge of the floor. Holding the letter above the brazier with iron chopsticks, he sets the blue flame of the lighter to the paper, turning it carefully this way and that, so that it is all consumed. Finally he breaks up the fallen ashes and stirs them into the charcoal. Mie watches this proceeding with some astonishment.

'It looks like your parents have rather a mess to deal with.' he says, straightening up and brushing ash off his hands. 'It would probably be best if you stay out of the way for now.'

He smiles at Mie's anxious face.

'I always appreciate your assistance here and I am sure the family of one of the other girls can look after you for a few days.'

Mie freezes.

'Don't look so worried! It's about time you had more friends of your own age to talk to.'

He smiles encouragingly.

'I hear things can be a little quiet at home.'

'Quiet' is not how Mie would describe her home life, but it is true that the social gatherings and committee meetings have become much more infrequent and, in any case, are mostly composed of people at least thirty years older than she is.

Mie returns briefly home to collect some things. She is not ushered inside. Instead, Mother meets her at the door with a bundle already packed. Her face betrays an underlying strain. For a moment, it seems again as if there is something she wants to say, but she presses her lips together and hurries Mie away with brief words of encouragement.

*   *   *

3 Yugamae

Setting the grip of first the right and then the left hand.
The archer's gaze turns toward the target.

I set out for Hiroshi's final lesson in a dispirited mood. True, he had given me the contact details of a London dojo, but that would mean long and expensive trips to get teaching. It still felt like something was being snatched away from me, just as I was beginning to feel its real worth. The idea of this melancholy farewell session only made the feeling worse.

As we entered the shooting area, I saw that Hiroshi had pinned a paper target to the board that caught our arrows. It was the traditional long-range kasumi mato, or 'mist' target, its alternating black and white rings reminiscent of the way autumn mists are depicted in Japanese art, as sharply defined bands. In spite of my low mood, I could not help a smile of wry amusement. At such a short distance the central spot was going to be hard to miss.

Confident by now, in my grasp of the movements, my breathing synchronised with each step, I maintain a calm and even rhythm. In the balance and stillness of a well-constructed draw, I let my gaze travel along the arrow and across little more than an arrow's length of distance, to the paper target. So much of this confidence, I know, is owing to Hiroshi's quiet faith. I look steadily at the target's concentric circles of black and white.

It looks back. A round, bulging, monstrous bull's eye. Swelling and staring, filling my whole vision, until I feel it is going to swallow me.

His large, hot hand gripping my chin, jerking my face up towards his. I want to close my eyes, but I know he will only force them open with his fingers, holding me, eyeball to eyeball, raging, 'LOOK AT ME WHEN I AM TALKING TO YOU!' in a voice so loud it makes my childish ears ring. I can see the red lightning bolts of broken veins in his eyeballs, the grey rivers of snakes wriggling and streaming out across the iris of his eye, the black, unfathomable disc of the pupil. I want, above all things, to look away.

I shut my eyes, desperately hanging on to the balance of the shot, but my arms have already begun to tremble. The perfect equilibrium of the draw is rapidly falling apart. In a few seconds more, it will collapse like Hiroshi's pile of stones, and I will drop the arrow or make a clumsy, dangerous release. I give in and raise my quivering arms, returning the bow to its undrawn state.

That final lesson had been a Thursday. I spent Friday and the weekend holed up in my flat, ignoring phone calls and messages. One thought went round and round in my head: *Now this too, this hopeful thing, is closed to me.*

When I had been unable to make the shot, Hiroshi had assumed I was unwell and had told me to go home and get some rest. Saying nothing to contradict him, I called up the cab early and left as quickly as I could. I felt an extra pang of guilt on the way out, to see a small sake bottle and two tiny cups standing on the desk in his office, awaiting some ceremony of farewell. I felt low and dishonest, leaving him standing there in the doorway, still dressed in his practice uniform, expressing concern for my health.

All through the long weekend, my feelings swung wildly between shame, embarrassment, anger at myself and a growing sense of fear. What if this panic attack in front of the target was yet another symptom of underlying malaise? Without Hiroshi's guidance and correction, I felt, it was going to be hard to keep my precarious stack of pebbles from collapsing.

* * *

Another new thing. A photograph, small, not black and white, but brightly coloured, has fallen out of the envelope in Mie's hand. A face she recognises from long ago, but transformed. Behind the glasses, no longer diffidence, but a happy self-confidence. It makes Mie smile in spite of her low mood, then sigh in envy.

The letter is cheerful too, full of a sense of forward movement she somehow cannot find in herself. She feels static, trapped in her comfortable city life. In this mood she replies, perhaps with more open gratitude than she might otherwise have done.

They meet, after her morning shift, in the top-floor cafe of a fashionable store in Shinjuku. The room is bright and airy. Pictures of Paris in white frames decorate the walls. They choose a corner table and after the effusiveness of their letters, Mie finds herself suddenly a little shy and cautious.

The waitress brings iced water while they consider the menu. European delicacies unheard of since the war, many of them new to her. The prices are simply alarming. It is as if there has suddenly been another outbreak of inflation, just in this cafe. Emi has noticed her discomfort.

'Don't worry, a cousin of mine runs this place, I get a good discount.'

'But these things … how?'

Emi's voice drops to a conspiratorial whisper.

'Glorious isn't it! My cousin has friends. From overseas.'

A slight hand gesture and a knowing expression is all Mie gets by way of further explanation. It is not enough.

Emi mouths '*Black Market.*'

'Oh.'

Mie stews in embarrassment at her own unworldliness. Emi chooses coffee and several very sweet cakes for them to share. Mie follows Emi's choice of drink. She finds it hard to relax.

'Well now! What have you been doing here in the Big City?'

So direct! Has Emi been consorting with Americans? Her

full-skirted frock, in a bright floral print, has been attracting disapproving glances since she entered the cafe. Her glasses are no longer utilitarian, but large and stylish.

Mie mumbles a few excuses for her dull, patchwork existence as miko and shop-girl. Seeming to sense her embarrassment, Emi covers for her by talking of inconsequential things. The cost of taxi fares, the spring weather, the problems of single life for single women. She points each topic with an anecdote at her own expense. Mie is soon smiling and even laughing a little, behind a cautious hand.

'Do you remember that day in the village?'

The sudden change of tone catches Mie unawares.

'It was so wonderful when you showed up. Like something out of an old story!'

Mie is horribly embarrassed at what little she can remember.

'I'm really sorry, I must have frightened everybody.'

'I'll say! Just about saved my life though, as a matter of fact.'

Mie is recalling the short girl in glasses who had seen further than the rest. Whose gaze had reached out to her, as she stood, swaying and exhausted at the entrance to the shrine, wondering if she still had the right to pass beneath the sacred gate. The friend who had reached out and pulled her scorched soul back amongst the living.

'I think it was you, your mother, everyone, who saved my life that day.'

'Pff! We looked after you as friends should, was all.'

Mie blushes painfully at the memory of a brush dragging ash out of her tangled hair. For a second of panic, she is convinced she can smell the acrid tang of smoke again, but it is only the coffees the waitress has just set down in front of them. She is suddenly on the verge of tears.

'Hey!' Emi's soft hand touches her wrist for a second. 'I'm sorry, I have the tact of an elephant – everybody says so, but I never seem to learn.'

Mie forces a smile.

'Did you really walk all that way? Such determination! – No, no, no. Never mind, you must tell me properly all about it some other time and I will listen sympathetically, I promise, but today the Elephant needs to tell you her own story. Please?'

Emi, it is true, is a little plump, but she refers to herself as 'The Elephant' with such cheerful self-confidence and dresses with such faultless, optimistic glamour and élan that Mie can only feel like some dowdy little mouse in her presence. It is as if elephants were suddenly revealed to her as the most energetic, fashionable, socially confident animals in the world. 'Perhaps,' Mie wonders, as a subtly colourful platter arrives at their table, 'perhaps, I should eat more cake?'

'I have to tell you by way of thanks. It's really why I've been trying to find you all this time. Things have been so mixed up since the war. I never imagined you would stay at that back-country shrine, I just assumed you would be here in the city, maybe with some relations, or a family friend. I wasted a lot of time.'

'I'm really sorry…'

'Hey! Not your fault! Silly me for making easy assumptions. I found out eventually from someone with a relative in the village. But of course, by then you must have already moved back here. Anyway, that's all nonsense.'

Emi waves her hand cheerfully and begins to cut the cakes up into little blocks the size of nigiri-sushi.

'No, all just nonsense. As a matter of fact, I spent a lot of time trying to chase up all the old crowd from that day. Would you believe the old dojo is a drapery store now? We should go there sometime, just out of curiosity! Anyway, the point is…'

Emi leans forward confidentially,

'… that day, at the village shrine, I was literally going out of my mind with boredom. You know how much I hated being trussed up in kimono? Would you believe as a kid I was always frightened I would fall over while tied up in all that hot silk, and I would never be able to get up again, and I would just have to lie there helplessly like a beetle until I got squashed?'

Mie laughs, covering her mouth, eyes wide at Emi's imagined plight.

'It was all coming to a bit of a head you see, what with the War and the stress of the housha ceremony and everybody so anxious about everything. I couldn't believe we were all still going through with the thing that year. I thought with a war on, we'd be let off all that just for once. How on earth they got the fuel to even get us there I don't know. I'd been training for weeks to do the kagura and then on the day, Mother insisted on this just ridiculous obi – she'd done it up so tight, I could barely breathe, let alone dance. I swear I lost five kilos that day!'

Emi laughs at the memory of her own distress and helps herself to more cake – not, however, before she has encouraged Mie to do the same.

'I am not exaggerating when I tell you I was getting close to ripping it all off and running naked down the road screaming like a maniac.'

Mie's eyes are wide again – this time with real shock.

'I had just had enough of everything. My family, my upbringing, the War, kimonos, ceremonies, dancing, archery, stuffy old priests and on top of it all – being photographed! I tell you it was touch and go. All of us standing there, pretending to be all happy and normal, when in fact, we all knew the world was going up in flames around us. I just knew that any minute, any second, there was absolutely, unavoidably, going to be the most terrific explosion. I was either going to faint, or throw up, or start foaming at the mouth and screaming, or my head would fall off, or I would sprout horns and turn into an ogre … or … or…'

Emi is holding her breath, her face quite pink.

'… and just at that moment, when I didn't know if I was going to live or die … you showed up.'

'Oh.'

Mie does not know what on earth to make of this. Is Emi quite … alright? A moment ago she had seemed so happy, so stable.

'I saw this … person … in the entrance – you. I forgot myself. It was like being lifted up out of reality into something utterly different. Like an old tale.'

Emi has turned to look out of the window. The lenses of her fashionably large glasses reflect the blue sky and the passing clouds. The other side of the sky.

'For me, that was the day my real life began.'

She turns back to look at Mie, with a serious expression.

'At first I didn't understand. But then, as I looked into your face, I guessed, just a little, what might have happened.'

Emi swallows hard. Looks down at her plate of cake as if staring into the depths of a well.

'And I began to understand, what you must have done, to be there with us.'

There is a long pause, in which the hiss of the coffee machine makes strange, incongruous music. Emi takes a deep breath.

'Mother was so frightfully cross with me. After she fixed your hair, she had to re-do my make-up, that she had spent all morning on. You probably didn't notice, but that's why everyone was tutting at me for arriving late at the shooting line.'

'I'm so sorry, I caused so much trouble for everyone.'

'Please stop saying that!'

Emi has taken her glasses off. Without them, her eyes are small and kind and look a little puffy.

'Mie, Mie-chan – I'm deadly serious. You really did save my life that day.'

Mie waits, in puzzled silence. She is at a loss to understand this. *I was just a bit of ash, blown off the fire,* she thinks, *I had nothing left, I was all burned up. How could I save anybody's life?*

'After everything that had happened to you, to your family – I'm sorry, I know I shouldn't remind you of such painful things. But it's because I have to tell you.'

Emi's voice, so glad and confident just a minute before, has dropped to a whisper. When she tries to smile, the tremor in her voice betrays her.

'I really was in such bad trouble that day, worse than ever before or since. Even if I had survived the ceremony, I think I might have gone away and killed myself soon afterwards. But then I saw what you had done. And I thought: *I* could be like that! Instead of being Emi the shy, Emi the useless, Emi the trivial, pushed about, short-sighted terrified little fool, trussed up in kimonos she hates, I could be – even just a little bit – more like … you. And at that moment, it was as if the sun came out from behind the clouds, and I felt a such huge, overwhelming sense of relief. Suddenly, I didn't care about kimonos or ceremonies or photographs, or even the wretched war. I thought: 'If Mie could live through that and still be here with us, then I can do all of this, it's nothing!' That day, my real life started. If you hadn't made that walk. If you hadn't been so utterly determined not to be the missing piece of our little group, I would probably not be here now. I would not exist. I would have exploded and all the bits drifted away into Hell.'

Mie is rigid. Emi suddenly reaches across the little table and takes both Mie's hands in hers. Her head is bowed so Mie sees only the odd view of the little whorl of hair at the top of her scalp. Something hot is dripping on Mie's wrists. Has the coffee been upset?

No. It is Emi's tears.

'Thank you!' she is whispering. 'Thank you, Mie-san!'

*　　*　　*

After three nights without much rest, I slept through my Monday morning alarm and found myself scrambling to get to the office by nine. Not that the agency was strict about hours, but Hiroshi was usually punctual to the minute and I felt it would be rude not to follow his pattern.

I clattered up the stairs and burst into our crazy little cabin of an office with thirty seconds to spare, only to find it empty. I dumped my bag and sat down, panting and out of breath, but relieved to have still beaten Hiroshi. At least I had few seconds more to rehearse some lies, or screw up the courage to tell the truth.

A quarter of an hour later I was no longer panting, but still alone. I abandoned my refuge and clomped back down to reception. Hiroshi, it seemed, had already gone. 'He's had to go back home, urgent family business apparently. He said you still had a lot of his stuff to re-write for the process engineering manual.'

It was true enough. Chemical engineering was not my usual territory. Looking up obscure words and checking things I was unsure about had slowed me down. Hiroshi had been running well ahead of me. At least it was something to do. I gathered up a coffee and some biscuits to revive me after the climb back up to the office.

An hour later, the coffee and biscuits were gone and I was still on the same page. My mind kept wandering off like a badly-trained dog. Sitting next to Hiroshi's empty desk, I came to realise how his silently industrious companionship had kept me focused.

At lunch time it was raining hard, so I sat and ate my sand-wiches in the office with nothing for company but the sound of the rain on the tiles above and the hiss of traffic on the wet road below. A couple of scruffy-looking pigeons came and sheltered on the window-ledge. They made a lot of fuss, flapping and cooing and strutting up and down, before abruptly flying off into the downpour, as if they had just remembered an urgent appointment somewhere else.

An idle and morally dubious thought occurred to me. I reached out a toe and tugged gently at the top drawer handle of Hiroshi's desk. I had expected it to be locked, but the metal drawer trundled open on its rollers, aided by the slope of the floor.

A new pencil, sharp and un-chewed. A half-smoked packet of proper cigarettes, with part of the carton torn away; but no sign of tobacco or papers for his usual roll-ups. One of those back-to-front Japanese glossy magazines, full of bright-eyed young women advertising trivial things. A small, black notebook, strongly bound, but very rubbed and worn. I flipped it open.

Lines of spidery characters, neatly written in pencil, ran across a faint grid, some in vertical and some in horizontal lines. Here and there, English words and phrases were carefully printed. Some I recognised as old friends. How could I forget the great controversy over 'AIR FILTER RETENTION RING'? Here were my measurements for the archery gear. What was happening about that now? I turned over more pages, wondering, rather vainly, if he'd written anything else about me, but it seemed to be all translation notes and a few scribbled maps and directions. Finding his way about in an unfamiliar city I supposed. I was about to close it when something fell out and fluttered to the floor under the desk. I got down on all fours to retrieve it.

An old black and white photographic print, quite small. It showed a young Japanese woman, shooting with a bow. She was standing in the moment just before release, the arrow fully drawn, its feathers brushing her cheek. Her face shone with calm concentration. Her white gi or practice shirt was slightly overexposed, giving it an inner brilliance against the black muneate chest-plate and her black hakama skirts. Her long, loosely tied hair was as dark as the emulsion could go. I turned the photo over. The address of a commercial photography studio was printed on the back in faded blue ink. A Tokyo address in roman characters. I looked at the picture again for a long time. Then I slipped it back in the notebook, replaced everything in the drawer and slid it shut. It refused to stay shut, rolling slowly open again as if determined to testify to my actions. Then I saw the neatly folded little piece of cigarette-packet that had fallen on the floor. I jammed the drawer shut again with it, feeling guilty of a small crime.

*　　*　　*

4 Uchiokoshi

Foundations complete, the first action of the shot.
Raising bow and arrow. Beginning the draw.

Younger Brother's wedding is not quite the quiet, low-key affair she had been anticipating. It is some years later than his breezy adolescent optimism had implied and the intended is not the original one. With so few of the immediate family remaining and the country relatives now so very old, it had seemed unlikely to Mie that there would be a big crowd. Nevertheless, although not extravagant, the turn-out is quite impressive. Perhaps thirty or forty people altogether. Some of the faces look familiar. Many seem too young to be people from the old days, but perhaps they are the sons, younger brothers and cousins of people her parents knew?

Mie is suddenly assailed with terror that the old gift-giver will be present. Sinking onto a seat, she sends her gaze flitting about, hunting anxiously for hidden faces. She relaxes a little. It seems that particular ghost no longer walks. At least, not here.

'You have the appearance of a person who is looking for someone.'

Mr Yanaga has suddenly materialised at her side, startling her. Sitting down in his presence makes her feel awkward. She stands, smoothing the dove-grey, calf-length skirt of the suit that Emi had helped her choose and prepares, with a sinking heart, to make conversation. He seems, however, a little less diffident than before. His face is rather flushed and he holds an almost empty wineglass in one hand.

'Your brother seems to have some very interesting connections.'

'Really? I'm afraid I know almost no-one here.'

'Oh? You perhaps do not read the newspapers very much!'

She smiles apologetically and looks down at her hands. Of course. That is why some of the faces seem familiar. It appears Younger Brother has indeed been quite astute in building on connections from their parents' circle. From the other side of the sky.

'It is true. I am disgracefully ignorant. It should not surprise me though. After Mother and Father, he was always the cleverest of the family.'

'Hmm. It's more than mere cleverness, I feel. You see gathered here before you a small group of people from business, academia and politics, who together could almost form the core of a new political party. Or at least, the support-group of a very effective politician.'

'Oh! You really think so?'

'I do. I'm no politician myself, but as you know, I have a great interest in social reform and progressive ideas. I recognise many like-minded people in this room.'

'Is my brother interested in politics?'

'Well, I suppose that's the clever part. When I first knew him – in my capacity as family lawyer you understand – I would not have said so. He seemed to be straightforwardly a very young but rising businessman, the sort looking simply to make a contribution to the management of his employer's firm. But since then… Well, if these are all just ordinary friends, I have to say he has an uncommon knack for choosing interesting people. But I don't think these are just friends. I think this is his war-cabinet.'

Mie does not like the association of war and her little brother.

'The thing is, though…'

Mr Yanaga is warming to his theme, becoming confiding in his manner, bending lower and speaking more quietly, his glass held carefully out to one side, away from Mie's fine wool suit and the little spray of cream-coloured artificial flowers on her lapel.

'The thing is, though, there is a fly in the ointment, a skeleton in the cupboard so to speak, as I am sure you are aware...'

Mie looks up at him blankly. He seems to be waiting for her response. She has no idea what he is driving at.

'Well, he is very young still. You feel he is lacking in experience?'

'Hah! I don't think that will hold him back for long. Politics needs new faces these days. That is what the newspapers like. And television. That is what the old reactionaries don't understand yet. It may be a while before he can have any real influence, but meanwhile he is going to be able to build up a following, a public image, in a way they don't understand at all. He will have the jump on them when the time comes to defend himself.'

Mie opens her mouth to protest, but it is already time for the next part of the ceremony. Her little brother does look rather ministerial in his suit. His bride, in her bulbous white headdress, looks like the Empress doll in a doll-festival display. They seem confident, assured of their future. What is Mr Yanaga holding over them? She begins to dislike his attitude. As soon as the formalities are over, she corners Mr Yanaga again. He smiles.

'Why must my brother defend himself? Against what?'

Mr Yanaga's cheeks are very flushed. He is perhaps, a little drunk. He draws himself up and intones:

'Who is wise enough to judge which of us is good or bad? We are all wise and foolish by turns, like a ring without an end.'

* * *

It is amazing how much of everyday life you can get through, but sooner or later, people always notice. And once they notice, they try to explain it to each other. Staring at my feet, while listening to the admonitions of teachers, was put down to sullenness, or lack of intellect. 'Shy', the more generous adults had said, 'A Passing Phase.' But it did not pass. It grew only worse. I found myself unable to meet even the glances of strangers in the street. Well, I wasn't the first painfully shy teenager in the history of the world, but it got so I didn't even like to meet my own reflection. Vampire-like, I avoided as far as possible, mirrors and windows. Slowly, the thing tightened its grip, until by the end of my student years, I had to reluctantly acknowledge the dozen follies daily, the catalogue of foolish subterfuges, all to ensure that gaze never met gaze.

In adulthood I discovered, the explanations become less generous: 'Lacking in self-esteem', 'Evasive', 'Untrustworthy', 'Cold', 'Arrogant'. Just because you are not looking at them, people think you can't hear.

I had once hoped it wouldn't matter, that somehow, I would always find a way through. The break-up with Jo had finished off that illusion. Sustaining a long term-relationship, marriage, parenthood, I came to feel, was probably always going to have been a bit ambitious.

I had clung to the hope that a normal life of some sort was still possible. But all the while, the old beast had been quietly stalking me. Now it had followed me into archery, driving me back to work as my last and only refuge. Even there, I had to confront my other loss. Was it my fault Hiroshi had left? Had he too, finally become impatient with my social inadequacies? That was my instinctive reaction, every time someone walked out on me.

Mother had been well aware that things were getting rough. She would fuss over me afterwards and make light of it, but I could see the desperation in her streaked eye-shadow and untidy hair. I could not avoid hearing the arguments either, because he used to shout at her with the same force he used on me. From my hiding place under the covers I could not hear what she said, but from the rise and fall of her voice I sensed she was trying to reason with him. I could also tell, from other noises, that it wasn't working. Finally, one tumultuous night, she had yelled at him in tones even I could hear: *'If you think we are so useless, why don't you just leave?'*

Later that night, I had been woken by the sound of the street door slamming. A sound I recognised, even from under the covers, as the note of final departure.

*   *   *

They meet in the park. The cherries are foaming, loose petals drifting on the breeze like pink snow. Everyone seems to be out for a stroll. Emi's outfit rivals the cherries in pastel gaiety. A long, white, full-skirted frock with a bold flower-print. A short-cropped jacket that emphasises her bust, in pale lemon yellow with pistachio green piping. A pillbox hat that matches the jacket and whose net fascinator is soon spattered with cherry petals. They stroll and laugh together under the trees.

After a while, at Emi's prompting, Mie chooses a spot and they settle on a mat she has brought. The stares her friend attracts are a trial to Mie's reticence. Emi chatters about her life, oblivious of approval or disapproval. The clothes are American it seems, but home-made. A pen-friend in the US sends her the patterns, in exchange for scraps of old kimono fabric. Emi pulls some out of her bag to show. They come in little paper envelopes with wildly exciting colour pictures on the front.

'This is the one I was wearing when we met at the cafe – I'm sorry about that by the way, I really didn't mean to come out with all that there and then, I was going to wait for a better time, but somehow, it couldn't wait. Anyway, this one is going to be my next project – isn't it fun?!'

The illustration shows a woman who looks as if she is about to dance. She has a long nose, high-arched eyebrows, a slender neck, and hair that looks like a shining golden helmet. Her arms and legs are impossibly long, thin and spider-like. Her laughing, freckled, red-headed friend swings a blue handbag and wears the same full-skirted outfit, but with little cap sleeves that show her bare arms, all in a different fabric. Staring at these strange figures, Mie is amazed at how beautifully Emi sews and how cleverly she has adapted the complicated patterns to her own very different figure.

'Clever! You are very clever with clothes. Is that your career?'
'Me? No! It's just a hobby. I have other ideas.'
'What are they?'

Emi smiles archly.

'Right now, I'm thinking of becoming a professional match-maker.'

'A matchmaker!?'

Mie is startled – and somewhat amused.

'Aren't you a little young for that, Emi-chan?'

'Well, it's something I picked up from my mother. She used to do it a lot, informally of course, for friends and family. Still does as a matter of fact.'

'Ah.'

'But these days, life is different. A lot of people lost connections in the war; family, whole groups of friends; – then made new friends. And modern life now is so much more complicated. I think people would like a professional service. An old schoolmate of mine and I are thinking of pooling our contact lists and taking a little office somewhere in town. We could offer a real service, something people would be happy to pay for – find out about people's lives and personalities, put them in touch with suitable friends, potential partners.'

'It sounds like a heavy responsibility.'

'Well it's a risk certainly, and I am studying to be more tactful – honestly. The Elephant is learning to dance!'

Emi smiles and twirls her fingers in the air with startling grace. Mie can well believe that if she chose to, this elephant could dance most beautifully, the cherry petals drifting and swirling around her, decorating her lemon-yellow jacket and hat.

'Really though, it's my partner who is the one to talk to people – my skill is the detective work!'

She tips an imaginary fedora. Mie smiles.

'Enough about me. Tell me about your plans!'

Mie is at a loss. She explains again her half-and-half life.

'Hmm. Miko is alright, but is that really you? And store work, well, shopping is alright, but working there is hard!'

Mie stares out through the veils of falling petals to the city beyond. Drifting. No real being, no roots, no community. All around, people are building: Younger Brother's political group, new office blocks, businesses, lives, this vast city. *Unless I do something*, Mie thinks, *I might cease to exist.*

'So, is there any one? You know?'

Mie shakes her head and looks at her fingers spread out in her lap.

'Oh come on, there must be somebody who's at least a possibility?'

Mie rallies.

'Oh stop it, I'm sure I can't afford your rates!'

'Ahh now, I don't charge for friends! Tell me about him!'

'Well, he's not really… He's just someone who…'

Mie explains about the family lawyer.

'So he has actually sent, handed you, a love-letter!'

'A love letter! No!'

Mie's hand is over her mouth, covering her embarrassed smile.

'It would be more appropriate to call it an academic history essay.'

Emi laughs at this. Mie feels warm in the spring sunshine.

'Look, I won't make any promises, but I will do a little digging around – with your permission? It will be good practice for me – please? All in complete confidence of course, you can trust me to be discrete – in spite of appearances.'

Mie looks dubious, but smiles.

'Come on, the worst that can happen is that I find out he's entirely unsuitable and then you won't waste any more time on him, ne?'

Mie nods. It seems indecent to actually speak.

'That's agreed then!' Emi bounces up. 'Now, where can we get some hot coffee and cake? I'm catching a chill here!'

*   *   *

I almost binned the message. After all, it did read a bit like some kind of scam:

'Urgent! Please collect your order from warehouse. My assistant hands keys to agent in 2 days.'

Even after seeing Hiroshi's name, it took me a minute to work it out. What 'order'? And then I remembered the night of the tape measure when I had been interrogated about the health of my bank balance. The archery stuff must have arrived.

A small, tired looking van was parked by the loading bay entrance. The big roller-shutter warehouse door was open, but I didn't fancy scrambling up onto the dock, so I rang the office doorbell as usual. An older man, looking as careworn as his van, let me in.

'Come for the parcels? They're just through here.'

The dusty brown tails of the man's shop coat were a sad contrast to Hiroshi's sharply pleated hakama, as I followed him along the familiar corridor.

Emerging into the warehouse, I stopped dead. As if in a theatrical trick, the space I knew had vanished, to be replaced by an entirely different room. The stacks of boxes had gone, revealing the corrugated metal and steel girders that outlined the true height and volume of the space. Hitherto unseen skylights trickled a dirty brown illumination into the dust motes below. The scratched and yellowed transparent curtain across the open loading bay glowed with the threat of more daylight and the outside world.

That lashed up arrangement of odds and ends, like a stage set in a studio theatre, had been a real place where something very important to me had happened. And where, at the moment of crisis, it had all been lost.

Shop-coat man had gone back to his interrupted task. The slow, methodical strokes of his brush erasing memories as he worked his way across the bare concrete floor.

'Over there mate!'

I turned, following his outstretched broom. A long, narrow, plywood packing case lay against the far wall. Next to it was a more conventionally rectangular package, smaller, but still quite bulky. The new life Hiroshi had tried to give me, all packed up and ready to go. Bending down, I hefted the long box. It was not exactly heavy, but soon would be, five minutes into a very long walk home. Because I certainly wasn't going to be let on a bus with that, and I couldn't see a cab driver being too happy either. I thought desperately of the skip I had passed on the edge of the estate. No good. Hiroshi would ask questions sooner or later.

I carried the boxes out on to the loading dock and stood there, wondering what to do next. The estate in daytime was a different place to the one I knew. Almost bustling. A refreshment van was parked near the entrance. Three men holding hot drinks were chatting with the owner. Social interaction. Give and take.

'Erm, I'm going to need a lift with these into town, could I get you lunch in exchange?'

'Tea, milk, three sugars, cheese and pickle. Gimme half an hour.'

When he'd finished and locked up, we sat on the edge of the dock to escape the pervasive atmosphere of dust.

'Friend of yours?'

Good question. What exactly was Hiroshi in the scheme of things? I could think of at least three options. It seemed to have depended on the time of day. Colleague in office hours, teacher by night and…

'Well…'

'I used to come in three days a week. Didn't see him much. He did all the paperwork, nights. He'd leave out lists of stuff to get ready. I make up the orders, see them onto the vans with the forklift. Get the driver to sign off, that was it.'

'Uhuh.'

'Interesting line of business. Sending stuff all over. This country, France, Germany, all over. Still carrying on. Got some firm up north to take over.'

'Oh.'

'No skin off my nose. Odd job man, me. Once you've done a job for a bit it's time to move on in my book.'

'Hm.'

'Interesting stuff though. Medical supplies. Special bandages and what not. Family firm he said. His big sister's the boss back home. Apparently.'

'Right.'

'Special stuff. For really bad burns.'

He gave the last three words lugubrious emphasis.

'My old Dad saw that during the War. ARP Warden. Had to go to a crashed plane one night. The guys in the crew, their skin was dropping off 'em he said. Like roast meat.'

I sipped my tea, picturing the pallets of boxes, stacked up into the gloom of the high roof.

'Some bedtime stories you shouldn't tell to kids, eh?'

*   *   *

It is only a day or two later and the cherries are, if anything, even more flamboyant. Emi, on the other hand, has toned down – a little. She steps lightly off the tram in a deep cerise woollen suit of a neat and conservative cut. She looks like she means business. They walk across the park, pausing only briefly at the bandstand to take in the spectacle. Two small children run past, throwing handfuls of petals into the air.

Children. Is that where this is leading? Mie shakes her head in disbelief, then glances at Emi who is talking about colours and clothes. What about Emi? What does Emi feel? Are future children running about and throwing petals in Emi's dreams? What is it like to be so confident of existence as to be able to imagine such a thing?

Emi suddenly becomes aware of Mie's puzzled stare. 'I know!' Emi says cheerfully, 'I talk a lot of nonsense!' Mie says 'No. Not at all.' but cannot think how to ask such a question. They walk to the exit on the other side of the park, while the breeze throws showers of petals at them.

Seeking out the same cafe as before, they settle into their corner table. It is warm and relatively quiet, for everyone is out strolling in the spring sunshine. When the waitress has gone, Emi carefully draws a yellow card folder out of her bag and begins to unlace the slender pistachio-green ribbons that hold it shut. As she opens it, there is a ghostly scent of flowers. Inside are sheets of pale lemon-coloured paper with feint grey lines.

'Mother let me have some of her old stationery. She used to get it from Kyūkyodō – you know? That very grand shop on Ginza? This was before the war. I've no idea what it used to cost – didn't dare ask!'

The rather exquisite sheets are covered in neat rows of hand-writing, the characters running horizontally, western-style. A small, passport-size, black and white photo of Mr Yanaga is clipped to the uppermost. He looks scared.

Mie is embarrassed. All this fuss.

'Now don't look so alarmed at my little bits of paperwork,' Emi says brightly. 'This is just me keeping things organised!'

'But, the photograph!'

'Oh, don't worry about that!' Emi's eyes have a teasing sparkle. 'I told him about my business and offered him a free listing. If you pass on him, he'll go into the files as a good catch for someone else.'

Mie's shame and horror suddenly become rather too deep to be expressed by any outward sign.

'I mean it!' Emi leans forward, oblivious of the turmoil she is causing. 'Because, let me tell you Mie-chan, this guy is a really good prospect. If you haven't been thinking about him seriously so far, then you really should. We are none of us getting any younger after all!'

Mie is sobered. Of course. She may not think she is moving forward, but that is an illusion. The river is flowing, whether she feels it or not.

'So, a few basics. A year or two younger than you, as you know.'

Emi has assumed an expression that is supposed to communicate professional tact and delicacy but succeeds only in convincing Mie that it is judgemental.

'And a rising lawyer in a good firm, as you also know. Father deceased during the war.'

Emi briefly slips down her glasses and fixes Mie with a meaningful look.

'Of natural causes.'

Then briskly continues:

'Mother, grandmother, one or two cousins, all resident on or near a rather delightful country villa in the upper reaches of the Awa river valley. So…'

Emi drops the glasses again.

'Property. Old money. Managed to hide it during the War and the Occupation. Probably an old merchant family, which is just as well. Aristocrats the world over are usually poor when it comes to cash. I haven't probed too far to be honest, but nothing to suggest the family isn't rather, how shall I say? Well set-up.'

Emi looks at Mie. Mie is not responding with much enthusiasm.

'But you know what? Never mind all that. This is a real love story! That letter he wrote you might have been as dry as a legal almanac, but it was meant to tell you how much he cares.'

'How do you read that in it?'

Mie would really like to know.

'Well, I don't need to really – and you only showed me a bit of it – because the most revealing thing is the sheer amount of time and effort he spent on it.'

'Oh.'

'Anyway, the big news is, I spent an afternoon with your Mr Yanaga.'

Mie's hands fly up to her face, muffling a small scream of shock. Just as she is about to berate Emi, the very expensive coffee and cakes arrive, and she has to forcibly repress her terror and indignation. Italian lemon polenta this time, with a small silver jug of real cream. When they are left to themselves again, Emi forestalls Mie's urgent protests with a raised spoon.

'I know, my cousin is amazing, isn't he?'

Emi drops her voice to a conspiratorial whisper.

'He gets his ingredients from the American Naval Base store in…'

'I don't care about your cousin! You talked to Mr Yanaga about me! I am so ashamed!'

There is a pause as Mie frowns darkly at her plate. Emi's smile of complacent satisfaction at her own cunning becomes uncertain.

'I don't know what he could have found to say about me. I've hardly spoken to him except about matters of business.'

'Hah! You don't have to talk, to be speaking to a man who is fascinated with you.' Emi's tone is infuriatingly knowing. 'And that's just how you want it to be! He's forced to use his imagination and see all sorts of interesting qualities in you. Of course you do have interesting qualities, which he will hopefully come to appreciate in time, but right now you have all the interest you need right there in his overheated imagination.'

This is not entirely reassuring to Mie. Mr Yanaga, (Tadasu, apparently), sounds even more of a wild card than before Emi started on her detective work. He represents a future she finds both hard to imagine and alarming. The exposure of her fragile sense of existence, to his bold certainties.

*   *   *

After supper, I unpacked everything and laid it all out on the floor, just to see the full extent of my predicament: all the paraphernalia of a student archer, no teacher, nowhere to shoot and an irrational fear of targets.

With a kind of bitter curiosity, I decided to at least try on the practice uniform. See what sort of a ridiculous figure I cut in it. The task had me poring over textbook diagrams of unfamiliar knots and wrappings for some time.

Eventually, tripping a little over the long skirts of my hakama, I stumbled through to the bedroom to squint at myself sidelong in the wardrobe mirror. Avoiding, as usual, my own surly gaze, I ran an eye over my new outline.

It wasn't me. It was someone else in a kyudo practice uniform. Someone with long, dark hair. In shock, I jerked back – and saw the black dressing gown hanging on the back of the bedroom door, just behind my head.

The following day, at work, I pulled open Hiroshi's drawer again. I picked up the black notebook and took out the photo of the woman shooting. It was evidently quite old. An original photographic print, not a reproduction. Even if it had been a chance find in a flea-market, I could see why Hiroshi might carry this. The essence of calm determination caught in that small image made me feel acutely my own lack of seriousness. Here I was, a grown man, daydreaming and hallucinating in a deserted bowling green, or having panic attacks in front of a target.

Which is how, one Sunday afternoon a week or so later, I found myself on a train to London in search of a new sensei. The 'dojo' Hiroshi had recommended, turned out to be a school gym in a dull suburb. Clean, well-lit and with pleasant changing facilities, it was nevertheless, a considerable step up from a dingy warehouse. Bows and equipment were available for new members to borrow, so for the first few sessions at least, I would need to carry only my glove and uniform on the train.

The senior teacher was an elderly man, with the kind of

powerful, charismatic personality that tends to make me immediately wary. The other students seemed very quiet and deferential around him, some to the point of appearing pathologically shy. Which was fine by me – I was a perfect fit.

Asked to wait at first, I watched with keen interest, while the teachers and senior students performed a group shooting ceremony. Finally, along with some others, I was invited to shoot at the short-range makiwara target. Not another improvised arrow-catcher like Hiroshi's foam pad, but the traditional cylinder of tightly packed rice straw, mounted on a stout wooden stand.

When my turn came, I was quite tense, but the teacher made no comment. Afterwards, he took me to one side, but still said nothing about my shooting. Instead, he asked searching questions about my former 'sensei' and his 'lineage'. What school, what ryu, was he trained in? Who had he studied under? What grade was he? Why was I no longer his pupil? I told him all I knew, which wasn't much. After that, it was time to pack up, and I left, feeling somewhat disappointed to have received no actual teaching, but relieved to have got through the evening without incident.

Still, it seemed I would be accepted, so I made arrangements to attend class monthly. The trips to London were expensive, but interacting with fellow students did not prove as difficult as I had feared. Everyone's gaze was on their equipment, their targets, or the back of the next person in line as we knelt, facing the right-hand side of the hall, waiting our turn to shoot. I began to take real pleasure both in the act of shooting and in all the quiet rituals of preparation and conclusion that surrounded it. For perhaps the first time in my life, I could enjoy being part of a social group. My damaged self-confidence began to revive a little.

After a few visits I was allowed to graduate from the short range makiwara to the long range kasumi mato – the 'mist target', with its concentric black and white rings of varying widths. This was a challenge I knew must come sooner or later. After a number of restless nights, I had hit on a stratagem for this moment, but I had no idea if it would actually work.

Of course, you can't just close your eyes and still expect to hit a target. Over the years however, if seeing someone's expression was absolutely socially necessary, I had developed a habit of focusing on the person's hat, or ear, or shoulder, anything close enough to the face to get at least an impression. By looking directly only at my left hand, the back of the bow, or even the arrow shaft, I could be sufficiently aware of the target to take aim, without actually returning its imaginary gaze. The fact that it was now nearly thirty metres away, rather than right in front of my nose, also helped.

Although it got me shooting again, this makeshift was not entirely successful. For a while, 'missed' target would have been a more appropriate spelling than 'mist'. It drove the teachers to exasperation. One even suggested I see an optician.

Vadim, the senior sensei, was morose and distant, often to the extent of being absent altogether. Even when he was physically present, teaching the basics was usually handled by Mayumi, a Japanese expat, assisted by some of the more senior students. She was, I was told, something rather grand in the London shipping insurance market. In the practice uniform of black hakama, with the black muneate strapped over her white gi and her long black hair tied back with a black ribbon, she cut a formidable figure in the dojo. Outside of actual shooting times, her loud voice whip-cracked across the room as she exercised her evident talent for marshalling confused people in baggy sleeves and long skirts, who are nervously clutching cumbersome bows and inconveniently long arrows, into some kind of order.

Between these two extremes of character, I began to accumulate some good advice. Nothing untoward manifested itself under the harsh neon lights to put me off my form. Even so, my shots never seemed to be quite as clean or as natural as those I used to imagine, practising with make-believe bow and arrows in the bowling green. In fact, I often finished sessions at the London gym-dojo entirely innocent of having inflicted any damage on the target at all. The backstop boards were not so lucky.

* * *

'The thing is…' Emi leans in confidentially again, for the cafe has begun to fill up around them. 'The thing is, he is an absolutely brilliant prospect – just right for someone like you! He's a little shy around women, but that's sweet, isn't it? Intellectually minded, but not a scatterbrain, he thinks to some purpose – that's the discipline of the law I suppose.'

Emi emphasises each point with a wag of her silver cake-fork.

'He already dotes on you, and his career prospects are very sound. I suppose there might be some conflict of interest at the firm, but I expect he would know what to do about that.'

Mie has a sudden image of Mr Yanaga being sternly shown the door by an infuriated boss, while she cowers in the background. Emi's brilliant picture is not what she had been hoping for. *Truthfully,* Mie thinks, *I suppose I was hoping she would find out something awful and rule him out of the picture altogether. Life would be simpler that way.*

Emi sits back and starts gathering up her papers. She closes the folder and rests her small delicate hands on top of it.

'Well, look, Mie-chan, I can see you are not altogether enthusiastic about this. I'm not going to meddle any further. I just leave this thought in your hands: this is absolutely as good a man', she taps the folder gently with a soft finger, 'as you are likely to get unless you really change your way of life – a lot. Don't forget, you can't be a miko or a shop-walker for ever!'

Mie pulls a face. It is a truth she has been hiding from. The role of miko especially, has been a refuge. The comforting routines of cleaning and preparing, of small ceremonies and observances. And at the big city shrine there is a rota, she is not in sole charge of the mop and bucket when it comes to purifying the halls. Although the faces of the other girls do seem to get younger…

Emi has fixed her with a slightly exasperated look.

'What have you got against him? He's not so terribly bad looking is he?'

Mie feels another surge of the vague doubt and discomfort Mr Yanaga seems to provoke in her.

'Who is wise enough to judge which of us is good or bad?'

'Mie-chan, what is that supposed to mean? You are seriously overthinking this!'

Mie lets out a sigh, pulls herself together.

'At my brother's wedding, Mr Yanaga was there. We were talking about the future. He said that one day, my brother would have to defend himself. When I asked him why, he just came out with that line – and something else about how everybody is wise and foolish, like how a ring goes around.'

'Did he now? How very intriguing!'

'He thinks my brother is planning to go into politics.'

'Yes, he made that pretty clear.'

'I'm not sure he approves. Of my brother.'

Emi licks a speck of cream from the back of her cake-fork.

'Mie-chan, this is a little more complicated than I thought. Give me a few more days. Please? I wont be bothering Tadasu again, I just need to think about a few things, OK? Meanwhile, you have a good think about what I have said. Whatever the problem might be, I still think he's a great prospect. Just think about it, and I'll come and see you in a few days time, OK?'

They emerge back into the chilly sunshine and part under the cherries by the park entrance. As she travels home and even after she has arrived there, Mie keeps finding more petals stuck on her clothes, in her hair. She is becoming entangled, with Emi, with Mr Yanaga, with her past, with dark dreams, with the world on the other side of the thunder-riven sky.

*   *   *

For a while, I held on to a hope that Hiroshi's absence wasn't going to be permanent. After all, he hadn't told me in so many words he wasn't coming back. Clearing his desk for other temps, I had stuck all his stuff in a carrier bag and taken it home with me ready to give back when he returned. Including the little black notebook.

But then, about a fortnight after his departure, the boss had called me in to her office.

'So ... your Mr Tanaka. Seems these family problems of his are quite serious. Looks like he will be staying in Japan for quite a while, maybe returning permanently.'

'Oh ... Right.'

The near finality of it hit me with a painful rush. A hole punched in my life. As I struggled to process this, I had my gaze focused on the boss's conservatively manicured fingers. With a decisive movement, she picked up a pencil. I tensed. Was this also going to be an 'I'm afraid we're going to have to let you go.' conversation? For a few seconds, it felt like my world was collapsing in on me.

'We've still got him on a retainer. He'll carry on sending stuff through from time to time for you to finish.'

I breathed out, trying not to let my tension show. The fingers were tapping the end of the pencil lightly against the desk.

'Do you and he talk much, I mean, apart from work?'

I kept my eyes fixed on the pencil.

'Well...'

Of course, if she meant the usual kind of social exchanges, the answer would really be 'No, not that much'. That odd, one-sided conversation, months ago now, was the only thing I could recall that really fell into that category. But how to explain the archery lessons? From brief instructions, through terse orders, to monosyllabic grunts of approval or disapproval and by way of variety, the occasional gently sarcastic or teasing remark. But most of all, the sense of shared presence in a moment of time. And of course, all those anxious messages. Since shortly after his departure, my inbox had been filling up with twice-weekly emails exhorting and encouraging me to maintain my practice in the bowling green. It was a bit one sided, but … it was the biggest thing I had. I took a deep breath.

'We certainly keep in touch.'

'I thought you were quite close? I heard you used to meet up after work.'

'Well, that was…'

The pencil was put down on the desk with a firm 'clack'.

'Look, I'm sorry, It's none of my business really, it's just that … I would really appreciate it if you kept in touch with him, generally. Even between jobs? Keep him on-side?'

'Well, yes. Sure.'

'He's actually quite useful as a contact out there. The fact is, I'm not sure I could afford to keep someone like you on without the extra volume of work he brings in.'

'Ah. Right.'

'I would like you to think of yourself as managing the relationship for us.'

'OK. No problem.'

'Good. So, I'm going to make a small investment in that relationship. The IT guy will be up tomorrow to set up video conferencing software on your PC.

'Ah, actually, I mostly use my own laptop these days. If he put it on there, I could use it to keep in touch from home too.'

I checked on the status of the pencil while she stared at me, no doubt with that shrewd look I had seen her bestow on other people who had said unexpected things.

'OK, good idea.'

The pencil rose swiftly into the air, hovered a moment, then descended with a decisive 'clack' to the desk. It was over.

Emotionally drained, I closed the office door behind me and sagged. Not a sacking then. Just the usual management mix of exhortations and thinly veiled threats. It was almost lunchtime, so I took myself off to a cafe and consoled myself with pie and chips. Which merely added indigestion to my bad mood as I wandered back and began the long ascent to my desk.

Hiroshi had gone, but why couldn't I stop thinking about him? All this effort in building a working relationship; then letting him boss me about with bows and arrows and now suddenly, that was it. Off he had gone, leaving me for the foreseeable future, peering at him over a no doubt flakey video link, while trying to find enough room on the screen for a one-hundred-and-fifty-page annotated document. And I was expected to spend time keeping him sweet as well, with a strong suggestion that my job might depend on it.

And then there was that other thing. Just before I left the warehouse for the last time, I had taken a quick look in the office, hoping that it too had not been swept away. It was just as I remembered it, including the old furniture, though Hiroshi's few personal effects had gone. Except, as I turned to go, I saw, hanging on the back of the door, a beige raincoat and a dark blue cap. The notebook I already had.

I had clutched the garments in my lap all the way home in the odd-job man's van. I hated how emotional the smell of them made me feel.

The IT 'guy' turned out to be called Helen and moreover, not an actual IT person, just another freelancer like me, but one who happened to know a bit about the software. Once the office PC was sorted, I proffered my laptop.

'You can download it yourself from here – look. It's free.'

'Oh.'

So much for 'investment', I thought.

Opening the video channel didn't seem to diminish the steady stream of nannying texts and emails coming from the other side of the world. All were something along the lines of: 'Are you shooting regularly? Are you keeping up practice in the park?' It was a link of a tenuous kind. I kept all of them in a separate folder and read through them from time to time.

Once I got settled in at the London dojo he seemed to calm

down a bit. The intervals became slightly longer. Sometimes he included snippets of family news about people I had no knowledge of, but as if he thought I ought to know them. If I tried to discuss any aspect of my shooting with him, his answer would always be: 'Ask your teacher about it.' It was still the same Hiroshi. Partly keeping me at a respectful distance, partly treating me as 'family'. I began to wonder if he was as uncertain about me as I was about him.

Practising had actually become a bit of a problem. I was still wary about the bowling green, and I certainly didn't fancy the open park. There were few bits of level ground and those very public. Instead, I cleared a corner of my sitting room by getting rid of a couple of chairs and a side table. As I never had guests, I wouldn't miss them. It didn't entirely work. My flat just didn't have the atmosphere.

The London gym didn't have much either, but shooting in company had reminded me of the thing I missed after Hiroshi left. How the mere presence of others keeps one focused, as they bear mute witness to struggle and progress.

This was perhaps the root of my reluctance to use the bowling green. It wasn't just elusive intruders or even illusory arrows. On certain evenings, in the shadows enclosed by its stone walls and overhanging laurels, I had felt a similar quality of attention.

* * *

It is one of Mie's rare days off, when neither the god nor the lingerie counter demand her attention. She is cleaning the flat, setting some flowers she bought in a vase by the open window, scrubbing the fly-screens before it gets too late to take them down without an invasion happening. While she is in the middle of all this domestic activity, embarrassing washing quite filling the small balcony, the doorbell rings. She has completely lost track of time! For a few seconds she seriously considers keeping very still and quiet until Emi goes away. But it is Emi. She cannot. Automatically, she reaches for the latch.

'Well! So this is where you hide yourself away! I love the area! That tiny courtyard full of plants and the little row of shops! Such a nice feeling, so friendly! Do you know all the neighbours?'

Mie drops her head.

'Not even to say 'good morning'?'

'Well – sometimes.'

'That's just typical of you isn't it! Saying 'good morning' is what it's all about! If you don't say 'good morning', you are never going to get anywhere are you?'

Emi's arch expression is only half-joking.

'Anyway, look, I brought these!' Emi carefully removes a crisp, white cardboard box from a crisp, white paper bag. Both carry the name and emblem of a very well-regarded and old established confectioner. With respectful care, Emi removes her white cotton gloves and folds back the flaps of the box to reveal a little tray of tiny, colourful, glistening cakes in the shapes of summer flowers.

'Got any decent coffee?'

Mie thinks a moment, then rummages in the back of a cupboard and pulls out a carton that Younger Brother had sent as a birthday gift. It is unopened. She never bothers with real coffee at home and usually just drinks cold barley tea in summer. Emi's eyes widen as Mie holds up the package for her consideration.

'Wow! When I said good coffee, I wasn't imagining super-excellent! Good taste!'

After some hunting about, Mie finds her percolator and some reasonable cups. Emi is fussy about the preparation and quickly takes over. It is half an hour before they settle down again, Mie, all the while, painfully aware of the homely flat and washing-filled balcony. Emi seems happily oblivious to the surroundings, lost in appreciatively sniffing the aroma of the slowly percolating coffee.

'Aaah! This is really good, Mie-chan! The real thing! Just exactly what these lovely sweets deserve. And just what my news deserves too! Now don't look so alarmed, it's nothing too bad!'

Mie is suddenly apprehensive. Is this going to mean she will have to take Mr Yanaga seriously now? Make difficult decisions? Has Emi let anything slip?

'Now before you say anything, Mie-chan, let me clear a few things up for you.'

Emi pulls out her pistachio-ribboned folder and consults some notes. Mie's apprehension shoots upwards.

'Let's begin with your worries over your little brother. That weird little speech Tadasu-kun came out with at the wedding…'

Mie's tension screws a notch higher. 'Tadasu-kun?!' Is it sarcasm, or is Emi already making Mr Yanaga part of her family?

'An interesting thing for him to say' Emi says, smiling, one eyebrow raised.

'What does it mean?'

'Oh, the meaning is plain enough: 'we all get it wrong sometimes' no puzzle there:

– what's interesting is who said it and where it comes from.'

'Eh?'

'Prince Shotoku, The Constitution of Fourteen Articles of 604BC, Article 10.'

'Emi! So clever!'

'Not really. I thought I recognised it, I just didn't remember the source. I asked an uncle of mine about it. Went to the same University as Tadasu. He seemed to think it was very funny that his little matchmaker niece should be interested in such a thing.'

Mie looks sympathetic. She is beginning to understand Emi's feelings about some subjects.

'He wasn't so amused when I made him look up the exact reference. Wanted to know where I had learned to get so picky. I didn't tell him about my own degree.'

'Emi, you went to university? You have a degree?'

'Don't sound so surprised please! Ochanomizu Women's University, Faculty of Letters. I enrolled as soon as I could after the war. I read English and American Literature. I wanted to look out of the window, see a bigger world!'

Mie smiles. Emi looks at her thoughtfully.

'It is such a shame your parents couldn't put you through university. You're just the kind of dreamy, thoughtful type it would have suited. Philosophy or something. Still, things weren't so good for women those days were they? Still aren't so great. Even so, have you not thought of studying?'

Mie finds an unexpected anger welling up inside her.

'Hm. I guess the war spoiled a lot of things, but it also fixed a few things. You could study now if you wanted to. I'm sure Tadasu wouldn't mind.'

Emi gives that last phrase a teasing note. Mie's annoyance makes her a little scratchy.

'Emi-chan, if you have a degree, why are you going to be just a matchmaker?'

'I didn't say I was *only* going to be a matchmaker! I said it was one of the things I had going on.'

Emi smiles, winks and tips her imaginary fedora, then puts on a serious face.

'To come back to the subject of our meeting, what quoting Prince Shotoku means is that your friend Mr Yanaga really does have a serious interest in politics as well as the law. He's a thoughtful man.'

'But what did he mean about my brother?'

'You really don't know?'

Mie simply looks at her friend, pleadingly. Emi sighs.

'Well, this is just a hunch – and to be honest, this is something I've never really associated with you personally...'

Emi pauses, frowning a little and sucks her lip.

'You do know that during the war your parents were widely believed to have assassinated a politician?'

Emi looks at the colour draining out of her friend's face.

'I am so sorry. The Elephant still has a lot to learn.'

Mie looks down at her lap. There is a long moment of silence, in which the percolator finally ceases to gurgle. Is this how people have been seeing her all this time?

'Mother! Father! They would not assassinate anyone!'

Mie's outburst is fierce.

Emi remains calm, serious

'It was war. At home as well as abroad. Many very lamentable things occurred. Still, perhaps it is better you should know. The Yanagas knew your parents quite well. Old Prince Shotoku says that harmony should come before everything else, but I think there is a kind of harmony that is worse than discord – the kind built on silence.'

'Silence?'

'I think perhaps you should talk to Tadasu.'

* * *

5 Hikiwake

Pushing the bow and pulling the string in balance toward the extremity of tension.

I hadn't intended to go home through the park so late in the evening. Hiroshi and I had been working together online to finish a job for a client of his in Osaka.

Surprisingly, I had got to liking the video thing. Because Hiroshi was not looking directly at his own camera, but at the image of me on his screen, there was almost no real eye-contact. The disconnect was just enough that I could relax and enjoy the novelty of observing someone's facial expressions as they talked with me. In a way, I felt I had got to know some aspects of Hiroshi better like this than I had in months of sitting side by side in the attic office, or being bullied on his makeshift archery range. It made me feel I hadn't completely lost him.

The receptionist had left me the keys to lock up, leaving Virtual Hiroshi and me comfortably settled in our old attic haunt. I could have gone home and continued on my laptop, but I didn't want to interrupt the flow, conscious that at his end it was still some ungodly hour before dawn.

Hiroshi's return to Tokyo had prompted me to invest in a self-study *Japanese for Business* course, and I was improving to the extent that I could do a few very simple bits of translation into English on my own. Of course, I always ran them past him just in case. It became a kind of game to see if I could slip even a few words past his laser sharp editorial gaze unscathed. It had become a less pleasant game, to find ways of reassuring him about my practice without admitting that I had almost stopped going to the bowling green.

On my side of the world, the sun was down by the time we finally hit 'send' on the Osaka document. Hiroshi logged off immediately with a curt nod and an equally curt 'Goodbye'. After all, I reminded myself, he had managed the whole session without a roll-up. I leaned back in my hard chair and massaged my eyeballs, unwilling for the moment to make a move. Then I stood up stiffly and began to pack up my few bits and pieces. The park was a convenient short cut toward home. The grass would be cool and delightful. I didn't have to go anywhere near the bowling green. I would just wander up the hill, slip out by my usual exit and perhaps pick up supper somewhere on the way.

It was a fine, still evening, the afterglow of sunset making the mist of buds in the trees glow green through the dusk. I slipped off my shoes and socks. The spring grass was indeed cool, moist and thick, filling the air with its cold and tender scent. Lost in these sensations, I drifted up the hill, unconsciously following my customary lunchtime route.

The sight of the little hawthorn tree by the horizontal path brought me up short. If I carried straight on, I would have to tackle the steep and tussocky bank beyond. I was tired and wanted to avoid a scramble. I would either have to turn right and go the long way round, or go left, taking the route I had intended to avoid. I stopped a little way short of the path, looking left and right, considering. As my gaze slid past, something pale glimmered in the grass at the foot of the hawthorn tree.

*　*　*

He has agreed to see her after work, Mie assumes, because her personal enquiry is not a professional matter. Already she feels embarrassed to have made this claim on his time, to have incurred an obligation.

He is waiting, in raincoat and hat, umbrella and slim lawyer's briefcase in hand, outside his office building. He raises the umbrella with a chivalrous flourish against a thin rain that scarcely warrants it and steers her through the sea of pinched and tired homeward going faces, into an intimidatingly expensive restaurant a little way down the street. He is evidently delighted that she has asked to see him. She had wanted only a matter of fact, business-like consultation, but now he is insisting on buying supper and has managed to make it seem like a date.

The restaurant feels oppressive. The masculine interior of dark wood and mirrors, the French film posters and even the menu, issue a challenge rather than a welcome. Mr Yanaga however, seems very comfortable, relaxing expansively in the Parisian-style bentwood chair. He has been talking solidly for what feels like three quarters of an hour, as the waiters bustle to and fro. She picks without enthusiasm at unfamiliar dishes neither wholeheartedly foreign nor wholly Japanese. As he talks, it feels as if she is being served cold, the shredded remains of her once warm and living childhood. A life, it seems, she had not understood, even as she had lived it.

'You have a lot to thank your parents for, I think.'

Mr Yanaga has, with a great show of seeking her permission, lit a cigarette which he waves now, with authoritative emphasis, while fixing her with an appraising stare.

'They succeeded in shielding you from a lot of unpleasant-ness.'

'You must have done a lot of research, to understand things so thoroughly.'

He seems not to notice the edge of bitterness in her words.

'It was somewhat difficult, but not excessively so. Many

records were destroyed, but I talked to my family and one or two of their friends. Your family and mine appear to have been part of overlapping circles. It seems fairly certain that the Imperial Government, or rather, some people in that Government, were convinced of your parents' guilt.'

'No!'

'You really did not know? I am truly sorry. I thought you must have known.'

He gives her that glancing look again, cool, appraising, perhaps even, a little conspiratorial.

'It appears your parents trod a careful line. They kept friends and contacts in many different factions. I think your father was as much a diplomat as he was a writer and thinker. In other times, he might have had a great career overseas.'

Mie is silent. This lawyer can only have been a child when the events he speaks so authoritatively about first began. Like herself, he had come of age amid the strange pretences of war. Not content to cut and slash at her childhood with his dirty blade of gossip and hearsay, now he is chopping at Father too. As a child she had naturally thought of Father as a great man. To think that he might have been a greater, that he too was diminished and degraded by the times, is a shock.

'Did you serve in the war?'

It is an atrocious question. He is visibly shocked. He blows a smokescreen to give himself time.

'Yes. In the Navy Yards, clerical section. For the same man my father worked for.'

'You did not volunteer to fight?'

His face darkens. She wonders where she got the courage, the cruelty, to ask that question, as she watches him suck the last out of his cigarette and grind it out in the ash tray.

'It was forbidden. Our Section Head insisted we knew too much to be allowed to go to the front.'

Mr Yanaga is looking at some distant point. He gives a wry smile.

'He used to say: 'The clerical corps keeps marching! Take them away and your man at the front will have nothing to put in his belly and nothing to put in his gun!' We were only a handful in our office. Even then it was a close thing. We were still expecting orders when the Emperor spoke on the radio.'

He is a little flushed. She has challenged him, a man. Questioned his courage. Forced him to justify himself. She waits, tense, to see what comes next. Without asking, he lights up a new cigarette. His hands shake a little as he holds the flame of his expensive lighter to it.

'To be honest with you I still find myself wondering sometimes if all this,' he waves a languid hand around the room, trailing smoke, 'is even real. Sometimes I wake up in the morning, wondering if those orders have come through.'

Mie stares. She had been cruel and aggressive because she had been angry with him. Now she wants to reach out, to say something, but he is looking at that distant other place, lost in his thoughts. Pulling himself back seems to be an effort. He turns slowly and points at her with the glowing end of his cigarette.

'I have often wondered how your father avoided conscription. A lot of men his age were called up, especially toward the end. He must have been doing something the government approved of. And it must have been something dangerous, that earned him the enmity of certain factions.'

Mie sits horrified. Tadasu is burning down the house of her childhood. Perhaps she has deserved it. Perhaps nothing was whole or pure. Perhaps she herself, in her ignorance, is as complicit as anyone else.

'The fact is, if they had not died in the fire-bombing, your parents would very probably have been arrested and executed. Many were and for much less. Sometimes for quite imaginary offences.'

Mie looks at her lap and says nothing.

'They survived as long as they did, because they had influential friends. I imagine that's how they kept your dojo going just when war shortages were at their worst. A lot of our parents' friends were high up in the government and the forces. I guess a few of them felt it was worth trying to preserve such things. Some of them leaned on your father and because he and your mother knew people who wanted to be on the right side of other people... Oh, you must know how it goes.'

Mie hides her frown behind a hand. It appalls her to think of Father, or Mother, like that.

'By the time the Americans started bombing raids, I guess time was already running out for them. Some old people my mother knows, felt that any members, or even associates of your family were in danger. In fact if you hadn't taken that little stroll into the mountains just when you did, you might not be here now.'

With a rush of chill, Mie remembers a boy in an ill-fitting police uniform, remembers shouts coming from the direction of her parents' ruined house as she walks swiftly down the next street.

*　　*　　*

A pair of geta. The indigo cotton straps made two dark arrowheads, pointing at the trunk of the little hawthorn under which they had been placed. The plain wood tops were completely clean of any sign of wear. Whoever left them there must have carried, not worn them.

I stood staring, while the sounds of the city drifted in from beyond the boundaries of the park. Looking around the grassy slopes, I could see only a few people, all hurrying home along distant paths, not loitering in the dusk like me. None of them looked like people who might have recently abandoned a brand-new pair of geta.

On a sudden impulse, I brushed my bare feet on the grass and tried to slip them on. The straps felt very tight and new, and I had to wriggle my toes quite hard to get them in. The wood felt smooth and clean. My feet are large, but these were evidently a man's pair and quite adequate. I turned carefully, conscious of having gained a couple of inches in height. Grinning at my own folly, I began to gingerly walk the level path toward the bowling green.

In the still evening air, the wooden teeth under the soles of the geta rang on the path with an odd resonance, as if I were walking between high walls. The tower lanterns were too high and distant to give any useful light, but the low cloud was beginning to reflect the glow of the surrounding city, so that even as the last of the day faded, few shadows were really dark. Even so, as I came up to the bowling green entrance, I felt a sensation of shade overhead. Glancing up, I could see only pale sky.

I stopped, looking anxiously around. A cliff-edge kind of feeling flowed through me. Fear, but with it, the irrational urge to lean into the abyss. I slipped the geta off, placing them side by side with my own shoes at the entrance and walked softly through.

It took a second for my eyes to accommodate to the deeper shadows. I scanned the space anxiously, the hairs on the back of my neck prickling. But there was nothing untoward. A few dry leaves, an empty crisp-packet, a dead bird.

Well, now I'm here, I thought, *I ought to at least go through the motions.* I put down my bag and began the preparatory movements, finishing with the gaze settled on the distant, safely imaginary target. All the foundations in place for a successful shot.

But at the moment of kai, of maximum tension, I suddenly reached the limits of my courage. The night air seemed to crackle with a feeling that the release, even of an imaginary shot, would trigger something irrevocable. I brought my hands slowly back up to the starting position, lowered them to my sides, bowed, and stepped back.

As I stoop to pick up my bag, the dojo I had been visualising as the setting for my shots seems to persist in memory. The polished wooden floor of the open-sided shooting hall. Between the hall and the target shelter opposite, a square of fine raked gravel, or a moss lawn, or even a delicately tended garden of stones, gravel and low-growing plants.

All I have to do is turn round.

* * *

He sees her to the tram stop, where she enforces as cool and formal a parting as she can manage. Once he has gone, she does not wait, but slowly walks two or three stops along the line. She needs to become calm and to think.

How is it that he seems to know so much? How did he know about her journey to the shrine? Emi must have betrayed her. But no. There were plenty of people there who may well have known his family. Word of such extravagant things soon gets around. Mie's insides shrivel at the thought of being … spoken of.

She chides herself. The question comes more out of her resentment at his manner, than from logic. She must stop being a child. Stop seeing other people as mysterious, immanent beings full of knowledge, as if it were the very substance they were made from. It is high time to ask questions.

Why does he speak so insinuatingly, so knowingly, about Father? Presumably, his own father was a visitor? Perhaps a spy even. *'Like a ring going round.'* She scans her memory, looking for a face that might have been that of Yanaga Senior. It is too long ago. The memories too infrequent and confused. Her parents had indeed sheltered her from much that went on in her own home. It is a desolate feeling. A double exile. She feels so much a stranger in this new world, and now he has made her a stranger to her own past.

Her eyes roam the busy evening street. In places like this, she has an uncertain sense of being close to something she has lost, wanting both to find it and to not find it. She cannot say clearly what it is. A memory that seems too strange not to be a dream. A recurring dream that feels like the illusion of a memory.

Is this how the dead feel? Those who should, but cannot leave the world? A punishment for the neglect of her parents' funerary rites? Perhaps tomorrow, she should visit one of the Buddhist temples and arrange a belated memorial. But even as the thought arises, she can hear Mother's snort of derision. Her parents loved to debate the intellectual ideas of Buddhism, but they had little good to say about the Buddhist establishment, of whatever sect. At every twist she feels thwarted, like a fish in a trap. Should she perhaps, not remain, but seek out death? But if she is already dead? She shakes her head. She can almost hear Mother's sarcastic, impatient voice, telling her firmly not to be so weak as to give credit to such perverted, nonsensical things. Her parents' strongest belief perhaps, had been in the importance of living in the moment. 'Be here now!' Father would say, when ideas too abstract or metaphysical were proposed. She halts, nose to the glass of a shop window, trying to immerse herself in the reality of the present, in all its mundane glamour.

And at that moment, she sees it. A company logo? A new but oddly familiar brand name? A half-recognised shape? Perhaps just a colour? Nothing that she can point to. Something that prompts a feeling, a sense of movement. It is not only the city and its people that are changing. It is everything. Time, at last, seems to have recovered its confidence. A certain direction of travel is beginning to assert itself, a certain spirit. It is all moving, moving like quicksand, moving like water, flowing like a strengthening tide. It would not take much for it to become more like the world of the dream. Perhaps it is the dream.

She turns to see a shady looking man in a worn-out military coat who appears to be taking an interest in her. The street is quieter than it was. Glancing around in a panic, she sees that the policeman, taking the air outside his box on the street corner, is also taking a detached, professional interest in both of them. Abandoning thoughts of the tram, she scurries away to a subway entrance.

In the silent flat, she takes off her coat and lies down in her clothes on the bed. She does not bother to turn on the bedside light. Staring at swirling images in the dark, she is swept by a feeling of suspended panic. It seems unpleasantly familiar. Her mind reels with a kind of vertigo. If only there were some rock protruding through the floor, to cling to.

*　　*　　*

146

Was it arrogant of me to think I was the only one passing through the park that day who even knew what geta were? But who had put them there? And what was really unsettling – who had reclaimed them? Leaving, I had found my own shoes exactly where I had left them. But not the geta. Had Hiroshi snuck back into the country? He was the one who had remarked on my shoe-size. Someone had to be fooling about with me. The thought that it might be Hiroshi kept me looking out for them, but it also made me resentful. Why was he playing games instead of making himself known? I found myself slyly scanning passers-by, or glancing behind me in the hope of catching him lurking.

But for all my vigilance there were, for a while, no more tricks with footwear and no more uncanny occurrences. Spring turned to summer, and evenings in the bowling green were a pleasant alternative to my flat. I ended up practising there almost every night.

The weather got steadily warmer and more humid, until an evening came, so hot and airless that you almost began to panic for breath. After work, I had gone home only long enough to get something to drink and to nibble listlessly at odds and ends of food. Then I had come back over to the park, hoping that as night came on, a breeze might spring up. Quite a few other people seemed to have had the same idea.

For a while I sat out on the dried-up grass of the hillside, reading newspapers and trying not to be eaten alive by insects. Gradually, the number of insects increased, and the number of people decreased, until just a few couples, aware only of each other, remained in the shadows of distant shrubberies.

It was one of those short summer nights that was never going to get really dark, but at last, as the twilight deepened, the faintest hint of a breeze began to trickle down the slopes of the hill. I got stiffly up, rolled up the mat I had been sitting on and began to climb. Coming up to the horizontal path, I glanced at the little thorn-tree, but the grass in front of it was clear. I stood looking at the spot, only half disappointed.

In the distant streets the soft rush of traffic was insistent even at this hour. The sound of a car horn and, further away, a brief burst of an ambulance siren, told of the city still busy with its nightlife. I was in no hurry, and the idea of a little late practice was attractive. Just at that moment, someone hurried past behind me heading for the bowling green. I turned immediately, but there was no-one on the darkening path. I set off to follow, hoping it had not been one of those couples.

As I approached, I had the odd impression of a gnarled old pine tree on my left, extending tortuously trained horizontal branches across the entrance. Had that always been there? But why would something so carefully cultivated be moved to such a neglected and overgrown spot? As I tried to make it out, I became confused, unable to trace it among the tangle of shrubbery and the branches of more distant trees against the sky.

I was about to take a step forward, eyes wide open, straining to make out details in the gloom, when a moth flew into one of them. Blinking tears, trying to wipe the thing away, I was blinded for a moment.

When I can see properly again, I find myself looking down at the geta. They are not alone. Across the entrance lies a large, smooth, flat rock, half buried in the earth. Lined up on it are not only 'my' pair of geta, but several other pairs with different coloured straps. There are also some rush sandals and a couple of pairs of rather old-fashioned looking western-style men's and women's leather shoes.

Disappointed that I do not have the place to myself, I step forward to see what is going on – and nearly fall flat on my face. Someone has laid a wooden decking or floor across the entrance, a few inches higher than the top of the stone with the shoes on. I step up, only to be brought to a halt again by pitch darkness. Surely I ought to be able to see something from here? A texture brushes against my hands and face: the darkness is material, a curtain hung across the entrance. I grope around until my hand finds a gap, push through – and stop dead again. It is, if anything, even darker. A dead acoustic suggests enclosed space. Have they restored the old clubhouse? Deprived of spatial cues, I have a sudden momentary sensation of falling. Throwing out an arm to save myself, I feel an uncertain contact. A faint vertical bar of lesser shadow to my left emerges, as if a door has swung half open.

*　　*　　*

Tadasu 'senses', apparently, that she did not find the restaurant 'altogether congenial' and would like to show her a much more attractive little place in…' She folds the notepaper in her hand. Looks at her own name on the envelope. Her name, in his hand. What does she own of herself anymore?

And yet, she does not want to be dragged back, reclaimed – either by the dim glamour of her dreams or the desperation of former times. She wants to escape this feeling of having only a temporary, provisional existence. Of not, somehow, having full title to her own being. It is a hard bargain. Which self to hold onto? The one that was lost, or the paper-fragile new one folded impossibly out of her own impulses? She thinks of that night she had wished for a rock to hold onto. Tadasu appears to be holding out a hand. She becomes suddenly filled with panic at the thought of what might happen if she does not take it.

The invitation becomes the first of several. She walks out with him, once a week or so. They do the very conventional things. They go to this temple garden, that new terrace bar, or contemplate the impersonal vistas of the Imperial Palace Park.

The park offers a neutral beauty on which to gaze. They sit, uncomfortably close, awkwardly distant, on a summer evening bench. Those for whom these Imperial walks and vistas were laid out all had, from the highest to the lowest, she thinks, a purpose and a place. The curve of the path before them is not a route, a way to an end, it is merely something to soak up the footsteps of people who already had goals and routes. It challenges her with her own emptiness. Beside her sits a man who seems to have purpose, a notion of the way forward. He has his doubts, as she does, but seems able to take his place in the flow of things.

That evening, as they part, she briefly reaches out and takes his offered hand. It is warm and solid. He makes no move, like a careful fisherman who does not strike too soon.

*   *   *

Beyond the doorway, the faintest suggestion of a long, narrow space. A soft reflection of light on something shiny, high up. If it is a bulb, it is surely turned off. It makes me think of those dreams in which you flick the switch, but the brain cannot conjure up an entire room in an instant and so it remains stubbornly dark.

There is something like light though. If I keep my gaze still and level, an impression of dim, blue-grey panels, high up on my left, just below ceiling height. I keep still, looking straight ahead. Although I can see nothing directly, the sense of a room softly forms around me. Low benches running along the walls. Some garments hanging above. A curtain strung across the far left hand corner. All of these, impressions rather than facts. Possibilities constructed out of shadows. Opposite the curtain, the sense of an opening, leading into some space that is again, a little lighter.

There is a queasy sense of disconnection from my surroundings, as if I were a little drunk. Although convinced I am not alone, I can see no-one. Turning, I step through the second opening as boldly as I can manage. The space beyond, again seems to take a few moments to coalesce. And then, recognising at last where I stand, I make, in reflex action, a formal bow.

A wide, high-roofed room. The long side opposite open, so that at last I can see out into what should have been the bowling green. Staring rigidly ahead, but with all my attention on the borders of vision, I walk softly to the edge of a smooth wooden floor and peer out into the gloom. A barrier to the right, that is not the stone retaining wall and shrubbery I am used to. To the left, instead of lower bushes and small trees, a tall fence. Puzzled by its construction, I forget myself for a moment and turn to look directly at it. The fence becomes a darkness, but what had been the hidden view ahead, now blooms softly on the edge of shadow. A shallow canopy, roofed with dark tiles, spanning the full width of the far boundary, rising gracefully to a small rounded gable in the centre. A strip of dark coloured curtain hangs all along the edge of the roof, gathered up beneath the central gable with a heavy tassel. Beneath it, five round, paper-covered target drums, their familiar alternating circles of black and white glimmering in the dusk-light. Between shooting hall and targets, not the conventional plain open space, but a miniature landscape of low growing shrubs, dwarf bamboo, mossy rocks, stepping stones and gravel.

As I look, the light seems to gently increase, rendering the scene in shades of silvery-grey. Low above the roofline of the matoba, the target shelter, a full moon hangs in a dark sky that softly shades down toward a lighter horizon.

Forgetting my manners, I look the moon in the eye. She vanishes, leaving the five eyes of the target roundels staring up from the lower edge of vision. Some shadow seems to be falling on the pale rings of the right-most target. Drawn on by a kind of unwilling curiosity, I step unsteadily down off the edge of the shooting-floor and work carefully from stepping stone to stepping stone, threading my way across like a man treading on thin ice.

A pair of arrows, frozen in flight. One, within a few feet of impact, the other close behind. Hai-ya and oto-ya. One arrow feathered to spin with a right-handed, clockwise twist, the other, its sinistral opposite, balancing the universe. There seems no doubt of the accuracy of these shots. The poise is perfect, completed.

A faint noise, like the shriek of an insect, makes me turn my head toward the shooting hall and in the same instant, the whole illusion collapses from under me with a sickening lurch, as if the floor of the universe has suddenly dropped away, to be replaced with another, a few inches below.

When I recovered my balance, I was crouching in my familiar, derelict bowling green, amid the weeds and cracked asphalt. In the shadows near the entrance, a couple were staring at me. The woman had a hand to her mouth.

'Who are you?'

I struggled to find words.

'How'd you do that?'

I started to walk unsteadily towards them, feeling like someone who has just fallen off a cliff but inexplicably survived.

'You jus' … like …'

The man made a despairing gesture.

'… Sh'zam!'

The voice was slurred and anxious.

'Where'r y'ur shoes mate?'

I was in no mood for conversation. I pushed past them and turning left, began to rapidly climb the flight of steps leading to the upper promenade. I was anxious to turn corners, to get out of range of unwanted curiosity. I heard footsteps coming rapidly up behind me.

'Hey! Mate! You lef' these!'

The voice had the dangerous, blearily insistent urgency that comes from trying to connect with the real world through the fog of drink, or drugs. I turned, warily. A pair of geta were being held out to me. The pair. I took them. They felt solid and hard.

'Thanks.'

'S'alright, no worries mate. You take care now.'

Feeling a twist of irony at being the concern of an apparent addict, I turned and hurried on up the steps, the geta slung from my fingertips by their padded cotton straps. It was not until I was out in the street that I realised the sensation of weight in my fingers was only a kind of after-image. I knew I had not dropped them, nor put them down. I simply no longer occupied a reality in which I held them.

* * *

From the moment she passes under the dark wooden portal of the covered gateway, treading the path that winds among brushstrokes of moss, rocks and gently mounded foliage, she feels acutely awkward and out of place. An elderly pine leans on crutches by the side of the sinuous path. A group of cherries shadow a corner of the artfully rambling, single storey house, sulking in dark green foliage after the outburst of spring blossom. A cluster of mossy stones stand ankle deep in a muddy-bottomed pond, like washerwomen who have forgotten what they were doing.

An affected informality, that feels anything but relaxed. Like a miniature Imperial villa, she thinks, or a minor daimyo's country retreat. Even out here, among the foothills of the mountains, it seems unreasonably large. Whether obtained through heredity or purchase, she does not venture to ask. Perhaps that is something Emi would know about.

Mie expresses conventional pleasure as Tadasu shows her around his family home, but in truth, the place seems made of shadows. It feels like a house from that other world, before time received such a shock.

Tadasu's mother seems to sense a challenge, though Mie offers none. In response Tadasu draws his parent out into the garden. Mie watches them, heads bent together. The pair spend most of the first day outdoors, discussing, Tadasu says airily afterwards, 'planting, weeding, pruning'. On the second day too, Mie is left largely to her own devices, barely acknowledged by anyone. Only the elderly grandmother greets her, with a gracefulness that seems positively warm by contrast.

A thin, bald, middle-aged man, dressed in formal kimono, arrives to join the family for supper. He is introduced as a former colleague of Tadasu's father. He greets Mie ceremoniously, but thereafter devotes all of his conversation to Tadasu and his mother. During the meal however, she notices that every time she makes a movement, he seems to direct a brief, appraising stare in her direction. She cannot shake the feeling that he has been called in to make some sort of livestock evaluation.

At night, she finds herself lying decorously alone on a futon spread on the floor of a chilly corner guest room. Under an antique quilt that feels slightly damp, she wonders at her own actions. Is this what she wants? To be part of this cold machine of family relationships? But it is reality. It is an invitation to join the world. And could she really expect an invitation to come from any other quarter than this? A place, that like herself, seems to only half exist in the present?

And Tadasu, for all his irritating attitudes, does seem to be consistently interested in her. At least, in a theoretical, legalistic kind of way. It is something. He seems reliable. A kind of security.

She wakes in the morning, somewhat stiff and cold. Oddly, in this ghostly house, she has not been haunted by dreams.

*   *   *

Although I dragged myself into work the following morning, I succeeded only in fidgeting restlessly at my desk, suspended between weird elation and dark terror. I went down to reception, mumbled some made-up excuse about having to go to a meeting and left.

My head was spinning with all the old anxious thoughts. Had my ridiculous sidelong way of living done something to my eyes? Should I be seeing an optician, having a brain scan, or seeking urgent psychiatric advice?

Crossing the park on the way home, I forced myself to go and stick my head inside the bowling green, just to see it in plain daylight. Although it was still exhaustingly hot and humid, a bunch of kids were having a noisy kick-about soccer game on the old, cracked square. I ducked out again before they noticed me. It really didn't seem like the same place. Then again, I didn't feel like the same person. Something, hard to name but disturbingly deep, had shifted.

I went home, had a long, cool shower and ate a salad I had bought in town. I turned on the radio, turned it off again, then looked up a weather forecast. More heat, more humidity, more 'risk of heavy, thundery showers'. I picked up a random book and sat fitfully reading by an open window with the lights off, until it got too dark. Then, finally, I did what I had known I was going to do all day.

Dressed in just a t-shirt and shorts and carrying my practice outfit wrapped in a furoshiki cloth, I drifted in sandalled silence along pavements and past walls still radiating the afternoon's sunshine into the dusk. After all, there was nowhere else so suitable and if I was going to practise in a proper dojo, it was only right to dress correctly. That was as far as I allowed myself to go in justifying this reckless enterprise.

The park entrance on the side nearest my place was in a poorly lit side street, scarcely more than a lane. I slipped unnoticed into the darkness under the trees and climbed the short, steep path up the back of the hill. As I emerged onto the promenade, I was momentarily puzzled by a strange, flickering light that seemed to come from above. Looking up, I saw that although the tower lanterns hung still, each was surrounded by a glittering, fluttering ball of thousands upon thousands of moths.

As soon as I began to descend the steps, I was almost sure I caught, even from this unfamiliar angle, the shadow of the pine tree, but it was hard to make out against the dark background of other foliage. Arriving at the bottom, I deliberately looked away and set off along the path to my left. As I had half-hoped, there was a hint of pale wood in the grass under the little hawthorn. I took a careful scan of the dusky park. I was alone.

I put down the furoshiki, untied it and laid back the four corners. On top of the pile were the white tabi, split-toed socks of strong cotton, worn for shooting on a dojo's polished wooden floor. It took some inelegant wobbling to get them on, and I had to stand on the edge of the furoshiki to avoid dirtying them on the ground. Then, the long, white kimono-shirt, wrapped over itself at the front and tied at the sides. Over that, the stiff cotton obi belt, wound firmly around the waist and secured with a special knot, which is then slipped around to the back. Next, the swinging pleats of the heavy black hakama, half trousers, half floor-length kilt, with long waist ties knotted in front. Finally, I slipped the geta on, wrapped my thin sandals up in the furoshiki and tucked it into the front of my shirt. I was ready.

The long hakama swing round my legs. The wooden geta ring and echo as if I am walking down a narrow lane between high walls, not an open path on a grassy hillside. I look up to see pine boughs making dark gestures across the entrance, inked-in against a building sketched in shadows. Below them, only a dark rectangular recess, the top two thirds closed off by a curtain of still thicker darkness. But if I look a little aside, a large round emblem, like a full moon seen through mist, is dimly revealed: pale against the darkness, a geometric pattern of three arrow feathers, contained in a circle. As I gesture aside the impression of fabric, the symbol shivers and splits.

I come to a stand in pitch darkness. For a second it occurs to me that, this being perhaps some kind of dream, I could break the laws of physics, pass through walls or even fly. I am not tempted to try. This already feels far too much like walking a long way out onto very thin ice. Instead, I follow my former route, pacing carefully through the dimness of the empty changing room, until I can step uncertainly into the slightly lighter space of the shooting hall. I make the customary bow, then stand a while, taking in this strangely persistent hallucination. The centre of my vision, as before, is a vague darkness, but looking steadily ahead, I am vividly aware of the polished wooden floor at my feet. It seems to reflect the light of a different sky, though just as muted as that of the twilit evening I have left behind. Stepping aside from the door, I arrange my skirts and quietly kneel with my back to the wall. The low position makes me feel like a fascinated child as, sidelong, I examine my surroundings.

To my left, against the wall, I recognise a barrel-sized cylinder of rice-straw on a stout wooden stand, presenting its round, flat end to the room. A makiwara target for short-range practice. Nearby, on the same wall, an old-fashioned bulletin board with criss-cross ribbons holding some hand-written notices and folded papers. A rack for bows, another for arrows, and a small cupboard.

All these things I see not only confined to the edges of vision, but dimly, as if in a tarnished antique mirror. I could say it is dream-like, but dreams shift and change and transmute and will not submit, as this does, to steady observation. Yet this is not like reality either. Perhaps some paintings have this sense of absent presence. It is like watching someone who is very deeply asleep.

Set into the right-hand wall is an alcove housing the kamiza, a low dais to seat the teacher and guests of honour on formal occasions. In the alcove itself, I recognise a kamidana, a small shrine to whatever deity or presence presides over this place. Somewhat old-fashioned, then, or perhaps a private establishment, since overt religious symbols are not today acceptable in public dojos. High on the wall at the back of the alcove, another old-fashioned feature: a black and white photograph of what looks like a man in western military uniform.

Hanging nearby, a calligraphic scroll bears three large, bold, black characters in a loose, vigorous style of brushwork. To memorise a decent range of characters is hard work, but I had been working hard. Even so, I struggle with the recollection of recent studies and the difficulty of making out even such large characters without looking directly at them.

The connection of shapes and meanings comes suddenly and makes me glance back in surprise at the pleasing arrangement of plants and stones that lies between the edge of the shooting floor and the target shelter. Such an ornamental arrangement is, I know from my obsessive researches, a little unusual. But when had I come to think of this illusory, yet curiously consistent apparition of a place, as having a name? Was that scroll only there because that was what I had imagined it might be called?

Ya no Niwa.

The Arrow Garden.

* * *

She can hear raised voices in another room. Tadasu. Trying to restrain himself, but … angry. His mother. Outrage, offence, exasperation in her tone, changing to resentful remonstration. The Grandmother's voice is thinner and quieter, but she is the one who is not ruled by her emotions. Calm. Analytical. A voice of authority that does not need to assert itself.

Mie stares unseeing at the book she has been reading. What has just happened? And why is she afraid, though she hears no mention of her name, that it is about her? Has her fate been decided in her absence? In another room in this house of empty mats and dusty screens, while she sits reading an idly chosen book about – she flips to the title page – *Buddhism and the Legal Profession*, written in … 1924?

She puts down the book and slips out to take yet another walk, as slowly as she can manage this time, around the garden. Little scenes and landscapes devised long ago, by someone who knew nothing of her feelings. And yet, her mind is quieted somewhat. Where did it go, that sense of purpose, of freedom to act, that she had discovered in the mountain village? That too seems a tale of long ago. But it had been hers. What is she doing here, among these people who seem so equivocal in their welcome?

She turns a corner, the furthest from the house. A fence of decaying reed-bundles, a small stand of arrow bamboo, and a view of the pond. The bamboo stirs softly. She stops, suddenly afraid to take another step.

Shades of ash, breathtaking in their subtlety, as pure and sad as snow. The garden has become a photograph of itself. A print in soft tones of silver grey. An emulsion refined out of the very bones of the city itself.

Can it really have been as perfect as she remembers it? A beauty absolute in its shutter-frozen horror. Staring at it, she had known that the present had become, in a single night, the past. A lost world, as irrecoverable and as irrevocable, as the world imaged in a photograph.

It has been a long time since she has cried. The heat sears her cheeks, then chills them as the rivulets cool.

'So many people.'

The old woman is standing nearby. Still as a statue. Out of the corner of the eye, her clothes appear formal, dark and plain. Mie turns to look and sees that the woman's kimono and obi are shot silks and muted brocades that swirl and shimmer like unquiet waters.

'So many tears. I sometimes think this pond must be filled with them. Every time it rains...'

The voice trails off into silence. Mie puts a hand up to her face, hesitates to wipe her western fine wool sleeve across it, like some ancient poet dressed in the wrong outfit. Tadasu's grandmother reaches into the breast of her kimono and offers her a handkerchief. An arm is slipped through hers. Unsure of who is guiding whom, she finds herself led into a little hidden arbour with a stone seat. Cushions have been set on it, between them, a little tray with tiny tea-bowls and a small iron teapot.

'I know it is not very pleasant for you here. My family, well, they are an odd lot. They like to think of themselves as intellectuals, but really we are all hopelessly conventional. No heads for real philosophy. Not like your parents. I remember their gatherings.'

The old lady pours tea with a decorous liveliness of spirit that gives Mie the ghostly feeling she is talking with a woman of her own age. Mie is grateful for the warmth even of this tiny bowl. It feels like the first real generosity she has encountered in this house.

'You must miss them dreadfully.'

Mie is suddenly lost again. What to say? The loss is perfect. Limitless. Beyond even tears. Only little sentimental things, like the garden, can make her cry.

'I think you should understand something.'

The older woman's voice is gentle, tender almost.

'About how important your parents were. I don't mean as

parents. I don't mean important in social or political ways. What I want to say to you, is not about status.'

An aged koi, huge, white and mottled with grey, blows a slow bubble on the surface of the distant pond.

'It is about how your father – and your mother especially, about how they held us up. Supported us. So many lamentable things… No, that is a conventional hypocrisy. Let me say what I really think. So many utterly disgraceful things were done and said.

All this humbug in the press these days. People scrambling to find some scrap of dignity. As if they had all come back from swimming to find their clothes stolen. Hah. We do not need Americans to tell us how to feel.'

The woman beside her seems to have stopped talking to Mie and to be immersed in her own train of thought, connected yet zig-zag, like the plank bridge across the corner of the garden pond.

*   *   *

By day I shunned my new obsession, not wanting to see the bowling green in its everyday aspect, even from a distance. I lived only for nightfall, the ambiguity of shadows and the occasions of finding the geta waiting for me.

A change in the quality of light would precede the apparition, the natural dusk of the park imperceptibly replaced by a different ambience, more like the echo or memory of light than the direct experience of it. In the spaces it revealed, especially in the shooting hall itself, I felt a deep, inner stillness, that filled the place like a solid block of invisible substance. Everything bathed in the same ambiguous light, calm and empty, as if I were somehow inhabiting an old photograph. The only sense of time passing coming from my own movements through the steps of the Hassetsu.

Softly however, as the summer nights wore on, it became the stillness and silence of an empty building, that, unoccupied by any noises of its own, is colonised by every little sound that drifts in from outside. Footsteps hurrying past? The now familiar ringing scrape-and-clack of geta? The rumble of a wheeled vehicle, although with no engine noise. The distant squeal and rattle of train or tramcar wheels? City noises, but not the noises of my city.

Even so, it was hard to be sure that these were real sounds. Often, it was like suddenly waking, to hear only the echo of the sound that woke you. But then the echoes began to come closer, within the boundaries of the dojo itself. Noises like running feet, half-heard impressions of shouts and laughs, made me think of children. Other voices too. Indistinct snatches. Half a word, half a remark. Then one day, the sudden shocking impression of a face peering through a gap in the darkness. A gasp, a single, breathy exclamation: 'Nani!?' – 'What?!' Staring wildly about, I could see nothing more and heard only my pounding heart and ragged breath.

After that, flickers of movement began to people the stillness. Fleeting shadows and outlines; shifting, reflected light.

Without being able to say I had actually seen or heard anyone, I came to believe in certain habitual presences. One, I took to be the Sensei himself. The quiet, dry voice of an older man, uttering fixed phrases of encouragement or correction. Some of them, I felt sure, directed at me.

*   *   *

'This country! We invented dangerous machinery, long before the West. Machinery of thought. Machinery of obligations. All too easy to get sleeves trapped in the cogwheels and then...'

Tadasu's grandmother shakes her head briefly and refills Mie's tea-bowl.

'Forgive my incoherence. We were all caught up in a terrible dance. And none of us, at least no one I knew, was brave enough to stop. It would have meant death. And so we all danced on and tried to pretend we were not terrified.'

Mie cannot help but be astonished at this old woman who talks like a young woman and who speaks more boldly than anyone she has ever met.

'Your parents, I think knew this. They cared about all of us. They did not label people 'good' or 'bad'. They held to their own ideas yes, but quietly. No dramatic fuss. And that gave many of us the strength to hold on too, not to our principles, if we had any, but to life. It was a time when it was easy to despair, or to hide your head in comforting nonsense. But in their house – your house – there was always a window open that revealed a freer landscape, a fresher air. 'For now,' we would tell ourselves, 'we must hide our feelings and eat crickets and frogs. But one day..."

Mie listens eagerly. This is the first time she has heard anyone talk about what it was like to meet the mother and father she thought she knew so well. It is like an invitation back into the home she has lost.

'Of course, it could not last forever. For them too, it was a terrifying dance of lethal consequences. But it was how graciously they danced that mattered. How they treated each person with the same consideration, whether they thought them an enemy or a friend. They were not saints. But I am certain they never sank to assassination, as Tadasu seems to have got into his wooden head. I am sorry he has been so in-sensitive as to bother you with such foolish notions.'

'It was my fault...' Mie begins aloud. *It was my fault*, she thinks, *for being so ignorant.* Tadasu's grandmother has led her through a maze of memories, only to suddenly break down the wall and show her present and past, standing side by side.

'When I discovered what Tadasu thought about you and your family, I considered carefully my own recollections. And I was convinced I was right. But to convince others, I needed more. Especially my mule-stubborn grandson. So I wrote to some old acquaintances. Women who had also been part of your parents' circle.

'Even today some were unwilling to say too much. So much fear. But all were sceptical that the politician died at your parent's hands. Because it would not have been their way. Whatever his politics, whatever his crimes, their way would have been to treat him just like all the others.

'I remember your father once quoting a saying of Lao Tzu – although I think he had learned it from your mother. Did you know she could read and write classical Chinese? Anyway, one day someone had been muttering in his ear about the wickedness of some other person, and he suddenly laughed and said 'What is a bad man? A good man's care.' And then he laughed again and said, 'Although it might be hard to find a good man to care for him!' That's typical of how he used to de-fuse things. And yet it speaks both to his morals and his modesty.'

Mie smiles a little. That is more like the Father she remembers.

'None of my friends had been much surprised that the man died when he did. But not because we suspected plots. Quite the opposite. It was no secret that he was having treatment long before the Pacific War, for a number of conditions, which, frankly, if you put them together, add up to alcoholism-induced liver failure and heart disease. He was a seriously sick man for a long time before that night at your parents' house.'

Mie is recalling the ashen face of the family doctor as he closes the door of the western dining room behind him. Now at last, she can read his expression. The man on the mat in there, who had behaved so boorishly at table the night before, is dead. Dead of natural causes, true, but the doctor knows there are enough who will not believe that, or who will find it convenient not to believe that. From now on, the family is in terrible danger. She remembers the atmosphere of tension, the strain on her parents' faces. She senses their sheltering arms above her, warding off this rain of calamities that threatens to engulf them, protecting her, keeping her distant, ignorant of their fears. Pushing her out of the path of their own oncoming fate. She remembers Sensei becoming, briefly, a diffident second father.

* * *

Loud, electronic-sounding noise fills the shooting hall. For a moment I stop at the threshold, confused. Then I recognise a sound known to me then, only from film soundtracks: the strident buzzing hiss of the min-min semi, a cicada that celebrates the heat of late summer with a noise that seems more appropriate to a machine than a creature.

Feeling sure no one is about, I dare to practise the kata in front of the right-hand target, the position usually reserved for senior members. I feel, as always, the exhilaration of the graceful movements, even though I have no real bow or arrows in my hands. But as I approach the moment of release, I am shocked to see an arrow already sticking out of what I was sure had been a pristine target.

I tiptoe across to examine the damage. Another mysteriously suspended shot, the head this time, less than a finger's breadth from the centre of the still unbroken target. There is something intensely harmonious about its perfect alignment with the paper surface, which it has not yet and yet must already have pierced. I gaze sidelong at it, trying to absorb the spirit of its imminent arrival in the target.

As I turn away, I glimpse someone standing at the shooting line. A broad shouldered, older man in a formal grey kimono and hakama, left arm and shoulder bared. Standing in zanshin, the position just after release, he seems as fixed and stationary as his shot, but the second arrow is held ready in his gloved right hand. With a cold sensation in my gut, it occurs to me that the target bank of a kyu-dojo is not a particularly sensible place to stand while shooting is going on. I drop my gaze and cross quickly to the left side of the target shelter. From there I return to the shooting hall via the arrow-collection path. When I look up again, I am alone. I kneel at the back of the hall to recover my composure, wondering what else might happen. But there is only stillness.

After a while, becoming a little frustrated at not having completed the kata, I stand and walk forward to the shooting line. Humbly taking the left-most target, I begin, tense and self-conscious, to move once more through the form of shooting. As I settle my aim the circle of illusion on the edge of vision seems to grow inward, until finally, it is only the target roundel itself that I cannot resolve. I am aiming my imaginary arrow into darkness.

Just at that moment I am startled by a light touch under my right elbow – it is still a bad habit of mine sometimes, to let it drop. Familiar with being taught in this way, I adjust the movement before realising that it cannot have been Hiroshi. I stand, frozen in shock for a few seconds. Then, not knowing what else to do, I mime the release of the shot.

I hear, quite distinctly, an intake of breath and a single word, softly spoken, as if the speaker were commenting only to themselves:

'So-o!'

I make the concluding bow and retire to kneel once more by the back wall. Trembling and a little breathless, I let my gaze sweep around the shooting hall, the garden, the target shelter. There is no one there.

The Sensei's touch had been a shock, but what had followed it, even more so. For a second, I had seen the target. Like a huge full moon that has just risen above the horizon. Unmissable.

The sound of a door closing triggers a sudden panic. What if I were to be locked in here? What if the illusion does not fade? I stand and walk swiftly, if a little unsteadily, to the exit, remembering my manners sufficiently to turn and make a hasty bow as I leave the shooting hall. The narrow changing room is empty, the door at the far end partly open. I hurry through into the lobby, still finding no other presence than my own. Reaching out, I pull at the curtain. The cloth seems to spill through my fingers as I step blindly out into darkness. For a second, I have a terrible sensation of falling through infinite space.

I knew by the smell that this was my own darkness. The damp summer night of the park, stained by street-lit clouds. The sharp grit of the rough asphalt as I stumbled and fell to my knees. The cold prickle of it through the soles of my cotton tabi as I stood up. I paused to slip them off before they got too dirty. I brushed down the front of my hakama, walked a few steps forward, then slowly turned and looked back. No building, no curtain, no pine tree. The great 'shoe drying stone' and my carefully deposited pair of geta, had gone too.

* * *

6 Kai

The moment in which one waits for the moment of unity.
To meet the shot.

In the shop window, a display of watches. Again, this dream. All carefully synchronised. On the left, needle-like hands, pinning down time, twitching as it fleets by. On the right, small, grey-green panels with dull-grey numbers. It had taken her a few seconds to recognise that the strange, blocky, stencil-like characters were, in fact, numbers. Silent, vague in their very precision, requiring calculation to give any real sense of time. Without movement or life, except perhaps, for a pulsating dot, or a tumble of tiny figures breathlessly gabbling out the seconds, too fast for the eye to catch.

Bewitched, she watched eagerly as the count approached sixty, a moment lost to the eye as the minute number transforms in a flick from past to present. With a ragged unanimity, the others echo, like a reef of anemones opening and closing at the bottom of the sea.

Was this what she saw? Was this the thing that had not happened yet?

Time. Date. It is the motion she remembers, the motion and the stillness and the impenetrable moment in between. The wrong time. An irrational, impossible date. Her mind had discarded it. Implacably displayed. Identical on every grey green face.

Something nightmarish in that insistence.

* * *

The weather had continued sultry and wearyingly hot. People in the streets looked tired. I had gone to bed without even a sheet and without much expectation of rest.

As so often in recent days, I dozed in and out of unsettling dreams, or lay awake feeling perplexed and afraid. It had become a pattern. After visits to the Arrow Garden, I would lurch into anxiety about how I was accepting as normal something that clearly was not.

About four in the morning, a bad-tempered thunderstorm did nothing to clear the air. At seven, I got up with a thick head and a dull desire to go to work, sit at a desk and lead an ordinary life. Fine drizzle misted the ground with damp, falling from clouds that hung low and thick. Even so, you could feel the heat of the sun behind them, bullying and knocking to be let in. I walked with deliberate slowness, through the town, across the corner of the park and up to the agency, trying not to break a sweat.

No new temps had been imposed on me for a while, and the day's work did not call for any contact with Hiroshi. I was resigned to solitude and burying myself in the safe world of some dry, technical text.

As I pushed open the street door it was obvious something was wrong. Nobody had gone up to their offices. A few still had raincoats on in spite of the sweaty heat. I squeezed in and sidled into a corner. The young man who looked after reception was staring into his lap. Everybody was trying to avoid catching the eye of everybody else. For the first time ever, I felt really comfortable about workplace social interactions.

The boss walked briskly out of her office at the back of the room and stood looking over our heads for a moment.

'Right, now everybody's here…'

I blinked as she flashed around a bright, sour smile,

'… I'm afraid it's not good news.'

She looked, I have to say, like someone who'd had a good night's sleep.

'As you know, with the downturn, business has been poor for a while. I've hung on for as long as I could, in the hope that things would ... stabilize, but the fact has to be faced ... they haven't.'

For some reason, the crack in the ceiling above her head seemed more important to me than anything she was saying. I could have walked out then and there and still have been able to guess the rest of it. But I waited, until the few frustrated questions had been asked and parried, the few wry, hopeless pleasantries said and the brown envelopes handed out. On the pavement outside, I had to push through the huddle as they stood exchanging embarrassed goodbyes, addresses and numbers. As I walked away, the rain started to come down hard. I glanced back to see only anonymous hoods, hats and umbrellas, already dissolving into the city.

The rain didn't seem to be freshening the air much, it was too warm, thick and heavy. I glanced up at the office block across the road where I used to work. Some of the small, square windows of the top two floors had giant red letters pasted to the glass, each letter filling a frame. They spelled out 'TO LET'. I felt rain trickling into my collar, seeping into my shoes, pooling around my feet. Someone was staring gloomily out through the letter 'O'.

I suddenly felt angry with everything and everyone. Squatting, I undid the laces and tore off my already sodden shoes and socks. Paddling a little way along the streaming pavement, I shoved them, with an impulse of rage that shocked me, into the overstuffed waste-bin by the newsagent's. Then I threw back my ineffective hood and let the rain run into my hair.

At first, as my anger cooled, it didn't seem like all that big a deal. I had just been awarded an early, indefinitely extended lunch break. Avoiding both town and park, I wandered aimlessly about for maybe half an hour, until I found myself in a lonely stretch of the docks the developers hadn't prettied up yet. Standing on the wet stone edge of the old wharf, looking at the pattern of the rain on the oily, dark water below, I told myself over and over, it was just a job, I'd soon find something else. I wasn't very convincing. The dreary facts of my life seemed to come swimming up at me out of the murky waters. A failed relationship, no prospect of any other, a lost colleague I couldn't seem to stop thinking about and now, a failed career.

I had done good work. Good, hard work at the sort of boring as hell, life-sucking tasks that keep the world going round. For what? People don't care about that stuff. They just expect it. I had done all that, for years, and all I had to show for it was a dull flat, a heap of bills, no friends, a weird hobby and hallucinations.

I turned, wondering morosely if it would really matter if I just happened to slip and fall in — preferably striking my head heavily on the coping stones of the edge as I went down. *'Poor fellow, he was probably dead before he hit the water!'*

Apart from my sense of balance, two things saved me. One was the stomach pump. They used to tell horrific stories about what they did to you in the local hospital if you were pulled out of those docks alive. Waking up to that was not an inviting sort of afterlife. The other was shooting. Once a month, in a West London school gym, I still, just about, had a life.

The other stuff I tried not to think about. In fact sometimes I amazed myself with how good I was at pretending it wasn't happening, or that it would probably never happen again and that everything was, in fact, perfectly normal. I guess that's how addiction works.

So I walked. By the gentrified docks full of marina pontoons and plastic yachts. Through the shopping areas, ignoring the odd looks I attracted. Into and out of parks. Restlessly treading down despair by putting one wet, naked foot in front of the other.

After a couple of hours, the clouds broke up. More out of habit than hunger, I stopped at a cafe that had dared to put out its street tables again, letting the wet clothes dry on my back in the fierce sun as I sipped coffee and brooded.

It would have been good to have someone to commiserate with. But where was Hiroshi these days? After our last job I had received a few more of his pastoral messages, exhorting me to keep up shooting practice, but he had stopped replying to my replies. And now, the messages had ceased altogether.

Maybe I should have done more to keep up my end of the conversation. Had I made him feel invisible too? I had a moment of desperate longing for those nights of chilly intimacy in the warehouse.

And how had I become so socially inept? It had to be about more than a reluctance to look people straight in the eye. I had read somewhere that in some cultures, looking people in the eye too much is actively disapproved of.

Was I really just using my own personal quirk as a scapegoat for more fundamental issues? Life, I decided, had got peculiar because I had been getting steadily more peculiar. Probably. Whatever the reason, I had come close to the edge in more ways than one. I had been reminded of the fear that always ac-companied those dreams in the bowling green. The fear of losing myself, of losing reality. From now on it seemed, such self-indulgences posed a risk to mental stability I could no longer afford.

I should give London more serious attention, I decided – maybe even move there in search of work.

Then, with as much confidence as a pathologically shy, barefoot, unshaven man in a damp shirt could muster, I ordered a sandwich.

*   *   *

From festival, to park, to temple, to cafe and back, their meetings continue, but something has changed. They keep it up more for the sake of pleasant routine, than any real purpose. True, his talk becomes less abstract, more and more about her. He tries to reach into her darkness, to offer a clumsy, legalistic kind of help. Somewhere, in the midst of all these meetings in which he never seems to actually meet her, he begins finally to lose hope.

Grandmother has been blunt with him, but it has taken a while for Tadasu to fully realise what he has done. His boyish enthusiasm for her father's ideas of social reform helped him create a heroine: the mysterious daughter of freedom fighters, in the darkest times of war and militaristic fascism! Assassins in the cause of democracy and progress! He grinds his teeth in embarrassment.

Emi has written him a long, serious letter, trying hard to rescue her ill-fated project. He tries to see Mie with fresh eyes. It is hard to see her at all. She seems not entirely uncomfortable in his company, but rarely meets his gaze. She listens attentively to his increasingly desperate talk, makes intelligent, if brief, replies, but no connection, no engagement, literal or figurative, develops.

It is Mie however, who eventually gives up. They are sitting on the viewing terrace of a new hotel bar overlooking the bay. He is trying to tell her a vital truth about life and experience. A world without obligations he insists, is not real. *But a world that is nothing but obligations*, she thinks, *is hell*. Already he is forgetting her, lost in the shine and logic of his argument. She knows that what he is saying is probably important – to him. She listens respectfully, as she feels obliged to do. But it is all words. That would not necessarily matter. One can appreciate, even love, a dog, without knowing what it barks about. An amber-gold dragonfly lands on the rim of her cup. How hard it must have struggled to fly this high. Or was it merely swept here by the wind?

* * *

Although beginning to worry about my finances, I kept to my monthly attendance with the London group. It still seemed strange to shoot in an ordinary school gym under harsh neon lights, but at least the discipline, the social ritual, was there.

Vadim, the senior sensei, had been making one of his increasingly rare appearances at the shooting line. His teaching had always been frustratingly minimal, and on this occasion he had said nothing at all until the session was over and we were packing up. He beckoned me to one side. My hopes rose.

'Your shooting has improved.'

I smiled diffidently; eyes fixed on the belt knot of his hakama.

'I thought you told me your former teacher had to give up.'

'Yes, he had to go back to Japan.'

'Then who else are you studying with?'

I flushed with embarrassment. It was a grave breach of protocol to study under two different masters at the same time. And yet I could hardly tell him I had been receiving the odd hint from... well, who exactly?

'I am sorry, but I can no longer teach you if you insist on studying with someone else behind my back. I know my senior students. They would not have moved you on in this way without consulting me first.'

The confidence in his voice was overwhelming. It felt pointless to argue.

'Evidently, you have found a good teacher. You have made real progress even since last month, but I can see a different hand at work. Since you have done so well, I suggest you stick with whoever it is. Good teachers are hard to find.'

He turned and strode away towards the changing rooms, his grey striped hakama swirling angrily about his legs. At the door he stopped and turned back. I was now the only person left in the gym.

'By the way, I would be interested to know the name.'

'I'm sorry,' I stammered, 'I don't know it.'

He stood still for a few seconds, then, apparently making up his mind that I was indeed an irredeemable idiot, he turned on his heel and walked out. The heavy fire-doors of the gym thumped shut behind him, a sound I recognised from long ago, as the note of final departure.

*   *   *

Tadasu sees at last and stops trying to find her. Stops trying to reach through the invisible curtain that seems to be drawn about her. Stops lecturing her about the responsibilities of being a real human being. She seems to him more and more like a statue, a doll. Conventional enough in appearance, but utterly unable to play a real part, and so, for all her conventionality, completely strange. Mie herself senses that something is wrong. Her manners, her dress, her speech, her behaviour are all, for the most part, accurate. But to be 'accurate', one must be an imitation. A very painstaking, effortful, exhausting, imitation.

But then the mask of accuracy begins to slip. She begins to talk to him of strange things. Dreams, memories, or memories of dreams? They make little sense.

'Things are going to get much smaller,' she says suddenly, as they stroll down a busy street of shops. A party of foreigners are passing them on the broad pavement, looking around with detached curiosity.

'Yes.' He smiles faintly. 'The world does seem to be shrinking with all this air-travel.'

'No, *things*. Things will get smaller.'

She has stopped and is looking with absorbed concentration at the contents of a shop window.

'Eh? What sort of things?'

A little spark of concern flares up in him. He does not like the slant of her shoulders, her downcast face, hidden by loose hair – or the way, the next moment, she flings it back, angling her face towards the sky, eyes closed, speaking in a faraway voice, a shaman seer in an office-lady's pastel cardigan and navy blue jacket.

'Radios.'

'Eh?'

'Radios, some cameras, televisions, even telephones.'

'What?'

'Some watches will have numbers, but no hands. Grey numbers that change.'

That evening, as they walk to the metro station, she is silent. It is as if she does not remember what she said, in that strange outburst that seemed to come from far away and deep down.

He does not call again.

* * *

I rode the train home in a state of shock. It was probably a good thing for my sanity that I got back to find a large and urgent job sitting in my in-box. I had been pestering local firms for odd bits, but this was from a former client of the agency. If I could get it done and they paid out on time, it would at least see me through next month.

Working long hours in a state of deadline anxiety helped blot out the pain, but I couldn't work all the time. Whenever I stopped to eat or rest, my mind went round and round Vadim's rejection like a hamster in a wheel. A feeling of panic, like walls closing in, drove me back to work, even though I dreaded the moment of finishing the job.

As it happened, when I finally delivered, the client not only wanted more, they wanted an ongoing relationship. It was a bit old fashioned of me, but after I had got the first contract I had written to the agency, asking permission to take their former account. I had addressed it to the old office, hoping it would be forwarded, but there had been no reply. I tried emails, but got only ambiguously worded auto-replies. I tried phoning, but only got 'number unrecognised'.

I suppose I had been hoping the agency might be revived one day and I didn't want anything to get in the way of being re-hired. If I went back to the boss with this promising account, she might be tempted to start up again. Maybe I'm lazy, or just not a natural entrepreneur, but I hated the whole business of chasing up my own work. It called for all those social skills I seemed to so conspicuously lack. But there was another, more fundamental reason. Certainly, I was concerned with financial self-preservation, but all this obsession with work was about more than that.

Before childhood had been even properly over, I had been made to feel only too clearly that my acute sensitivity to something as simple as another person's gaze was considered a shameful, disabling deficit, even as I was desperately trying to pretend it wasn't happening. It was hard not to see my strange experiences in the old bowling green in the same light: another guilty, furtive secret. What, rationally, could they be, other than symptoms of a similar mental peculiarity?

Worse still, after each episode I had felt ever more disconnected, ever more disengaged from my own reality. Each time, in reaction, I had thrown myself into work, into household tasks, into the everyday details of waking life.

As a last shot, I decided to walk down to the old premises to see if I could find someone who had contact details. It was at least an excuse to get out of the flat and forge some link with reality.

I strolled round one morning, deliberately avoiding the park and keeping to the streets. I almost walked straight past without recognising the place. The recessed doorway between the windows was full of dead leaves, litter, and a rough sleeper's abandoned bedding. I leaned over the debris and peered through a gap in the thin whitewash that had been applied to the back of the glass. The interior was empty and unlit. Not even the carpet remained, just the bare pine boards, dark with age. Toward the foot of the door, the whitewash had been carelessly applied and I could see a drift of mail lying on the floor. It looked faded and curled, mostly junk. My letter was probably in there somewhere. Stepping back, I looked around for any scrap of evidence of the building's former life. To the left of the door, a notice was stuck to the inside of the glass. It began 'Thanks to all our...' But the rest was a dark bruise of spreading printer-ink, dissolved by condensation.

Back home, in a last-ditch effort to find a contact address, I looked through Hiroshi's notebook, but it was no help. I gave up and sent a message confirming the contract.

*　　*　　*

For some time after her return to the city, Mie had continued to take up her bow, but only for ceremonial duties. The resonance of the plucked string, a warning to evil that it should be gone. Even this is not often required. Emi asks her about it one day and is surprised to discover Mie no longer shoots.

'I used to hate it as a kid, but now I find it essential.' Emi says, sounding, Mie thinks, like a precocious child. 'A kind of meditation I suppose. It slows me down, stops me scheming and plotting for an hour or two.'

Emi attends a new club in a city school gym. Mie is persuaded to accompany her. The club is busy and cheerful, the room, somewhat echoing and noisy, even during shooting. Mie finds it hard to connect what goes on there with what she used to know. The teachers are correct and rigorous, lit from within by an evident eagerness to pass the spirit of shooting on to a new generation. But this is a different spirit. This is shooting in a new world. There is no garden here.

Sometimes, club members do participate in organised visits to traditional dojos out of town. Places that were part of the old world, or have been rebuilt in the old forms. Except there is no kamidana, no portrait of the Emperor. Word has come down from on high. Archery, like everything else, is to be free from the bonds of state ideology, state religion.

There is another change Mie notices. Archery it seems, has reached out beyond the seas. From time to time, foreigners from many countries visit, wearing the practice uniform, participating in grading examinations. Some are rendered silent and childlike by lack of language, chaperoned and minded by their carers and translators. Others speak quite good Japanese.

Mie does not attend very regularly and usually only as a result of Emi's exasperated encouragement.

'But you are so good at it, Mie-chan! And it is good for you! I can tell!'

Mie bites her lip, holding the phone away from her ear to dilute the force of Emi's enthusiasm. She can no longer find in herself, at the point of release, that intensity of focus she once had, that moment of life or death. She cannot find even the easy, ordinary, confident, relaxed enjoyment that Emi seems to take in the process of shooting. Besides, as time goes by, she becomes more afraid. She knows perfectly well that it is irrational, foolish, shameful even, but there it is. Her mind is playing tricks with her. She has become anxious that one day, one of those foreigners will turn to speak to her and he will have no face.

One of them has certainly spoken to Emi, although that one did definitely have a face. Quite a handsome one, for an American. A tall man, big-handed, slow in speech and manner. He seems genial and open-minded and yet with a proper respect for courtesies and ceremony. Mie sees Emi appraising him carefully, as if he were a client, cleverly not giving anything of herself away, while still expressing her natural ebullience.

Mie stops attending altogether. It seems there is nothing left for her in the Way of the Bow.

* * *

When my message accepting further work from the new client brought no immediate response, I became concerned and sent a polite reminder. When the reminder 'bounced', I became alarmed and searched for information. My worst fears were confirmed. The company had gone into administration, another belated victim of a still rumbling economic crisis.

I sent a message to Hiroshi, calmly expressed, but born of desperation, to see if he had any more jobs like those we had worked on at the agency. That too elicited only an automated reply: he was 'away from his desk until further notice' in order to deal with 'family matters'.

There came a morning when I sat down at my kitchen table, coffee in hand, to write a list of possible options – and had no earthly idea what to put on it. My client had vanished, the agency had vanished, Hiroshi had, at least for the foreseeable future, vanished into his own concerns. The London dojo wanted no more to do with me, the bowling green had frightened me off, and the flat had become too depressing, with the result that I now had nowhere to shoot, even in mime.

It felt like some implacable opponent was shutting me down, across the board, move by move. The life I had tried to construct for myself, the very traces of my existence, were being erased, one by one.

That night I had twirled Hiroshi's business-card in my fingers, I had made a free choice. Perhaps my first ever. Almost everything in life up to that point, I had done because someone had leaned on me. My father. A girl who needed some company and a flatshare. Managements who wanted me to take on this or that project. Even joining the agency had been a reaction to pressure. All of them had painted me into a corner and left me no way out that would not result in fuss, conflict and the thing I dreaded worst – attention. Only Hiroshi had not leaned. In spite of his blunt invitation, I had sensed no pressure from him other than a kind of negative pressure of positive expectations. He seemed to accept me for who I was. He seemed to have no doubt that archery was a thing I could do – if I wanted to. How could I act freely like that again? How can one be real, if one cannot act? What meaning would my actions have, without a companion to witness them?

Of course it was irrational. There were plenty of things I could have done. I could have lowered my expectations and looked for other kinds of work. I could have signed up for training to update my skills, or just spent time researching some industry or technology to present myself as expert in. I suppose it was because my confidence had taken some knocks, but I found it impossible to have faith in these or any other possibilities. I had become convinced that anything I tried would, sooner or later, crumble to nothing and slip through my fingers.

I went round and round in my own head like this for a week. Unable to concentrate, or settle to anything, I ended up lying all but continuously in bed for two days, unable to take any meaningful action.

Finally, with considerable effort, I got up. I knew what this was. I had been here before. 'Depression' is not a great name for it; it just makes it sound like you're a bit low in mood. It's really nothing like that. It's a severe malfunction of the ability to initiate action. A willpower-cut, if you like. Clinging to that knowledge, I literally forced and cajoled myself onto the phone, out of the door and up the road to the doctor's surgery.

But the trouble with depression is that it is not always just a piece of bad luck like a cold or a sprained ankle. It sometimes happens for reasons. The doctor listened. The doctor wrote a prescription for anti-depressants. But the doctor did not concern herself much with reasons. How could she?

* * *

It is a dark afternoon in the spring rains. Mie is leaving the city shrine, having changed from her miko's vestments of white kimono top and red hakama into a dark blue skirt, white blouse and fawn raincoat. Shoulders hunched beneath an inadequate umbrella, she scurries out through the curtain of drops falling from the crossbeam of the high red torii arch to merge with the crowds on the wet city street.

A shadow slides over her. She glances up. An alternative sky of cheerful blue, with, instead of a cloud, a company logo floating in it. A man in a very dry looking camel raincoat has fallen into step beside her, covering her with his own much larger, sky-blue corporate umbrella. She feels a rising panic, an instinct to run.

'Miss Tanaka? Excuse my rudeness, but may I, on behalf of my company, beg a few moments of your time?'

She flushes with anger. Creepy salesman! She looks ahead to where the policeman in his glass box sits, surveying the traffic, while outside, the rain beads and dribbles on the chrome headlamp of his motorbike.

'We have a mutual acquaintance, you see...'

She risks a glance at his face, suddenly afraid it is the old man she snubbed, or one of his minions.

'... in Mr Yanaga – the lawyer? You are acquainted I believe?'

She stops, as irritable commuters jostle around them.

'Yes,' she admits, still wondering if this is some kind of confidence-trick.

'Can we go somewhere out of the rain? I would like to explain and introduce myself properly.'

Reluctantly, she remains beneath his guiding umbrella. They turn into a shopping mall and stop at a small coffee-stand. She relaxes a little. It is not the place someone intending to make a bad move would choose. The man's face seems worldly, but does not strike her as dishonest. And if indeed he does really know Tadasu... She decides to reserve judgement.

He folds and arranges his dripping umbrella. The logo, she

realises, is repeated in many of the glittering shop windows around them. Is that why it seems familiar? He goes to the bar, orders coffees and brings them to their tiny table.

'I'm so sorry, this is not our usual standard of corporate hospitality – but this is not a bad little place. I've known the owner a long time. He started up on the street during the last year of the war, you know. That's business vision! Now he has this place and a whole chain across the south of the city. Forward thinking! I used to come here in my lunch breaks when... well, never mind.'

He smiles and they sip their coffees.

'So, I hear you are a miko at the shrine here. That must be interesting.'

'Not really. Most of the time it's like being a tourist guide,' she ventures.

'Oh.'

'And the rest of the time it's like being a cleaner.'

Momentary disappointment seems to flick across his face. He dabs his brow with his napkin.

'But it must be a very spiritual place, sometimes?'

Mie looks dubious.

'What is this about, please? I don't even know your name.'

'Oh, forgive me, I was so wrapped up in... Please forgive me, here you are.'

He presents his card, respectfully, with both hands and a little bow. It is a company card. That logo again. His name with some roman letters after it. An opaque job title.

'I had a conversation a few days ago with your friend Mr Yanaga. He told me about some ... interesting things ... things you had said to him. About clocks and watches and radios?'

Mie winces. She remembers just enough of that awful, awkward afternoon to imagine what this man's conversation with Yanaga, so elliptically described, might really have been like. She is fiercely angry and ashamed to think of Tadasu talking about her to other men.

'To be honest, I didn't think about it again until a day or two later. I was in my office, reading some reports from America and Europe on the latest advances in our field.' He indicates with a deprecatory gesture, his business card, still in Mie's hand and by a vague extension of that gesture, the many electrical products in the windows around them, bearing the same badge. He drops his voice and leans a little closer. 'I saw … remarkable connections between what I was reading and some of the things Mr Yanaga told me you had said to him.'

He looks at her seriously, almost accusingly. Mie stares back at him in blank distress. She is really beginning to dislike coffee. So often it seems to be the accompaniment to awful moments. He smiles confidentially. She suspects it is probably meant to be reassuring, but the actual effect is deeply unsettling.

'I haven't told any of my colleagues about this. They would probably tell me I was losing my sense of proportion.'

Mie lets him hang out to dry. He has, surely, got to explain himself, sooner or later and then she can slap him, scream, run, laugh, sign a document, or whatever seems to be called for. He does not seem to notice the pause. His eyes wander over the nearby shop windows before he speaks again.

'One paper, I remember, had almost the very phrase in it that he told me you had used: 'Things will get smaller'. I was startled. Astonished. It seemed so unlikely that a person such as yourself could have read the reports I was reading, internal company documents from our own laboratories and from our offices in the USA.'

He looks at her. Is she being accused of some crime? He must have seen the anxiety in her face because he smiles and rubs the back of his neck with one hand.

'I was just wondering how it is a person such as yourself gets to hear about things that are only just becoming generally known in my industry?'

He leans further across the table, though not offensively close. Glances to one side.

'Does the kami never whisper things to you?'

'Mr,' she glances at the card, 'Mr … Miyamoto, I think you may have been reading too many comic books!'

She is pleased with her rebuff. She does not read comic books, but the children who are brought in large parties to visit the shrine sometimes drop them. She has been mildly astonished at the range of unfettered fantasy to be found in them. So free.

*   *   *

I can't completely blame the pills for the way reality seemed increasingly determined to hide its face from me. That gap between consciousness and 'real life', I recognised, had been widening for a while.

I was signed up for some sessions with a therapist. The appointments were, if anything, confusing. A voice calling me back toward reality, but I had no idea where it was calling from, or what I was supposed to find if I got there. 'Dissociation' was discussed. It probably didn't help that I was reluctant to talk openly about my experiences.

Meanwhile, I went through the motions of life. A bad, jerky, puppet imitation of a real person. Nobody else seemed real either. Through the cool, neutral veil of the anti-depressants, life and everything and everyone in it, had little more sense of presence than a faded advert on a decaying billboard.

My sleep pattern became even more disrupted. I did laundry and cleaned house, but at anti-social hours. One night, I came back indoors from putting out my rubbish, glanced at the clock and saw it was three a.m. I filled the fridge from trips to an all-night convenience store.

These simple chores were my last remaining investment in the idea of a future. Picking out a packet of frozen peas in the shop, implied that I would, at some point, eat them. I was living from one shopping trip, one meal, one filled bin-bag to the next.

Then, glancing up from a book I had been reading one evening, I had a truly terrifying experience: the sudden, horrible and disorientating sensation that I had somehow wandered into someone else's similar but different flat and sat down in someone else's chair. The TV was on low, just to give some sense of life to the room, but nothing on the screen seemed to make sense either. It was just shapes and colours and noises.

For a long time, I suppose, the image in my head had been of the flat as I had shared it for several years with Jo. When she left, she had of course, taken most of her stuff. Maybe I had never updated my mental perception of the place to include her absence. That evening, perhaps, the illusion had finally worn thin and dissolved, leaving me sitting in a set of rooms I barely recognised. Her presence, her things, had given meaning to the place. In the time since she left, I had added almost no associations of my own other than poor housekeeping and half-filling one empty bookcase.

On my first monthly review, the doctor wanted me to continue the prescription. She wouldn't say for how long. I went home clutching the piece of paper and wondering if I agreed with that. I walked past the pharmacy without actually making the decision not to go in. Decisions were hard work. Arrived home, I crumpled the prescription form and tossed it into the wastepaper basket. It hit the rim and bounced on to the floor, where it lay, tauntingly. I stared at the ball of paper, unable for the moment to conjure up the motivation to retrieve it.

Just to do something, anything, I dug out my practice uniform and put it on. I examined my diminished form in the mirror. The waist-ties of the hakama had a lot more spare ends to tuck in than before. I shook my head and sat down on the bed. Maybe, I thought, it would be stupid not to carry on with the pills. But what then? Keep taking them till I drop dead? Some people had to, why not me? I became possessed with the idea that my life was being lived somewhere else, by someone else, and that I was occupying only some fragment of soul that had somehow got lost and left behind, haunting derelict and abandoned places.

There was one remaining option. Perhaps not a free choice because every avenue except this last seemed to be shut down. Nothing else, not even Hiroshi's invitation to shoot, had ever given me this intense feeling of being ... called.

* * *

Mr Miyamoto had been persistent. He had also been somewhat indiscreet. Last week she had looked in the mirror and made up her mind that Emi's advice must at last be followed. But the meeting with the Head Priest in the wood-panelled quiet of the shamusho, the shrine office, had not gone well. In testy, almost wordless grunts, he had refused, point blank, to accept either her resignation or her apology for remaining on the premises for so long.

In fact, he had, she later discovers, quietly increased her nominal salary as a miko to something more substantial. With that and the income from the property, she has been able to give up the shop-work, although not without reluctance. It offered immersion in, if not connection to, the tides of humanity, and that odd sensation of watching the stream of ten thousand things become more and not less familiar in its forms.

Thanks to Mr Miyamoto, she has acquired something of a reputation: 'The Miko Who Sees in Dreams the Future of Things'. He had pestered her with phone calls and with meetings, although in rather more comfortable cafés and restaurants than that first bar in the mall. He had been too good a questioner and too good a listener. She had been persuaded to tell him a little of what she had tried to tell Tadasu.

She is not sure exactly what Mr Miyamoto made of it. She is not sure what she makes of it. It was irresistible to tell someone, to unpack a little, her heavy burden of dreams. At the same time, she could not help feeling ridiculous and also, after the last such meeting especially, that something had somehow been stolen from her.

Now, it is Mr Miyamoto's friends and business associates who pester her. She is invited to speak to their boards at meetings and conferences, which she does, although with some diffidence at first. She realises, with a flush of shame, that it is more than possible she is not always being taken altogether seriously. But she finds in herself an unexpected ability to amuse, to entertain with teasingly dry reflections on progress, the modern world and her own odd reputation. She remains carefully elliptical, mysteriously oracular. This only has the effect of considerably enhancing her appeal. She predicts nothing, forecasts nothing, but rather, gently enhances a few people's confidence in things they had wondered about or suspected. Her roundabout reflections on progress enable a few boardroom discussions, so often fraught with awkwardness in this culture of cautious harmony, to move forward with just a little more confidence, a little less friction.

But the more she does this, the more she dreams of future days; the more restless her nights become: harrowing pursuits, desperate flights, moods of terrified anxiety haunt her dark hours. Sometimes it is too exhausting.

Nevertheless, she does well, in a quiet way. 'The Miko of Radios and Digital Watches' becomes a small media phenom- enon. She is interviewed by women's magazines on all sorts of unlikely topics, appears briefly on TV once or twice, and is ap- proached by advertising agencies. Shaking her head at her own presumption, she writes small magazine and newspaper columns in her signature dry, self-deprecating style and occasional little jokey feature articles for technology magazines. And all this brings a stream of curious visitors to the shrine, although they rarely set eyes on her – at least, not knowingly. She is good at cultivating the anonymity of the miko's uniform.

*   *   *

7 Hanare

The moment arrives and is past.

The first big Atlantic storm of autumn was coming ashore. The sky was crowded with low clouds, charging out of the west like a herd of stampeding Zeppelins, pale bellies catching the light of the city beneath.

The wind was funnelling up the river-gorge, humming through the chains of Clifton Suspension Bridge and bouncing over the Downs. It ruffled the hair of Brandon Hill, grabbing armfuls of leaves from the trees and throwing them all over the park. As I hunted for the entrance in the dark perimeter lane, the ground was flickering with wild lights and shadows. It was much cooler than it had been, with little shivers of rain in the wind. A cat skittered past, leaping after delusory birds among the flying leaves.

I took a last look behind to check I was alone, then started up the steep path into a dim firestorm of yellow leaves. Walking briskly through the little wood, I tried to ignore the running and jigging and gesticulating things in peripheral vision and pushed out onto the open promenade. The four electric lanterns, after a summer of sober illumination, were dancing drunkenly with the wind, sending flashes of light and shadow running down the walls of the tower, to scurry about among the branches and shrubbery at its foot.

I came to a momentary halt, bracing myself against the gusty wind. The steps down to the path were an erratically flowing waterfall of leaves, making it hard to keep balance. Reaching the bottom, I ignored the shadows that seemed to gather in the entrance to the bowling green and turned left instead for the thorn tree. The geta were waiting, the raw wood spattered with dark raindrops. I peeled a big, wet, mottled leaf off the left-hand one and slipped them on.

A low building, its flat roofline broken here and there by the ink-painting flourishes of the old pine tree. As I walk towards it, the darkness filling the entrance resolves into the indigo-dyed curtains and their large white mon of three arrow-tails, standing like plants, enclosed within a circle. The symbol, like the heavy curtains, hangs perfectly still, and there is no answering sigh from the millions of pine needles to the bluster of the westerly wind.

I leave the geta on the drying-stone, pull the curtains aside and pass through. As they fall back into place, the noises of the storm are shut off, as if a bank-vault door has silently closed behind me.

In the dimly lit shooting hall, I hear only the whistle of heavy silks. Some very formal ceremony is taking place. I sink into the shadows by the back wall, peering through forms that seem to be a row of students kneeling in front of me. An elderly man in white robes, wearing an odd, backward-curved black hat, begins chanting as he walks up and down the shooting-line. He carries a short stick topped with zig-zag pieces of white paper. From time to time, he pauses to shake the tassel of paper strips. A young assistant, similarly clad, follows a few paces behind, fitfully banging a pair of wooden clappers together.

The activities of these two continue for quite a while, but finally they are escorted to positions of honour in front of the takemono, and the grave dance of archery begins.

The Sensei's style of shooting is solid, graceful, treating the target with reverence. The shooting of the students, as each follows in turn, is likewise a lesson in character. The younger kids, eager, but not yet fully controlled. The young women, serious, precise, sometimes a little diffident. The old men, practical and workmanlike, but a little long-winded.

The last in the sequence, a young woman, seems to notice me as she turns to take her place in the shooting line. She hesitates for a second in her step. I keep completely still, but see Sensei give her a sharp glance, as if warning her to pull her concentration back together. She goes on with her part of the ceremony as if nothing has happened.

Finally, it is over. The old man with the hat and his little assistant take their leave with many bowings and formalities, and the students file out into the changing room. I remain where I am, hoping to have the place to myself for a while when these shadows have all dispersed. But the Sensei remains behind, settling bows in their racks, tending the flowers in the takemono and then slowly and methodically drawing across the shutters that close off the open side of the shooting hall. By the time he has finished, the last goodnight calls of the students to one another have long since faded down the street.

* * *

Dappled sunlight shifts across the page. Mie realises she has been, not asleep perhaps, but certainly no longer immersed in the arguments of the text. She leans back in the library chair, gently flexing stiff arms, legs and feet. It has been something of a holiday. A few days in a pleasant country hotel, a few hours of each day spent here, on the leafy campus of a prestigious university, checking proofs of a new edition of another of Father's works. It contains a long section on the education and social status of women in a future society. A future, it startles her to realise, in which she is now living.

Had he been thinking of her as he wrote? But there is something about the language, a characteristic phrasing, that makes her wonder how much of the text before her is in fact Mother's work. She would definitely have been thinking of her daughter, Mie reflects with a smile, and perhaps admonishing Father, with a wave of her editorial pencil, to buck up his ideas on the subject.

With a little help and advice from Tadasu, she has built a modest but solid wall of security for herself against any future money worries. By the time her brief fame began to fade and it really was time to retire from the shrine, a new career had already begun. It had started with another excited letter from Tadasu. Not a declaration of love this time, but an openly academic communication. Winding up the estate of one of the families who made up her parent's circle, he had unearthed an unsuspected archive of Mie's father's papers, hidden by sympathetic friends in the strongroom of a remote provincial bank. With both Emi and Tadasu's encouragement, Mie had signed up at last for a degree and, with the support of her university, became editor and curator of the archive. Interest in her father's work was reviving. Sorting, cataloguing and talking to publishers and researchers quickly became a full-time occupation. Rediscovering, or perhaps discovering for the first time, her father in this way, she is astonished at the range and scope of his ideas.

For Mie, the half-comic 'Mysterious Miko of Technology', is soon forgotten, a brief, curious flower of an already passing age. Instead, she becomes quietly known in certain academic circles, as the somewhat formidable curator of the Tanaka Papers, the gate guardian whom all interested researchers must placate in their quest for knowledge.

Now, as she works, memories of a different kind emerge. Moments when she had glimpsed her parents at work. More than once, entering their shared study on some errand, she had, she realises, found Mother waving an admonitory pencil at Father. He would often be listening, with an expression of anguished concentration, to what was probably, Mie now sensed, a lengthy and formidable dissection of the logic of his argument – of *their* argument – as they worked together on yet another book, doomed never to weight a bookshelf in their own lifetimes. Now at last, under her watchful supervision, one or two of those books have begun to move towards publication.

Mie sets her studies on course for higher levels. Invitations to speak arrive, from universities abroad. There are introductions, prefaces and explanatory essays to write. Conferences to address, interviews to give, in which she is still self-deprecatory, but does not need to be humorous and can relax into documented fact and well-founded opinion.

Yet, in the middle of this stable, productive life there is still a dark uncertainty. Nights shot through with restless dreams. Images of fire. Formless things in shifting darkness. One night, she wakes up screaming, at the sensation of a pale, cold, hand clutched in her own.

* * *

The Sensei bolts the last shutter into place with deliberate care, closing the shooting-hall off from the night.

'I am expecting rain.'

He could easily be talking to himself. I keep still. He does not look straight at me, but walks slowly and purposefully to within an arrow's length of where I sit. He kneels, a little to my right, with a grace and lack of stiffness you would not expect in a man of his age. For a few seconds, he sits quietly, staring at a point on the floor a little in front of him. Outside, heavy drops of rain are indeed beginning to fall against the shutters. Suddenly, he lifts his head.

'Miss Tanaka, would you come in here, please?'

I look around, startled out of my stillness. A young woman, who must have been waiting silently in the changing room, comes diffidently into the hall, stopping just inside the door to bow. It is the girl who had hesitated during the ceremony. She keeps her eyes on the floor.

'Miss Tanaka, would you come and join us for a moment?'

The syllables are clear: 'watashtashi' – 'we', or 'us'. I am present.

The young woman comes forward reluctantly, walking softly in white tabi, a little incongruous now she has changed out of her shooting uniform into a dark, western-style outfit. She kneels, with a slight awkwardness caused by the narrow woollen skirt, settling with eyes firmly cast down, hands clasped tightly in her lap. I feel uncomfortable. She seems very nervous – or very frightened. Another interval, filled with the steady hiss of rain. It has become a real downpour.

'Miss Tanaka. Do you think this gentleman might be your brother?'

The girl's eyes flick up for a bare second. Then she drops her head and makes a slight motion of crossed hands in her lap.

'You are sure?'

'Mn.'

She does not look up again.

'Thank you, Miss Tanaka. It seems that your honoured brother is not expressing any anger about the manner of his death by visiting us.'

The small hands, pale in her lap, squeeze tightly together.

'Goodnight, Miss Tanaka.'

The girl makes a rapid bow, fairly shoots upright and nearly runs out of the room.

'Oh, Miss Tanaka! There is an umbrella in the porch, please take it!'

There is a short squeak of acknowledgement, the closing of the lobby door, then, only the hiss of the rain. My legs are beginning to go numb.

'Her family have suffered. I also, feel a certain responsibility toward her.'

He subsides into thoughtful silence. I wait respectfully. After a while, I become aware of a noise that is not the rain. The old man is chuckling softly.

'Eheh! That old fraud of a priest! I pay good money for an exorcism but before he's even half finished you walk calmly in, sit down and watch the proceedings as if you had been invited!'

He laughs out loud; a short, dry laugh that subsides into grunts of amusement.

'It was a good joke!'

He drops into silence, and for a while, the rain takes over the conversation. When I try to speak, it is as if my voice is coming from another room.

'I am sorry to have caused so much trouble – and expense.'

'Hm! Laughter is scarce these days.'

He looks at me earnestly. For some reason, I do not feel a need to look away.

'I am sorry to have subjected you to this indignity, but when the ceremony failed, it seemed the only way.'

I make a bow of acknowledgement.

'It was preying on her mind. Miss Tanaka has recently lost her older brother... She respected him greatly.'

He sighs, pinching the bridge of his nose.

'These days, I teach only old men, young boys and women. Even poor Noburo has been signed up. He's a good boy, but things must be truly desperate if they accept him. It will kill his mother.'

He looks up at me again.

'I can perhaps, speak to one such as you in confidence.'

I make a small bow.

'Is it so bad to wonder if the path we have taken is one that can never lead to a harmonious conclusion?'

I bow again. There seems nothing I can say.

'Shall we be seeing you again? As far as I am concerned, you are welcome, the exorcism was purely for Miss Tanaka's sake.'

'I have been told that my shooting has improved since I began practising here.'

This seems to amuse the old man greatly. He grins broadly, his eyes vanishing in a maze of wrinkles.

'Is that so! I am pleased to hear it!'

He bows. I bow, taking care to go lower.

'Well, I am happy to continue giving what help I can.'

He looks down at his knees.

'Who knows – perhaps before long all my pupils will be ghosts.'

He sits silent for some minutes, as if he cannot trust himself to speak. Then he bows, rises gracefully and walks slowly out of the hall.

* * *

That date, ringed in her parents' calendar, had been an act of faith in the future. A stepping stone. And yet they could not follow. The annual gatherings at the village shrine had probably owed a lot to Mother's romantic ideas about her own past and to the impulse of other nostalgic families, to hold on to something beautiful amid war. That final year also perhaps, a commemoration, for all those absent young men.

It is curious this, that she should be the one to recover, re-instate and re-inscribe her parents' thoughts, their life together, their relationship. To weave it back into the present as a living thread. Why is it Mie that lives? They would have been elderly, but they could have had their say. And why is it Mie that works to carry their hopes forward into a present she hardly dares to own and not Younger Brother who inhabits it so confidently?

His face was in the newspapers again only last week. Some manoeuvring over a vote in the Diet. What was it? Tax reform? How proud and thrilled they would have been to have a politician for a son. Their books portray a shining, optimistic future. It would have been hard for them to sit back and leave him free to follow his own lights. Perhaps it is better this way.

She looks down again at the summer-dappled page, wondering if she should ask the librarians to pull down the blind. The small breeze wags the leaf shadows to and fro, as if they are waving, trying to attract her attention. What was that vote really about? What does it mean for women? Mr Yanaga seemed to have thought of Younger Brother as a social progressive in her parents' mould, but was that true? The press coverage of his political career makes little mention of ideas. Does Younger Brother even know what his parents thought about women's role in society – or about any other matter? She has been sending him, of course, complimentary copies of each new edition, but do they do more than decorate his book-shelves? What are his actual policies? How does the party he is affiliated to stand in relation to the great issues their parents once explored with such muscular enthusiasm? It is embarrass-

ing to realise she has almost no idea. Handing their parents'
legacy on in this academic way is all very well, but should she
not also be seeking more direct means? Outside the library, the
breeze shifts, the shadows that have been to the left, swing to
the right, pause, shivering, then flow slowly back across the
page. This way and that, a slow debate of shadows. She sighs
softly, gathers up the proof sheets and gets ready to leave.

'Each of us is wise and foolish by turns, like a wheel going round'.

*　　*　　*

Eventually, not wanting to spend the night in an empty dojo, I get up to leave. Or rather, I form the intention to rise and walk out, but somehow cannot convey it to my limbs. An appalling sensation grows, that mind and body do not occupy the same space or time and that a dreadful gulf between them is widening. If anyone else had been there, they might have found me staring into the dark, paralysed and wide-eyed, trying to see through into my own world. They would not have heard my voiceless scream.

I am assailed by unaccountable impressions: that I had gone home again and returned without knowing it. That I had been walking in the nighttime park. That I had been standing by the little hawthorn and heard distinctly, two loud handclaps.

In the darkness to my right, a flickering light. Two tapers burning on a low shelf. A square of matting. The Sensei is kneeling with his back to me, facing the kamiza. A small paper lantern glows on the mat at his side. The folds of his fine, silver-grey silk kimono, the one he had worn at the exorcism, shine softly in the dim lights.

'You are late.'

'I am sorry, sir…'

'Hm. I thought ghosts were supposed to haunt at regular hours. You seem to come and go as you please!'

Somewhat shaky, I get to my feet.

'Please forgive me sir, time here does not seem to…'

With an impatient gesture, he motions me to join him, indicating the opposite side of a low, cloth-covered table that conceals his knees.

'An old man like me has to take care of his joints.'

Although I can feel nothing, I guess that the table, a *kotatsu*, conceals a charcoal heater. He has seated me with my back to the takemono, in the position of an honoured guest. I feel embarrassed. He reaches down to the side of the table and I see the lantern illuminates a little spirit stove with a small iron kettle on it. Slowly, with the same quiet, confident finesse with which I had seen him shoot, he prepares tea. He sets two small bowls on the low table, and for a moment we contemplate the rising steam together.

'I do not know if a ghost can take tea, but I felt I should offer hospitality.'

It sounds almost as if he is making fun of me. I bow.

'I do not know either, but I appreciate your kindness.'

He bows and reaches for his tea. I follow his lead, gently curling my fingers around the little bowl. A fleeting, distant sensation of heat surprises me. The shooting hall seems to become a little more solid.

'We have often seen you, though I think you did not always see us.'

I make a brief, embarrassed bow in acknowledgement.

'The idea that you might be her brother ... I felt it unlikely. You have the build and manner of a foreigner ...'

I bow again.

'It is understandable. In these times, it is easy to become anxious.'

He seems more to be musing to himself than expecting a response.

'Some of the little ones here thought you might be an ogre. On account of your feet.'

I am at a loss. Is he making fun of me?

'I pointed out that you did not have horns. That seemed to reassure them.'

'I am very sorry to...'

He cuts across me, with a small wave of his hand.

'And you do not look like someone who has been granted leave from Hell to improve their archery. Your clothes appear clean and unscorched.'

Again the twinkle of humour.

'And why would someone who had attained the Pure Land, return to study in my humble establishment?'

'I...'

'I do not recollect instructing anyone like you, but perhaps you had not been coming here long … before…?'

'I am a stranger here, sir. That is, I have never been an … official … student.'

The old man shows no reaction.

'Then how comes it that you attend here?'

*　　*　　*

What is it you want, eh? To be famous again? All that women's magazine chatter and nonsense? Have you any idea how embarrassing that was for me?'

Younger Brother seems angry. She is reminded uncomfortably of the prickly reception he at first gave her, when she went to find him after the war. Mie is apologetic, despite her nominally elder status. She is painfully aware that a lot of it *was* nonsense. She knew it at the time and played along with it, because... because it had been so long since she had played. It had been an opportunity for a little humour, a little fun. Some recognition of herself as a person with a reason to exist, however trivial.

'I suppose it's compensation for not having found a husband and having no kids.'

Mie is stunned. Is this what politics does to people? Hours later, in the solitude of her apartment, she is still brooding on the injustice of his remarks. Has he really torn away some self-deceit of hers? Exposed a pathetic inadequacy? She cannot stop herself chewing over and over on the bitterness of his words.

There is, after all, another view of things. While he and his wife may indeed have children, it is not as if they allow themselves to be much inconvenienced by them. He seems to pay them little attention, and during the whole days they regularly spend with her, the children barely mention him. And as for fame, well, he doesn't seem to mind having his own face in the paper every other week. How many people even know they are related? She has rarely spoken of it to anyone. And all this... rage, because she had had the temerity to ask him a few straight questions about his political ideas.

In the midst of her anger and shame, a strange feeling occurs: in the past, she might not have had the confidence to withstand such an onslaught. Now, she senses a sullen kind of strength in herself. The years of editing and curation, soaking herself in her parents' words and hopes, have shown her another world than the one her brother seems to inhabit. Mie blinks involuntarily, startled at her own thoughts: Mother and Father are and always were, firmly on this side of the sky! Already living in the future, they seem to have had – no, to *have* – far more in common with their grandchildren than with their children. Mie has always felt broken into two people: one whole, but lost in the past, a flake of ash; the other living nominally in the present, but shadowy, uncertain, cut off from real life. Torn out of one generation, she has, it occurs to her in a flash of awareness, been reborn into the next. To find, a little miraculously, her parents alongside her in thought, present more in this new world, than she has ever allowed herself to be.

Mother's hand, leading her down the corridor outside Father's study. Her eyes and legs heavy with sleep. The door slid open just wide enough.

Mother's hand, guiding her through, then closing it softly behind her. Bronze brown silk glowing in lamplight. Warmth as she kneels by the man's side, watching with sleepy anticipation, as he opens a book.

A soft click awakens Mie from her brooding. She twists around in her chair, realising she must have failed to latch the door. Dusk has fallen while she was lost in thought, and she cannot make out the figure in the doorway against the light from the hall.

'Mie! What are you doing sitting all alone in the dark like this?'

Emi waves a paper bag.

'Do you mind if I cook supper for you? Arlen is being impossible; I need to get away for a bit and cool off!'

Mie blinks. Emi has snapped the light on and is looking round at the paper-strewn room.

'Honestly, Mie-chan! What sort of a recluse are you turning into? – Are you sure you don't mind? I just need the company of someone familiar and sensible for an hour or two! Please?'

Mie nods, smiling, and Emi bustles into the kitchen. It is a relief to see her.

'Will noodles be alright?'

'Mm!'

'Mind if I put on some music I brought?'

'Nn!'

Soft American folk-rock pads out the silence between them.

'It's serious, then?'

Emi's laughter rings out.

'You can tell, huh? Yes, this time next year I will probably be living in Colorado!'

She sticks her head round the door, waving a spoon and looking anxious.

'You won't mind too much will you? I will keep in touch, I promise! And you must come and see us!'

'You are really going to do it then?'

'Yes, I'm afraid it's come to that – lovers' tiffs notwithstanding! I am going to become one of those shameless women who runs off with a foreigner. And yes, that is just what my mother always said would end up happening and it grieves me deeply to have to admit that she was right about something!'

* * *

There is a silence. Sensei takes a delicate sip of his tea as he waits for my answer. I cradle mine, wondering if I can lift it and suddenly feel a real warmth in hands and knees. Simultaneously, the dojo and everything in it, including the man before me, seems to swell into more vivid life. For the first time, I feel I am really here, able to see, even in the dim light of the tapers, the warm sheen of the oiled wood floor, feel the texture of the mat on which I kneel, and hear the whistle of his silk sleeve as he sets down his tea bowl.

Why *do* I come here? Do I have an explanation that makes sense, even to me? I try to buy time by drinking. The bowl seems to follow my hands as I lift it, but there is still that odd feeling of disconnection. The old man is watching me intently. I lower the bowl, embarrassed to try to drink under his surveillance.

'I live in an ordinary city, sir. A long way from here.'

He waits, still betraying no surprise.

'There is a garden, a public park, and in the park there is...'

I hesitate, realising I have no idea what the Japanese for 'bowling green' might be.

'... a place, a level ground. I go there sometimes to practise the kata.'

He gives a grunt, encouraging me to continue.

'And sometimes, when I go there ... I find I am here.'

'Aaaah ... Is that so?'

There is a long silence.

'Yes. Now I see. The eyes of a foreigner.'

The Sensei drops his gaze and sits unmoving. I begin to think the whole scene has frozen around me, like one of the suspended arrows. Only the occasional flicker of the tapers reveals that time is still flowing.

'Tell me something. If you will. Where then, is your ... home?'

'Igirisu-jin desu.' I reply without thinking. He starts back momentarily, as if I have prodded him.

'An Englishman? Hm!'

It is a little jarring to be called an Englishman, but I don't have enough confidence in my vocabulary to dispute it. He has been staring down at the table, but now he looks up again, with a small gesture of his right hand, as if turning the page of a book.

'And how is it, may I ask, that in an enemy country, there are people, ghostly or not, studying the Japanese way of shooting arrows in the public parks? I would have thought it was somewhat … unusual. Forbidden even.'

'It is a little unusual, true, but it is not forbidden.'

Even as I say that, it occurs to me that there probably is a bye-law. He scratches his cheek, staring at the tea bowls on the little table as if thinking his way through a difficulty.

'Here, at the moment, foreign things, especially enemy foreign things, are somewhat disapproved of. If your face were to be seen, for example, it could be…unfortunate.'

In the silence that follows, my understanding begins to ripple wider and wider. Beyond these wood and plaster walls, beyond these bamboo fences, beyond this unseen city, beyond this moment. For thousands of miles, in every direction, the insanities, the cruelties, the legendary atrocities, the hardships, tortures and miseries of global war.

I am indeed, very, very far out on the ice. I bow down, more under the weight of horrified realisation than of etiquette.

'So how can it be, that in this time of war, you are permitted to study the Way?'

'My country is not at war…'

I stop. That is rarely true. Britain is nearly always at war with somebody, if only itself.

'You said you were an Englishman.'

I try again.

'I think, that the war you are talking about, has been over for some time … on my side of the curtain.'

He seems to be trying to look into my eyes. I keep my head lowered.

'Over for some time?'

To say it aloud seems cruel. I nod.

'A long time?'

'More than fifty years.'

He lets out a long, slow, soft breath. Then he slowly picks up and sips his tea and, equally slowly, replaces the bowl on the table.

'It seems that after all, it is I who am the ghost.'

In the long silence, I wonder at his calm response. Then I realise he is softly chuckling to himself. After a few moments more, he lifts his bowl and takes another sip of tea. He is staring at me intently. Glancing up, I glimpse for an instant my own face reflected in his dark pupils.

'If I call, will you come again?'

'Yes.'

'More punctually I hope.'

I make a low bow.

Seemingly satisfied, he takes a sip of his tea. Inspired by his example, I raise my tea-bowl. Now I can feel perfectly the heat, the smoothness of the porcelain. The scent of the tea is a clear note. I put it to my mouth and feel the warmth begin to kiss my lips. Only as I hear the bowl shatter against the floor, do I register the blow that has dashed it out of my hand. Only as I become aware of the impact, the hot liquid splashing on my clothes, do I understand his shout:

'Yamé!' – *'Stop!'*

* * *

Later, they settle down to the meal. It is consoling and warming, and they eat in happy silence together. Afterwards, Mie plucks up the courage to ask what the quarrel was about.

Emi lets out a long sigh, but it sounds more like contentment than exasperation.

'Well, in the years since we married, I couldn't count the number of times I've got Arlen out of embarrassments and scrapes he will get himself into because he thinks he knows all about our culture. Couldn't count! I'm always running around after him clearing up messes and smoothing ruffled feathers. Some of his business clients over here have stopped calling him altogether, they just ask for me. You'd expect him to be grateful wouldn't you? And maybe listen to what I tell him just once in a while? But no, on he goes! A great big moose crashing through everything and getting his horns stuck in the branches!'

Mie smiles. Emi has got Arlen precisely.

'He means well, but he just doesn't see it. Odd, for someone so infatuated with this country. Honestly, even when we do emigrate, I'm betting we will be spending half the year back here, he loves it so much. You won't be losing me altogether, really.'

Mie's smile has settled into a slight, unconscious ache. It will be sad all the same, this change. It still feels like a loss.

'Anyway, the point is, this afternoon, after all my efforts, after all his blundering, he has the cheek to start lecturing me on how Japanese women think and behave! Me! Hah!'

Mie manages to keep her face from betraying amusement. Emi whisks back into the kitchen and emerges a minute or two later with a box of tiny jewel-like mochi sweets and a pot of green tea.

'The trouble is, I can't stay angry with him for long. Somehow, even when he's being outrageous, he's always so charmingly innocent and polite about it!'

Emi smiles to herself, staring at the mochi with a far-away

look. 'It's so strange isn't it? The unsuitable people we fall in love with. And here's me a professional matchmaker! It's a real comedy!'

Mie looks down at her fingers. Emi notices; her face becomes serious.

'Mie, what were you brooding about when I showed· up? Sitting all alone in the dark like that! Even forgetting to lock your door! It's not a man, is it?'

Mie smiles, still looking down.

'It is!'

'No! ... Well, sort of ... Younger Brother.'

'Oh, him! How's he getting on? I thought you scarcely ever talked.'

'I asked him what his policies were.'

'Really? ... Wow! ... I bet that didn't go down too well!'

'Mn.'

'What happened?'

'He shouted at me.'

'Brute!'

Mie frowns. It feels wrong to criticise family. But under Emi's concerned stare she cannot help giving details.

'Look, I hope you won't be offended by my saying this about your kid brother, but a rising politician like him doesn't have policies, only strategies. You probably touched a raw nerve, and he has enough decency left in him to feel bad about it.'

Mie gives Emi a look of grudging admiration. All his bitterness towards her. It really was as if she had said something equally stinging to him. Was it her fault after all?

'I just wanted to know. I didn't mean it as a criticism.'

'I know that. You know that, but...'

Emi frowns, studying the air.

'You know what though, reacting like that ... it really gives one the impression that he is anxious about what you think of him. Getting so defensive straight off the bat!'

'I should not have asked.'

'Oh, come on! He's a politician! He must get asked far harder questions every single day! You have every right to ask!'

'Well, perhaps he gets fed up talking about it all day and resents having to discuss it with family as well.'

'Hmm. You always give people the benefit of the doubt. But why this sudden interest in politics, Mie-chan? It's never been your thing before.'

Emi's eyes shine with a warm, steady interest that Mie cannot help notice, even as she pours out the complexities of her past few years. The strange immersion in her parents' lives and dreams and her sudden realisation of... of what? It is hard to explain, but Emi is patient as she tries.

'It is as if I am living the life they ought to have had. They should have seen it, this world. It is so much the world they dreamed of, argued about.'

Emi remains silent, listening.

'They imagined it all, the problems and difficulties as well as the good things. Not the way things really are of course. Not the little details. The phones, the screens, the clocks, the shapes of buildings, cars, trains. The way we keep old traditions going in a world that looks nothing like it did when they began. But they saw the spirit, the mood of things. It's as if they imagined a future for me and here I am in it.'

'Good.' Emi nods approvingly. 'But I still don't understand why this leads you to suddenly challenge your politico brother about his policies.'

'Because I have lived like a sleepwalker, hardly able to believe I am here, not able to trust that I am really real. Am I sounding crazy? It is crazy, the life I have lived. A life apart from life. I made it through the war, yet I have never felt confident that I had really escaped, that I was not living in some great illusion that might burst like a bubble at any moment.'

Emi says nothing for a moment, then looks down at her lap.

'For the first time since I met you, Mie-san, I have the feeling that perhaps I begin to understand you a little.'

'Perhaps it is because I cannot remember, that I feel this way.'

'Remember?'

'How it happened. How I survived. I can't remember. Not in any way that makes sense. It is as if I fell asleep and dreamed a dream of a whole other world. A 'dream of a single night.''

'I think a lot of us, our generation, feel a little bit like that.'

Mie is disturbed. Is it not unique then, this feeling of fragility? Of a provisional existence that might fade at any moment? She thinks of Tadasu. Is he still anxiously waiting for orders?

'I suppose we move along.' Emi shoots her a penetrating look. 'But perhaps, for you, it was more serious.'

'Sometimes I wonder if I am still dreaming.'

'Tell me what you can remember.'

Emi props her chin on her hand.

'Are you sure you want to hear my ramblings?'

'I expect no one has ever asked you before, have they? Perhaps that is why you cannot remember.'

* * *

Staring upward, I could see only the night sky. Shocked by the Sensei's sudden display of violence, I picked myself up off the ground and made my way slowly home, grateful perhaps, that the spell of illusion had been broken.

Was this what happened when you suddenly stopped taking the pills? Half-formed phantasms turn into detailed hallucinations? It felt like I had had a lucky escape from what I had always feared: becoming trapped in another world, or – which amounted to the same thing – in a permanent psychosis. And yet I had not escaped. I had incurred an obligation.

The thought left me suspended in a state of anxious tension. At three o'clock on a particularly restless day, I went shambling around the park in a pretence of jogging, trying to shake the fog of anxiety out of my head and the tension out of my limbs. It was a damp, chilly afternoon and panting in the cold air was making my throat sore. I gave up running and started to climb slowly toward the summit, taking my customary route home. As I came up to the little hawthorn, I was startled by the sound of two loud handclaps. I spun around. There was no-one in sight, except a distant high-visibility jacket emptying a bin.

Two claps. In Shinto, the opening of a prayer. And a prayer is also a call. It was still light. There were no geta under the tree. I went home and ironed my practice outfit. As I put away the ironing board, the cold thought occurred to me that this banal magnolia-walled flat and its contents might, sooner or later, be left as my last mark on earth. I got out the vacuum cleaner and harassed the dust for a bit. I washed the crockery and put it away. I stuffed dirty clothes into a laundry bag.

As soon as darkness began to fall, I hurried out, my shooting outfit mostly concealed under a long overcoat. Entering the park, I bundled the coat into a carrier bag and tucked it out of sight in some shrubbery. When I got to the thorn tree, the geta were waiting. I pulled out a pair of clean tabi I had tucked into the front of my gi and slipped them on.

Standing, I momentarily lose my balance, as if the earth has shifted. Then I see that the geta had been placed, not under a thorn tree, but at the foot of a little wayside shrine. Squeezed into a narrow gap between dark wooden buildings, a Buddha-like figure sits cross-legged on a small stone plinth. A red bib is tied around its neck, while tumbled around the base, wedged onto the top of the plinth and even piled in the figure's lap, lie little offerings: tiny jars, bottles, coins and plain, smooth pebbles. Small bamboo plants in pots are clustered round the plinth. Little twists of paper tied to the branches flutter in a blustery wind that is sometimes cool, sometimes warm but always thick with a foul-tasting haze. Covering my mouth with a sleeve, I set off down a street made of echoes, toward a doorway of shadows.

As I enter the dojo, time is flowing with a sound like a river in spate, formless, directionless, threatening. The side of the shooting hall is open onto the night. In the arrow-garden, the leaves of the low-growing bear-bamboo are rustling angrily and ripples chase from side to side of the long target-shelter curtain.

The Sensei is standing at the edge of the shooting floor, looking up. There are no lights. Only a dull orange glow to the sky and a reddish-brown moon make it possible to see anything. The old man is holding an empty water bucket. Others are lined up by the edge of the shooting floor.

'Good. This time you are prompt!'

He puts down his bucket and turns to look at me.

'I am sorry to have sent you away so rudely. I feared you might become trapped.'

I am about to bow, when there is a sudden thumping from the changing room. A boy in long shorts, clutching a peaked cap in his hands, bursts into the hall. Straightening up from a hasty formal bow he sees me and takes a sudden step back. Sensei turns and strides toward him.

'Hiro-kun! What is it?'

The boy is breathing hard. He points at the roof.

'Fire! … Coming! … More … Planes!'

I hear it. Above the roar of flame, the drone of a monstrous swarm of approaching insects. Sensei hurries the boy out of the hall, speaking urgently. From the street outside I hear his parting shout:

'Hurry! Tell your mother to leave everything and run to where the river joins the canal. Perhaps there the fire will break!'

The Sensei turns back into the hall.

'The boy tells me more districts are alight.'

* * *

They have finished their meal and cleared away. Emi takes off her glasses and with them, her air of dashing confidence. Instead, she pours tea with quiet solemnity. A small lamp on a nearby shelf casts a soft glow as they kneel together at the electric kotatsu table, the blanket draped over their knees. For a few minutes, they share the silence, holding the warm tea-bowls, savouring the tea.

Emi lowers her bowl to the table. Her voice is soft but level, like someone beginning a seance.

'I survived the war, because my wealthy parents made damn sure I was out of harm's way, up in the mountains, in a quiet little town, with plenty of root vegetables.' She pulls a face.

'How it was for you, Mie-chan?'

Mie smiles and shakes her head.

'Nothing like that!'

'Did your parents not send you away?'

Mie sighs.

'They had fearful arguments about it. Father had fixed ideas that the Americans were all humane and rational and would never kill civilians. Mother told him he was being a fool and that no-one could predict what would happen in wartime. After the islands began to fall, he agreed to my little brother going to live with relatives in the country, but it was felt they were too old and poor to support two children.'

'Ah!'

'There were more arguments. Father felt it was already setting a bad example to the neighbours. When Mother pressed him about me, he got quite angry and said she should be pestering someone else about it, not him. Maybe Father was being obstinate. Maybe he just didn't want to face any more decisions. He certainly refused to move himself, but so did most people. It would have been disloyalty.'

'So many lamentable things.'

'When they did send me away it was nothing to do with air raids. I never knew that politician had died. I thought they wanted me out of the house because he was sick and they were too busy looking after him. Sensei arranged for me to stay with a family whose daughter I knew, because she also went to the Arrow Garden. They were not very welcoming.'

'Probably afraid.'

'Afraid?'

'Of being seen as suspicious by the authorities, because they were sheltering you.'

The coldness of that time seizes Mie's heart, in spite of the warm tea. The chill of that awful morning, as the family starts to pack. The girl, the servants, everyone, avoiding her gaze, none of them speaking to her. Perhaps if she had made a fuss, they might have taken her with them, but she is silenced by shame. Soon her former hosts are all gathered by the front gate. The father is loudly justifying himself to the curious neighbours. He is an important man in the railways. They must be kept running at all costs. He is moving the family near to a strategic junction up country, where he can keep a closer eye on things.

He barks orders, organising bags into the car that has arrived, then having them dragged out again to re-pack in a different order. Even the maid is being squeezed into the back seat. Inside the house that is already falling into silence, Mie gathers up her few belongings and creeps away by the back gate, burning inside with feelings of unworthiness and shame. Having had no word from home, she returns to the Arrow Garden, step by reluctant, bitter step.

It is too painful to relate all this in humiliating detail. She gives only the bare facts of the family's departure, but Emi's face shows a dark understanding.

At the sight of the distraught girl, clutching her few belongings, Sensei's eyes flash with something like anger. For a moment she is convinced he will turn her away. But he recovers himself quickly, welcoming her with tea and kind words. With many apologies, he makes up a bed in his spartan room beside the shooting hall, moving his own to the corridor outside. He will not hear her protests. Finding, after some enquiries, a young street-runner, he sends a message of reassurance to her parents. Mie finds the courage to ask, a little tremulously, if he too is going to leave the city.

'So, you stayed with him?' Emi frowns. 'But how was it he did not come with you to the shooting ceremony?'

'No! I mean — I don't remember.' Mie waves a hand as if batting away an invisible insect. 'More things happened I have not told you of yet.'

'More tea,' says Emi, firmly.

*　　*　　*

The roar of time is not a river in spate. It is a raging fire. My mouth is dry.

'Most of my students will be defending their homes … if they have not already been killed.'

The old man looks suddenly haggard and exhausted.

'You are a sincere student of archery?'

I am not sure if it is a statement or a question.

'Yes.'

'You are an honourable person … I can trust you?'

I make a bow. I feel ashamed to be here.

'I have given you teaching which has been effective?'

I bow again, lower.

'Good. Then it is time for me to ask something of you in return. Two days ago, I effectively became Miss Tanaka's guardian. She is my … responsibility.'

I force myself to wait and listen, though my instinct is to run.

'This attack seems to be much bigger than anything we have experienced before. I do not expect any of this…' he gestures around the dojo, '… to remain.'

We can both hear, mingled with the approaching thunder of flames, the strident, swelling drone. A dragon-roar, and a gleam of monstrous silver crosses the night sky high above the target shelter. Moments later, trees of fire erupt in its wake. There is an ominous pattering on the roof above us.

The Sensei raises his voice above the din, but his tone remains calm.

'I am an old man. If I were to try to lead the girl to safety, I should only slow her down. It may already be too late. I sent the boy away because he is his mother's only hope, but I fear for both of them.'

He is staring hard into my face.

'For myself, I was long ago prepared. But for my… For this girl… Perhaps it is wrong of me, but I cannot help it.'

For the first time, I sense emotion in his voice.

'I am responsible for her existence. It is not...'

He is still staring urgently at me, as if seeking some response.

'Take her with you!'

I am so shocked I forget to close my mouth, let alone respond.

'Follow me.'

In the changing room, he throws aside the curtain that blocks off the women's section. The girl is crouching on the low bench. She looks up, and I see her jerk back, eyes wide with shock, as she sees me standing at his shoulder.

'Miss Tanaka, our friend has agreed to look after you. It is time to go.'

The roar of aircraft is a remorseless, swelling lament. The old man reaches out and takes the girl's hand, pulling her gently to her feet. He turns to me, speaking quickly as he ushers us into the porch. The curtain is dancing wildly in the gusty wind.

'Take her to a quiet place and keep her there until tomorrow – no longer! Then, bring her back, at least as far as the shrine, if you can get no further. Do not let her eat or drink anything, do not let her touch or see things more than is absolutely necessary. Do you understand?'

I nod.

'Good. Now go!'

He thrusts her hand into mine, closing my fingers over hers. For a second the three of us stand, connected by his firm grip. I look him in the eyes.

'What about you?'

'I am the archer, not the arrow.'

*   *   *

Mie crawls across the worn tatami mat on hands and knees, feeling her way in the dark. In the silence, a strange, inter-mittent muttering flutters round and round like a trapped moth.

She had stayed with Sensei for several days before the raid, awaiting word from home. At last, a messenger returns. The house is watched, he says. He has been too afraid to risk a visit.

'Everywhere is watched. Here too!'

Sensei tries to console, suggesting she remain at the dojo until the day of the her birthday and the shooting ceremony, when her parents will surely collect her and they will all go together to the mountains and stay there.

'So many influential people, friends of your father, are involved – a good few of them in the military. They surely cannot be interfered with without loss of face for powerful people. Your parents are safe.'

Mie is grateful for these crumbs of comfort, but privately dis-traught by any thought of further delay. There were rumours almost every day in the household that had abandoned her – word from the street and from who knows what shadowy networks, that the Americans were getting closer. Island by island across the Pacific – soon, close enough to attack from the air in numbers. For those who dare to think, the end begins to be visible.

After a meagre supper, they had talked for an hour or so before going to bed. Or rather, Mie had listened to Sensei telling stories of his youth. His time as a temple novice, and how he had been punished for doing spear-exercises with the broom he was supposed to be sweeping the courtyard with. How, as a young man, he had once had the honour to be con-descended to by the daughter of a noble family, who had mistaken him for a servant. Mie had crept at last, under the coverlet, her homesickness and anxiety quietened a little by his gentle, reassuring manner. Later, she wakes up, cold. A dim light from the street and the moon illuminates the bare, masculine room. She ventures out from under the coverlet in search of something to lay over it. In a corner, a kimono-hanging frame. A silk haori, its bronze sheen just catching the light from the window. It smells … of childhood. She is puzzled. How is it here? She lifts it off the frame, drapes it over her bed, crawls back underneath, warmed by its presence. A garment she never saw worn by daylight at home, never saw hanging on frame, or folded in a cupboard. As she lies, puzzling over memories, she becomes aware of the sound. A sound like prayer, or incantation.

Slipping out of bed again, she crouches by the door, listening anxiously in the darkness. The muttering is coming from outside. Softly, she inches open the sliding frame and peeps out. The corridor, lit by a tiny oil lamp, is a little lighter than the room. She sees the kneeling figure of Sensei, facing the far wall, like a monk doing zazen meditation. Perhaps it is the nembutsu, the name of Amida Buddha, or some mantra or piece of scripture? There is indeed a little image before him. But it is not the Buddha. She peers into the shadows. It is a tiny counter-part of the figure in the alleyway shrine opposite the dojo entrance. The bodhisattvah, Jizo Bosatsu, guardian of travellers and of children in the afterlife. It has been tenderly wrapped in a scrap of plum coloured silk streaked with gold. Another strange echo of childhood, it reminds her of the little padded jacket Mother used to keep as a memento of Mie's babyhood.

She strains to hear. It is not the nembutsu. The old teacher is repeating a single phrase, over and over again, his body rocking slightly with the emphasis of the words.

'It is not appropriate!'

'It is not appropriate!'

*   *   *

Sensei pulls aside the curtain. The noise of aircraft engines fills the night sky from horizon to horizon. With the vague, cold sensation of an unwilling hand held in mine, I nerve myself to lunge out into the street. The next moment, I am stumbling, flying, pulled fiercely and urgently forward, by a hand that has become in that instant, very definite and full of an urgent will.

The street outside the dojo is no longer deserted, but busy with dark figures, all hurrying past in the same direction. Between these flickering shadows, the park seemed to struggle to come into existence. When it did, it was dark, deserted, and dusted with a glitter of frost. We staggered to a halt, catching our balance, to find ourselves already near the little thorn tree.

My first instinct was to take the direct route home, up over the summit of the hill, but the thought of that busy quarter of restaurants and nightclubs gave me pause. Instead, I set off downhill, towards the grand wrought iron gateway that opens into quiet, respectable Great George Street. It would be a detour, but I had an idea I could avoid many, if not all, of the brightest, most distracting parts of the route.

I did not try to take Miss Tanaka's hand again but led the way out of the park, past silent office buildings and tall, dark, stone-built eighteenth-century town houses, their blank, unlit windows staring out the plane trees opposite. As the lights of Park Street became visible at the far end of the street, I suddenly became self-conscious. I had forgotten to retrieve my coat from the park. I hoped that my odd quasi-clerical garb might at least distract attention from the wayward shadow following me.

Once past the dark neoclassical bulk of St George's Church on our left, I had intended to turn left up the service lane that runs behind the shops of Park Street. As we came level with it, I saw that my plan had failed. The narrow pavement was almost completely blocked by large rubbish bins, while higher up, a truck was making a late-night delivery, all but filling the width of the road. Even more concerning were a couple of early drunks coming slowly down the hill toward us, weaving between the bins and the unlit stockroom and garage entrances. I gave up and plunged on toward the lights of Park Street. My caution had led me to the worst possible route.

To my relief there were relatively few people about and those we did pass, were wrapped in their own concerns and did not appear to notice either of us. Although the shops and most restaurants were closed, almost every window was lit, a couple even glittering with early Christmas decorations. More than once, I caught my companion turning her head toward things behind glass and impatiently encouraged her to keep up.

At the top of the hill, the Wills Building tower and its gothic traceries, seemed to momentarily entrance her, and I was relieved when we finally escaped into the leafy streets of big old villas by the university and, at last, the nondescript side road that led to my flat.

Without thinking, I automatically turned the lights on as we entered. They were savagely bright compared to the forty-watt bulbs of the dojo. I snapped them off again and cautiously led the way through to the sitting room, where the glow of street lights through the curtains made it easier to see. I was glad I had tidied up in here at least. I wished I had done it properly. I wished, for the first time in my life, that I had friends or relatives to hold me to higher standards.

It seemed wrong not to offer food or drink, but I was mindful of the Sensei's warning. While my strange guest perched unwillingly on the edge of a sofa, I restlessly circled the room, looking for ways to limit her experience of my alien place and time. I turned the radio and TV off at the wall, waiting impatiently for their standby lights to die. I slipped a digital clock and my laptop out of sight.

I tried to follow Sensei's example and make calm conversation, but she barely responded. She seemed to merely endure, eyeing everything around her with suspicious curiosity. I hesitated a little longer, but then decided I was as disturbing a presence as anything else in the room and that it would be kinder to leave this ghost to the terrors of loneliness, than to haunt her any more with my presence. Having quietly closed curtains and blinds, I went and sat in the kitchen and tried to read.

It proved impossible to concentrate, so I ended up just staring out of the window, conscious of every tiny noise outside and wondering whether it would be strange to her. I ate and drank nothing, even secretly, feeling it would be wrong not to share my guest's enforced fast. Eventually, I slipped into my bedroom, set an alarm on my bedside clock and lay down in my clothes to wait. I may have fallen asleep.

*   *   *

When she returns from the kitchen with hot water, Emi takes the little lamp down from the shelf and sets it on the table, making the tea-vessels shine cheerfully in the dark room.

'I was so frightened,' Mie continues. 'Only a few days before, Sensei, my parents, everyone, had still been making plans to go to the mountains for the annual ceremony. We were all prepared to go. When the planes came that night, we had to stay. Everyone had been ordered to defend their homes in such a case. Sensei was a warrior. He would remain because he was not afraid to die. I was not a warrior at all, but as I must follow the same orders, it seemed death was coming for me all the same. I was terribly frightened, lonely and homesick, but so ashamed of feeling that way, when Sensei was being so kind to me. I was even more ashamed because I could see my presence was disturbing his mind. I thought seriously of slipping away and running home to relieve him of the burden of caring for me. But I could not bear to leave him alone, and it would only have caused him even more anxiety.'

Emi nods. 'A dreadful situation – and none of it your fault. You must have felt so desperate.'

'You know, I'd forgotten until now, but it was almost a relief, after we heard the alarms, when the first wave of planes came over. It was better to do something and not sit fretting in the dark, even if I was going to be killed.'

'What did you do?'

'I got dressed, and we filled buckets and pans with water from the river and carried them up onto the roof. Then we sat waiting on the tiles, with blankets round our shoulders. The noise was terrible. The glow of the fires was spreading wider and wider. We heard the roar of them, it was like the sound of a rough sea. We felt gusts of hot wind rolling through. And the sirens. The city became a wounded animal howling in pain. Then they went quiet, one by one. I dared not think what those flames were eating to make them so vigorous.'

Mie is silent, face in hands. The slight steam from Emi's refilled tea-bowl rises, like incense before a statue.

The red glow on the horizon is in the wrong direction. Dawn is still hours away. What light there is, is dimmed by bitter smoke. A wet cloth tied over her face, Mie breathes with difficulty, conscious that she is breathing houses, gardens, shops, cars, trams, men, women, children.

Sensei has remained calm, seated and silent. A buddha contemplating hell. And yet their street, their district has been spared, for now. They have witnessed only the outward signs of destruction and slaughter and that has been terrible enough. Brought up to value sympathy and compassion, from this day, Mie will always be a little afraid of those things.

'Oh, Mie-chan! So that is how you came through!'

'Oh no.'

Mie's voice is small, flat, distant.

'That was only the beginning.'

*　　*　　*

A hauntingly familiar little tune was playing over and over again in my head. After a few repeats I realised to my horror, that it wasn't in my head – I had left my phone in the sitting room. I softly pushed open the door.

Miss Tanaka had risen from the sofa and was bending over the side table, examining the alien object as it glowed and buzzed and played its little tune. Hesitantly she reached out a hand and patted it. As she turned to look at me, I glimpsed a shadowy suggestion of an expression. Surprise and … eager curiosity?

I snatched up the phone, silenced it and scuttled back into the kitchen, heeling the door shut. It was Hiroshi. In the first instant of connection my spirits leapt, but in the next instant I was plunged back into anxiety. His voice sounded faint, frightened even.

'You remember my aunt?'

The sudden connection to real life was jarring. It took me a second to realise what he was talking about.

'The one I never met?'

'She is the reason I had to go away. She is very ill, in hospital. The whole family are here.'

'Oh. I'm so sorry.'

'Did you throw away that old picture? The photo of the girl shooting?'

So, he finally remembered.

'Er, no actually, I…'

'Have you got it?'

'Well, yes, I think so. I didn't throw it away. It should be here.'

'Can you find it please?'

'Now?'

'Yes, please!'

His voice seemed to be becoming more distant.

'Please, you just have to do this! … Please, just do it, now – then tell me you have it!'

'Sure! OK. Just a minute.'

'Please do this for me!'

'OK, ok! I'm doing it now.'

He sounded terrified, hysterical. I went to the drawer and fished about with one hand. I began to panic myself, remembering that I had not been able to find it the last time I looked. But this time, my hand found the notebook's soft cover. I pulled it out and extracted the photo. The resemblance was like a slap in the face. This was, without a doubt, Miss Tanaka.

On sudden impulse, I pressed the phone against my chest, took the photo through to where she sat and held it out.

'I think this is yours.'

She looked up at me, shrinking back, but then leaned forward, studying the photo carefully, as if short sighted. I wondered what I should say next. Hiroshi's voice was a tiny but urgent vibration, like a little bird held against my breastbone:

'Do you have it? Have you got it? Make sure you put it somewhere safe!'

'I have it.'

My guest was staring at the photo. I wondered if I had done the wrong thing. Then, quite suddenly, she relaxed, her shoulders dropping. She settled back into the sofa, still staring at the little photo clutched in my hand. I put it down on the coffee table where she could see it. She made no move to pick it up.

'It's OK,' I told Hiroshi, as I moved back to the kitchen 'it's safe.'

'Thanks, thank you so much. Are you sure? … Good, good, I have to go, now, I have to go. I have to go!'

His voice was wavering, as if he was walking quickly.

'… later, OK?'

'Later,' I said, but he had already rung off.

I sat for a while, cradling the phone in the dark, trying to hold on to something in this strange web of connections I found myself tangled up in.

Some time later, unable to sleep, I crept back into the sitting room, looking for something to read. Miss Tanaka was herself asleep on the sofa, her back to the room. Untied, her long, black hair had slid across her shoulders in a great dark fan. For a few seconds, I stood and watched her steady breathing, wondering in what world her dreams were.

The photo was still on the table, exactly where I had left it. I picked it up and returned it to its place in Hiroshi's pocket book. In that image, she was the archer. Now, as she slept, out of her own time and place, she was the arrow. Suspended, frozen in flight, the moment on which all the other moments depend, forwards and backwards.

*　　*　　*

Sensei stands swiftly up and looks at the smoking horizon. The noise of the planes has been replaced by the roar of the burning city. He motions Mie to climb back down into the building and he passes her, one by one, the water pails. Together, they venture out into the street, carrying between them as much water as they can manage. With this meagre supply, they help neighbours in streets on the edge of the district to damp down a few small, smouldering fires. Then they walk a little further. Reaching the edge of the burned-out area, they see how fortunate they have been. For now.

Mie can see that Sensei wants to go on, to see what if anything can be done. But after a minute or two, he takes her firmly by the hand and leads her back to the Arrow Garden. She understands. He is trying to protect her. But it is already too late. In imagination she has already seen. What lay in the few blackened streets beyond the edge of fire only confirms her fears. A once existing city, now made illusory, is burned into memory. They stumble back across the edge of destruction, into undamaged streets, as if stepping back into a little part of the past that still exists. But they have seen the future. The moment after, and the moment before.

Mie shakes her head and squeezes her eyes shut for a moment. The memory is too raw and vivid. To Emi she can only describe the barest skeleton of events. 'We did this … I did that … Sensei said…'. Facts that had been footholds as she had clambered from minute to minute up a desperate slope of revulsion and horror. But not the feelings, not the stench of emotions. For that, she can find no words.

Emi speaks, with quiet, careful emphasis:

'He was quite a man, that Sensei!'

Mie's shoulders relax a little.

'It's true!'

A pale, fractional smile.

Emi speaks again, a shade warmer and more natural in her tone.

'I only got to see him a few times – you studied with him quite a few years, didn't you? What was he like?'

'I was a little frightened of him.'

'Oh?'

'He was very kind, but he seemed never to be afraid of anything. Somehow, that made me afraid. Silly, isn't it? I couldn't help it. It was like watching somebody walk a high beam as if it were solid ground.'

'Hm. I can see how that would be scary.'

'He was really afraid of nothing. Once he even...'

'Go on.'

'I can't. It's too...'

Emi's upturned face is steadfast.

'It must have been some friend of his, some actor. Or perhaps I was already going a little crazy even then.'

Mie's hands are bunched tightly in her lap.

'I have a memory... No, it must have been a dream ... of him talking to a ghost – that can't be right, can it?'

'A ghost, Mie-chan?'

Emi does not mean to sound skeptical, but her question plunges Mie into confusion.

'I don't know. It must have been some ridiculous delusion of mine. I was half out of my mind.'

Once more, nothing but Emi's sympathetic, patient gaze. Mie sighs in resignation. It must be spoken of, or it will always be between them. Diffidently she asks:

'Did you never hear about the Arrow Garden Spirit?'

'Pff! I heard some talk about the place being haunted, but I never paid much attention.'

'It was faceless.'

'A Nopperabo? You saw it?'

'Mn!'

'How many times?'

Emi cannot help herself. She sounds a little shocked.

'Three ... four ... And the most terrible thing. He called it again, that night. *Called* it!'

'Mie-chan?'

Oh yes. Mie tries to face the recollection steadily. The

shadowy figure who would sometimes startle them late at night, or on summer afternoons, or clear winter mornings, when the ghost-moon showed bone white in the blue sky. Walking down the alley toward the entrance of the dojo. Silently sitting, unbidden, at the back of the shooting hall. Standing, as if entranced, in front of the targets, among the dwarf bamboo and mossy stones of the arrow garden.

*　　*　　*

Knowing my alarm was set for the early hours, I found it impossible to get back to sleep and lay restlessly worrying. Time crawled by as it does in an illness. Sensei had seemed very anxious that his charge should not remain too long in my world and I had made my not very scientific calculations accordingly. Even so, I began my preparations far too early, fretting about what to wear. It felt like trying to decide what to wear after death. In the end I left the practice uniform folded, pulling on instead the plainest shirt and trousers I possessed.

As one does, when setting out on a journey, I ran through all the possible things I might need. 'You can't take it with you.' seemed the only relevant answer. In the end I pocketed only my house-key, as an act of faith in my own return and even that, I decided, I would leave under a stone in the park. So many times I had set off for this destination. Only now did I begin to feel the full seriousness of it. With a lump of anxiety in my stomach, I gently knocked on the door and went into the sitting-room.

I took the direct route to the park, hoping that in the pre-dawn quiet we might slip by unseen. Last time, we had had to wait at pedestrian crossings next to people with phones glowing in their hands. This time, there should be no such distractions.

In fact, to my distress, the area around the top of Park Street seemed unusually busy for such an unearthly hour. No one paid us much attention, but many seemed to be going the same way as us. Then, as we turned into the quiet street leading to the back entrance of the park I saw, to my horror, flashing blue lights and reflective clothing. Cursing inwardly at my bad luck, I backtracked to the main street and began a desperate quest for alternatives. Alas, each entrance was easy to spot by its cordon of police. The iron gateway of Great George Street we had used the night before, seemed to have the biggest police presence of all. After breathless minutes I finally brought us to a halt in a quiet residential street at the far side of the hill. The little flight of stone steps I had used, a seeming lifetime ago, on my lunchtime escapes into the park, stood unguarded.

I hurried my charge up onto the perimeter path, only to stop, staring upward in disbelief. A fire-engine and other emergency vehicles had been driven onto the promenade around the top of the hill. Police and fire-crew were milling about by the entrance to the bowling green. Smoke seemed to be billowing up from behind the trees and shrubbery, but it was a strangely uncertain, misty phenomenon. Sometimes it seemed to have stopped altogether, but then you caught it out of the corner of your eye, full and flowing.

To my left and right, along the borders of the park, small groups of local residents were hanging over railings or peering from windows. Quite a few had also found ways to enter un-challenged and were standing on the lower slopes of the hill, watching the show. More were joining all the time, pushing slowly up towards the action.

There was a strange, edgy, almost festival atmosphere. Up nearer the lights, by a cluster of trees, a small group seemed to be doing a wild dance to the rapid beat of a drum. A couple of police officers started to walk slowly down the slope, one talking into their radio, the other holding arms wide, as if projecting an invisible force to roll people back down the hill.

Desperately, I scanned the hillside, looking for some way to get closer. Towing my charge along, I hastened left along the perimeter path to where the bushes of the wildlife reserve offered shadow and cover. As we got nearer, I recognised, running up the hill, the line of the old Civil War defences, its ditch and bank topped with small trees and bushes. Stumbling through the tussocky grass in its shadow, we got unnoticed to within a few yards of the bowling green path and in sight of the little thorn tree.

As I peered through the shadows and the raking lights of torches, I saw, at the foot of the hawthorn, not the pale wood of the geta, but something dark, lying in the grass. From old habit, I looked sidelong and caught an impression of movement. Definitely a curl of smoke drifting up – and in the opposite direction to a leaf that blew past. On impulse, I ran, ducking low, pulling my shadow companion up and onto the path. I did not even look to see if anyone had seen us.

*　*　*

It had been the Sensei's notion to make a gift of geta, Mie explains, a placatory offering, when all else had failed. He had joked that the apparition had saved the dojo's fortunes, as it had attracted several curious souls to join, in hopes of a sighting – although they had nearly always been disappointed. Sensei bought a fine new pair of geta in a large size and laid them reverently at the foot of the little figure of Jizo-sama that stood in the alleyway, opposite the incense shop.

And sure enough, one night, someone said they had heard the echoing scrape and clatter, and the geta were found neatly lined up on the drying stone by the entrance. Sensei returned them to the shrine, but they never seemed to remain there long. He would often find them in the morning, lined up neatly in front of the entrance, or lying discarded in the street a few doors away. And he would retrieve them, wonderingly and return them once more to the shrine with prayers, only for the process to repeat itself again.

Exorcism had been tried. Only herself and Sensei had seen, in the middle of the exorcism ceremony, the ghost quietly enter and sit down at the back of the hall. She had nearly run away in panic, but Sensei had actually been amused! Not only that, with a calmness that had made her skin crawl, he had made her wait, then called her in to confront the thing!

He had been doing it for her of course, in the mistaken belief that the strange figure might be the lost spirit of her Older Brother, reported missing in action. But it had been clear to her that the idea had been a mistake. Why would he return as a faceless nopperabo? And yet, undaunted, the old man had continued to hold converse with the dead, or undead, thing, eventually persuading her that this was a spirit of a very different kind. He had gone out to return the geta once more to the foot of the shrine, gruffly announcing: 'This is not to keep him away you know! I have invited him back. I fancy he must have some business with us. I am determined to find out what it is!'

The night of the raid, a strange and wild notion had taken hold of her, as the drone of the aircraft began to fill the night above, that by sheer force of will, she could break out of this hopeless, terrible world of fear that was relentlessly closing in on her from every side and flee into the unknown. Into Hell itself, if necessary, rather than suffer this unbearable tension a moment longer.

And that is all she can remember, that tension. As if standing with the bow at full draw, waiting for a release that never comes. And yet, it must have come, for here she is. Somehow, she must have found the courage to let go, found the moment when the water-drop slips from the tip of the slender bamboo leaf, and the future crashes into existence in all its shattering complexity.

* * *

I stare at the charred lumps that had been the geta. One more burnt offering, among a holocaust of little gifts, smoking and crumbling at the foot of the cracked and blackened statue.

My hand suddenly closes around nothing. Miss Tanaka is picking her way unsteadily towards the junction at the end of the lane. I start to go after her, then stop. The lack of any human noise is eerie. Just a continuous sputtering and crackling, close and sharp, far and soft. The sound of a desert of slowly cooling embers. The heat is still intense enough to make me flinch, and the acrid smoke, blown about by a blustery little wind, makes my throat burn. Blinking through stinging tears, I see that, of the buildings to either side of the shrine, nothing remains but the stumps of corner-posts. The little cobbled lane in which I stand looks as if someone had started to sketch it in charcoal, but had only got as far as the foundations of the buildings and a few hints of framework. Instead of close walls, there is a wide, smoky view, as if of open fields, but these are the farms of hell, in which only black wreckage, trees of smoke and the baleful flowers of distant fires grow.

My face is burning. The heat is relentless, pressing in from every side. Across the road, opposite the end of the lane, a fragment of the charred curtain of the dojo still hangs across a blackened doorway, part of its three feather mon, still just greyly visible. The building itself, like a few others on that side of the street, is partly intact. Through the gaps between the ruins, a winding watercourse can be glimpsed, its sluggish surface reflecting the ominous sky. A little river, that had lent the street its sinuous curve and which had perhaps formed a slight firebreak. The old pine-tree must have gone up like a torch. Only a stump remains, scarcely bigger than the shrub in the bowling green hedge.

Miss Tanaka has disappeared into the remains of the dojo. I follow, wondering a little at my own persistence. Abandoning her to her fate in this wilderness of ashes feels wrong and I certainly can't stand still, the ground already feels unpleasantly hot beneath my feet.

Inside the dojo the damage is extensive. Large parts of the roof of the shooting hall and much of the back wall between it and the changing room, are gone. For a second, I think I am looking out onto the bowling green, but the cracked and blackened ground is all that remains of the carefully tended arrow garden. Peering through the smoky air, it seems the target shelter is mostly untouched. The bank of damp river-sand it sheltered, which had held the targets and trapped stray arrows, has dried out and collapsed, exposing the brickwork that supported it and leaving ragged miniature cliff-faces and wind-blown fans of debris.

Miss Tanaka is kneeling near the edge of the shooting hall floor, nervously patting at a pile of cloth. Sensei lies on his side, his body unburnt. The heat of the firestorm must have killed him, scorching his lungs, sucking all the oxygen out of the air. His bowstring has snapped, and the bow itself, partly trapped beneath his body, is charred and split at the tip, where it hung out into the arrow-garden. I look to where the target must have been, before it tumbled from the dried-out sandbank, imagining the fragile wood and paper drum flaring to ash in an instant. I wonder if, mingled with it, are the remains of an arrow.

A thin, dry, keening sound pulls at my attention. Miss Tanaka is rocking on her heels, plucking at Sensei's sleeve. I walk away from her, towards the bow-rack. In the capricious destruction of the fire, a few bows remain, seemingly undamaged. The equipment-cupboard, though badly charred, has also shielded the gloves and other things. I gather together two sets and carry them to the back of the hall. Gently, I lift the old man's shoulders and lay him in front of the remains of the kamiza, placing his bow on his chest and folding his hands over it. Picking my way through the wreckage, I rip down what is left of the entrance curtain and cover his body. Miss Tanaka has not moved. When I try to attract her attention, she seems unaware of my presence.

'We will shoot in his memory.'

For a long time she makes no response. Then slowly, she stands up, moving like an automaton to the back of the hall, where I have laid out bow, arrows and equipment. She slips off her jacket and begins slowly tying on muneate and deerskin shooting-glove. Ignoring the bow I have set out, she goes to the rack and picks out what is evidently her own.

None of the paper targets have survived. Even if they had, the collapsed azuchi would no longer hold them. I remember the second arrow, still clutched in Sensei's gloved hand. Lifting the edge of the cloth and muttering a prayer for forgiveness, I gently pull it free. Walking carefully across the ruined arrow-garden, I wedge it upright in the remains of the azuchi.

Miss Tanaka kneels in second target position, facing the kamiza and Sensei's body. I kneel behind in third position, hand at the waist, tip of the bow resting an inch above the floor in front of me. She makes no move.

'You are the senior student here,' I whisper. 'Please begin.'

Slowly she rises to her feet, a wisp of smoke from a dying fire. Lost in the action of shooting, pouring every ounce of spirit into her two shots. The first thwacks into the loose sand so close to the mark that it pushes it a little to one side. The second makes the feathers of Sensei's old arrow fly apart, the bamboo shaft split and broken by the point of her arrow. She makes her concluding bow, steps back from the shooting line and resumes the kneeling position, carefully laying her bow on the floor beside her.

*　*　*

'Mie? … Mie-chan!'

With a start of embarrassment, Mie realises Emi has been calling her and is now reaching across the table to touch her hand.

'You went away there for a little while!'

'Sorry, I … was remembering.'

'Tell me what happened then.'

'I can't. I can't remember.'

'You said he called the ghost.'

'Yes. Later the same night, the night of the raid. We had only just got back to the dojo, when we heard the planes again and we knew they had come to finish off the job. All I remember is the terror, and…'

Mie drops her face into her hands, whispering.

'It came, Emi. It answered him.'

'Eeh?!'

'And then, as if I had been sleepwalking, I was in the garden at home and it was all burnt and grey and Mother and Father were gone. I knew they were dead. Someone must have told me, but… I can't remember anything of how I got there. I remember my face felt all hot and sore, I must have been near some flames, but…'

'Maybe you just ran away and had a lucky escape?'

'I thought I had died. I thought I was a ghost, lingering in the ruins. Sometimes, even now, I still think that. Because of the dream.'

'Dream?'

'I dreamed I was somewhere else. A different town. A different place. A different feeling. Cold, calm, dark. Like a fairy world. Everything different. A dark tower on a green hill. A pale tower in a city, tall enough to catch starlight. It's all nonsense of course … a ghost world with shops full of strange things.'

'It's what you wrote about, isn't it? Those articles? I have to admit I looked them up and read a few. I thought, "Here is a new side of my old friend!" You kept quiet about writing them. I thought they were witty. You seemed to be slyly sending up all those men and their gadgets. But now, I see them differently. I confess, I am even a little afraid.'

'Emi!'

'Was it his world? The Arrow Garden Spirit's?'

'I don't know!'

Emi is silent for a long moment, looking down at her own hands.

'Who are you, Mie-san? You went away, but did you come back the same?'

Emi! Even Emi!

'Ah, there I go again, always too honest about my feelings. But that's my special skill isn't it? You won't say it to yourself, you can hardly bear to say it to me, but something happened to you Mie, something bigger than I can help with. All I can do is listen and be your too honest friend. You must speak to someone who has more authority in these things than me.'

And Emi, who has never before betrayed the existence of a religious bone in her body, briefly adopts the blessing pose of a buddha.

* * *

When my turn comes, I shoot as well as I can manage. There is no question of hitting a target, but I don't think I disgraced my old teacher in the manner of shooting. Bowing, I turn to see my fellow archer crouching, head almost touching her knees, hair draped across the ash-powdered floor. After a long silence, she at last lifts her head, takes a long shuddering breath and begins to cry. Not the thin keening of a few minutes before, but a more open grief. I step away, pressing a gritty sleeve against my face.

Looking around through the gaps in the building, I see in the distance, a small group of people with a handcart, moving along the street. Sensei's mourner becomes gradually quieter. I go over to her, bending down so I do not need to raise my voice. 'I must leave ... and you must find help.'

She makes a brief nod. The first real acknowledgement she has given me since the evening before. I turn to go, but stop, realising I am still wearing the shooting glove. I kneel to remove it and then, I don't know why, return it and the bow to their places in the tattered shell of the dojo. When I look round from this task, I see Miss Tanaka near the exit, facing me. She makes a deep bow. I return it. And then I am alone in the ruined shooting hall.

A sudden loud groaning and a little avalanche of ash makes me glance up to see the flame-eaten corners of the roof lift and drop. A hot, restless wind is getting up. Fires could easily re-start at any moment as the embers are blown about. The whole roof could fall in.

Moving in the dry, oven-baked air is exhausting. My throat is raw and my eyes are constantly smarting. In a rising panic I stumble through the ruined building and out onto the street. Blinking against the hot smoky wind, I look desperately for any sign of my cool, green park. The empty, fire-stormed street remains stubbornly real. I look back at the dojo, wondering if somehow, somewhere in there, I might glimpse my old familiar bowling green.

As I watch, the corner of the shooting hall suddenly lurches in the rising wind, then falls in a slow, twisting collapse. A cloud of sparks shoots up, and tongues of new flame begin to lick up from the debris. I turn my attention back to the street. At least Sensei will have a decent cremation.

Far to my right, a straggling group of survivors with a handcart are picking their way towards the hills at the edge of the devastated city. One of them seems to be carrying a bow. It really is time for me to leave.

I cross the road and enter the little lane. As I pick my way through cracked roof-tiles and charred timber, a rich over-powering perfume suddenly wraps around me, a thick coil of grey-white smoke that smells like a bonfire of a million dead roses. Just as I am about to choke, the wind whips it away again. The smoke is fountaining up from the floor of what must have been an incense shop. Bundles and bundles of incense-sticks, wedged together on collapsed shelving, or tumbled across the floor, smouldering steadily. I bend to pick up a bundle that has fallen into the street. The charred paper wrapper breaks and the sticks fall, scattering from my hands, each with its little trail of white smoke, as if I were some divining demon casting the yarrow-stalks in hell.

I pick up one stick, walk on the last few yards to the shrine and wedge it upright among the charred debris at the foot of the cracked stone figure. Then I make a deep bow, clap my hands twice and offer a silent prayer for Sensei's soul and Miss Tanaka's future. I don't know what deity it is to, or what religion I think I am following, but I hope my improvised offering might somehow help to release me. I close my eyes, but it only makes the sounds of crackling destruction press more vividly around me. I open them and focus instead on the few square inches of ground between my feet.

It seems like hours have passed. Hours of dry feverish heat, cramped legs, watering eyes and arid mouth. Only the fear of being trapped in a world where Hiroshi does not yet exist keeps me from wandering off into the ruins in search of water. Instead, I stare at the tiny patch of ground under my nose as if it is a zen koan I am trying to solve, or a target I am trying to hit. Mostly I just crouch and like a lost child, wait for my reality to find me.

And then, complete in memory, though only ever heard in fragments, the old Sensei's teaching:

Don't try to grip, to hold on, or to let go.

Neither gripping nor letting go.

Just release.

Just...

... release.

* * *

Had he bundled her off into the underworld, poor child? Or merely sent her to die in the street, a victim, like himself, of both war and illusion? What if he had? It was a better exit than... It would in any case, not be seemly, for her to have to share, alone with him, these last minutes. A momentary pang twists at his heart. The memory of another girl, a girl both very like and not at all like Mie. Haughty, reserved, standing on her admittedly considerable honour in a chrysanthemum furisode, one summer afternoon long, long ago. He shakes his head at his own folly. What use at a time like this, to disturb one's composure over such things? A time to let go, to release, to hold on to nothing.

And yet, once more, he had allowed compassion to become attachment. Before he knew it, it had settled gentle fingers into his heart. And as a result, he had again done something quite unaccountably foolish. Succumbed to a temptation. What use? It was done. But what was done?

Meeting that proud girl again some years later, he had found her still proud, but distressed by a marriage she did not know what to do with. One child already and a husband pre-occupied with work. He had only sought her out because he knew of her inherited wealth, her interest in archery. He had been seeking subscriptions to help build a dojo on a plot of land leased from the city, to begin teaching in his own right. She had seized on the idea. Become not merely a subscriber, but chief funder and enabler. They had met, planned, worked. He had even formed a genuine friendship with her husband, that brought the couple a little closer to one another. Until one accidental night.

The steady drone of multi-engined aircraft is filling the depths of the sky, broadening above him, horizon to horizon. Already he can hear the other sounds creeping closer – a dull roar like ground-level traffic, spattered with small explosions, crackling noises. America is here. The wasp's nest has been poked and now the great silver insects have come, in their hundreds. It is decided.

When the pregnancy became apparent, he had been profoundly troubled. An awesome responsibility, to cause a life to begin, to call someone onto another turn of The Wheel. Let alone in such circumstances. She had not dissembled, but confessed frankly. For a while her husband became angry and withdrawn. Until he saw the child. He would adopt her as his own, on condition she was not told of her parentage. Her blood-father would be permitted certain visits while she was still small. Later, he would be allowed to be her teacher. For the world she would never be other than a true daughter of the Tanaka house. For the Master of the Arrow Garden, she would always be a wild arrow, loosed into the night.

From what he has seen, there is little sense in fleeing, or hiding, or seeking refuge. At least, not within the city. He feels oddly calm, now that he finds himself, after a lifetime of merely practising with weapons, a veritable warrior on a real battlefield, though facing certain defeat. Odd to think of that politician – what was his name? At the Tanaka's. Evidently the poor man had been staring death in the face himself, perhaps without even being aware of it? Or perhaps he knew only too well. Perhaps that was why he got so drunk. Each of us is wise and foolish by turns. One can only hold on to what seems right in the moment in which one finds oneself. It is of no use to judge others.

Almost without thinking, he makes the preparations for shooting. Whatever he has done, there is nothing more to be done. Except, to send the moment flying to its fate, to loose the string, one last time. It is not so hard after all, to let go of the past, to let the present drop away, to allow the urgent note of the aircraft to fade into insignificance, a mere diaper pattern behind the figure of an archer in full concentration upon a target, reaching out to harmony with a universe far beyond any city or war.

As the bow approaches full draw, he feels the tension drain out of him, to be replaced by an inner calm and strength.

Finally, after a lifetime of struggle, there is only this to be done. Without deliberate intention, the moment forms itself, water gathering to a drop at the tip of a bamboo leaf, until, inevitably, it falls.

The arrow flicks into the future.

He never sees it reach the target. It never does. Vaporised, halfway across the arrow garden, as the shockwave of the firestorm tears through the fragile streets, sucking away in an instant all the oxygen in the air, to feed its insatiable flame.

*　　*　　*

8 Zanshin

The final position. Inhabiting the new reality.

A tiny, brown hawthorn leaf blows onto the little patch of ground beneath my nose. I stare at it, amazed. How on earth has it escaped the firestorm? I shiver, suddenly feeling cold to my core. I must have caught a fever along with everything else. Am I condemned to live through season after season of a life that is not my own? I look up at the shrine in despair – and see the small, black, thorn-tree, a few brown leaves still clinging to its lower branches. At its foot, the last stub of white ash falls from an invisible incense-stick, the last trail of smoke wavers and fades, along with its scent, in a direction contrary to the early morning breeze.

I stood up slowly. The sensation of dry heat on my skin was already a memory, but I waited a few seconds more, allowing myself to be completely present in my own damp, grey morning. Then I dared to turn and look. The bowling green shrubbery was just as it always had been, except for a last strand of police cordon tape strung across the entrance, vibrating a little in the cold breeze. There seemed to be no-one about.

I walked home, unhurried. Everything, from an orange peel lying on the pavement by a bin, to the tiny silver airplane slipping out from behind a cloud, thousands of feet above, seemed to jump out at me as if newly made. I had to stop and stand still in the middle of the street, overwhelmed by the flow of reality. A whole city and all its teeming life. Not burning.

For perhaps the first time in my life, I was thinking, *I am living in the present. Living in this moment now and not some fantasy elsewhere.*

And yet, once you have seen, even in imagination, a rent in the veil, you cannot help but be anxious of its thinness. Of the provisional, hesitant nature of the moment. How things we think we have all put behind us, are still there, waiting. I have only to look at the news after all, to see the fields of Hell. I no longer so easily and thoughtlessly assume that today follows yesterday and precedes tomorrow. The days of course, stumble on one another's heels as they always have. It is their content that does not flow as steadily or as straightly as we like to imagine it does. Because that content is us.

Memory seems less a sequence of events to be confidently narrated, than a rising and falling of impressions. The coming into being, the fading away, of perceptions and occurrences. I do not say that things are not exactly as they always were. But that the time after those events was a time and was after, I can tell only by the flavour, the tone of memory. I cannot even be sure that they were 'events'. As if life was itself a confusing memory, even as it unfolded. There is a before and there is an after, but the moment of the shot always eludes.

At first it was like living in a blaze of brilliant light. A light so intense, it made it all but impossible to see anything clearly, because everything was seen too clearly. I moved cautiously through the necessary actions of maintaining life, like someone whose skin has become excruciatingly thin.

Slowly, this first rawness faded, and I found myself living instead, in a strange empty calm. I found comfort, then, in an old Buddhist parable I had discovered during that year of first taking up the bow. Idly searching for understanding of some of the language and images that the books and teachers used, I had strayed into the all but infinite maze of Buddhist ideas. Fortunately, in my unsystematic and unguided reading, I had also stumbled across this simplest of all exits from that maze.

A boy loses an ox. He searches for it. He finds it. He leads it home and ties it up in the stable. He goes off to town, whistling, empty hands in his pockets. Everything has changed. Nothing has changed. Everything is just as it was before, but everything that was before, is no longer the same.

Before, it seemed nothing more than a banal folk-tale. Barely even a story, although there was something oddly satisfying even in its seeming lack of point. But now it spoke to me directly. This was where I was.

Yes, of course, something big had happened. What it was exactly, did not seem to matter so much. I had been part of something, I had acted a part. I had anomalous memories that made no sense. But something had been resolved. I no longer felt pulled toward whatever had been going on in those shadows. I began to understand that this new and strange emptiness I felt was the emptiness of potential. The void out of which all things arise.

* * *

The dry cold of a winter's day. Christmas has become popular. The shops are full of sparkly things. The children are running a little ahead of her, stopping every now and then to look shyly back, to see if they have ventured too far.

In fulfilment of Mr Yanaga's prophecy, Little Brother seems comfortably settled in the mainstream of politics. He and his wife often ask Mie, with hasty apologies, to take the children for a morning, or an afternoon, or a day. The fact that she also has work to do never seems to occur to them. But then ... the children!

Running from window to window in their brightly coloured coats. Ghosts of the future. They will become citizens of that world. One day quite soon, she thinks, glancing in the shop windows, that world will be here and now. Perhaps it is already here. She and they will be alive – and dead – together.

But it is not really her dreamed or remembered ghost-world in which they will live. It is this world. The real world. The world she was not meant to have seen. *'Watashi wa ayakashi desu,'* she whispers to herself, her very tongue fearful of the words. *'I am a living ghost'.*

'Auntie Mie! Auntie Mie!' They are calling, pointing eagerly at some spark, some glitter in the flow of things, that they have found, captured and exhibited behind the retailer's glass.

There never was anyone else after Mr Yanaga. So strange in this world of so many million souls. And now, in any case, it is becoming too late for children of her own. In her own mind, it was always too late. To bring someone else into being, when she can scarcely believe in her own existence, feels reckless. She stops to buy soft, sweet mochi rice-cakes from a place Emi had said was good. Emi is visiting from Colorado for a few days. They are going to meet her in the park, and she wants to have a gift, as well as a treat for her nephew and niece. The children will like Emi, she thinks.

The girl is the older of the two. Sometimes, Mie catches her niece staring at her appraisingly, as if uncertain what to make of her moody aunt. *She knows.* Mie thinks one day, *She knows I am not...* The boy is different. He does not stare, but is attentive, open. She has the feeling that he accepts her for whatever she is. If only she could explain herself to someone like that, to shout across the gulf of sky, to tell them what it is like to be dead, but also alive.

Summer. A hot morning, prelude to a hotter day. She lost her temper with the children. That was not fair. Looking at their cowed, puzzled faces, she had felt ashamed. Are they becoming spoiled? She cannot help giving them gifts, drawing their attention to things. She wants them to notice, to see the world that is coming into being all around them. A world that is theirs to dwell in. But is it not foolish, this desire to give them what is already theirs? It is fear. She wants so much to tempt them with the toys of the future, out of the burning house of the past.

Walking along a street of shops, looking at things in the windows, she had been trying to point out to them things that showed the way to the future. Not understanding the urgency, they had made it into a game, not hearing, as she did, the flames of the past crackling somewhere behind her, consuming the street wherever she did not look at it. It was difficult, but necessary, she thought, to realise that for them war was only a picture. But how could that be?

A display in a toyshop window: 'Popular Toys of the Past'. An eccentric thing to do in this age of progress. The owner was perhaps, making a point, or perhaps just cleverly appealing to parents and grandparents. The children had been briefly fascinated by things that Mie recognised with a stab of sadness. A paper balloon, a top, a wooden dog on wheels. Things from the world that had ended in flames. She felt glad of the glass between them, convinced in imagination that if the children could reach out and touch such things, they might be terribly burned, seduced by hell-toys made only of flame. It was then that she had lost her composure.

Later, after a conciliatory lunch in an air-conditioned cafe and shaved ice with syrup, they meet some family friends in the park. A group of three boisterous girls, two sisters and a friend who has joined them, are in the care of grandparents, an energetic, enthusiastically chatty old couple. Another child, a boy, is accompanied by a young foreign woman whom he treats with ill-disguised contempt. The foreign girl looks strained and unhappy.

Her niece and nephew know the other children well, and all are soon playing together under the shade of the trees. Mie finds herself forced into awkward conversation with the other adults. The grandparents, in particular, make Mie feel very uncomfortable by their polite but insistent friendliness. Eventually, thwarted by her reluctance to respond, they give up on Mie and become engrossed instead in learning all about the foreign girl's life, culture, family, dreams for the future, boyfriends, etc. etc. Although there seems no limit to the scope of their enquiries, the young woman does not appear to be daunted or offended. In fact, answering so many personal questions seems to lift the unhappiness from her face and she soon looks like quite a different person. *How wonderful,* Mie thinks. *How wonderful to charm away someone's pain like that, through merely talking.*

She is left free to observe the children. The girls have a clear-eyed openness and a frank, logical, approach as they negotiate among themselves the terms of play. They seem to relish the world. The boy with the foreign au-pair is loud and bossy and seems to have an obsession with inventing rules for everyone else to follow. The girls blithely ignore him. Younger Brother's son, Hiroshi, is cautious, diplomatic, evasive. He does not seem to want to play the game of rules.

The bossy boy becomes angry, shouting commands with increasing urgency into the air. He seems to be trying to ensnare the others in some tedious, infinite warfare of status and strategy. The grandfather intervenes, speaks quietly to him. He becomes silent, furious, unexploded. The au-pair will have a hard time with him on the way home, Mie fears. And yet she is smiling happily, laughing and nodding with the grandmother.

When the time comes to part, the foreign girl thanks the older couple effusively.

'I will follow my dreams!' she declares, the words oddly accented, but clear and emphatic. 'Thank you for encouraging me.' The grandparents look briefly anxious, but then smile, 'I hope it works out well for you!' The grandmother says, an edge of concern in her voice. 'It will!' the young woman replies firmly, 'I will give my notice this evening and tomorrow, buy a ticket for the North!' Her face shines with happy determination. The boy looks up at her with a sudden sense of uncertainty.

Will the girls, Mie wonders sadly, grow up to discover the world they face with such candour and logic has been twisted into a dark forest of obligations, pressures and limits? How is it possible to be apparently so free, like the foreign woman? Yet, self-evidently, it must be possible. There she is, seemingly off to tender her resignation and buy a ticket to some long dreamed of adventure. To release the moment and fly toward the future. And it hits Mie with a sudden shock, that that is just what she herself once did. Everything which surrounds her now is the result of that moment of release, of destruction, when she left her old life to burn and set off, through some dark dream, to the mountains.

That it is how it is done. At the moment of extremity, one lets go the tense balance of the present and releases the future to fly into existence.

*　　*　　*

Night. A white eel, swimming steadily, nose pointed at the sky. The warm breeze from the sea ripples the dark indigo banner on which it is printed. A breeze that has wandered here through city streets from Tokyo Bay. Above it, a colossal mural of a tuna leaps ten storeys into the night.

Early morning. A tiny coffee bar, little more than a wooden cabin in a street of cabins near the old fish market. Behind the counter, an elderly woman with strong, brown, well-spaced teeth. She vigorously pumps up the pressure in a small brass spirit stove under a black iron kettle and brews, in an old-fashioned percolator, coffee black as tar. Satanically strong, it makes my tired head spin.

A night-time visit to a top floor skyscraper lounge with panoramic windows, lined on walls and ceiling with glitzy mirror tiles, furnished with an even glitzier mirrored bar and mirrored tables and chairs. A vulgar spectacle – until the house lights are dimmed, and the teeming lights of the city outside invade the darkness, doubled and redoubled to infinity in Indra's endless net of jewels.

Early evening. A ride in a rattling suburban train. I stare abstractedly out of the window at the passing castellations and tessellations of office and apartment blocks and the misty grey cathedrals of baseball park nets. A sudden glimpse, purple in the horizon's orange haze: the paper-cut outline of the distant God-mountain.

Arriving somewhere for the first time, you visit a place that you will never see again, however many times you return. An impression, fresh as dew, that evaporates in the first few hours or days of your visit, to be replaced by an everyday familiarity.

The first thing to arise from my new-found calm had been a determination to return to the London dojo. As my therapist had pointed out during our final session, no-one had actually *told* me I couldn't continue as a student there. That was an inference I had made for myself. Vadim's parting words could be read as a challenge to shape up, as much as condemnation and final excommunication. Which way to take it was up to me.

Under the neon lights of the gymnasium, I had found a new regime in place. Vadim's last words to me had, I was told, been among his last on Earth. Mayumi Harding was now in charge. Although I deeply regretted not being able to resolve things personally with Vadim, I soon found myself swept up into the life of the club, assisting with committees, translations and general organising.

Some years back, the All Nippon Kyudo Federation, the governing body of Kyudo, had issued a decree that all gradings above the level of 5th dan must take place in the mother country. As 5th dan is the minimum level at which one may instruct others, and higher gradings are desirable for the prestige of a teacher – as well as for other reasons, this meant a good deal of expense and organisation for members of clubs such as mine.

I wished to progress and I also hoped one day to teach, so, after a good deal of taking on extra work contracts, weekly journeys to attend practice sessions in London and much general effort, I at last found myself suddenly surrounded by the tranquility of stratospheric flight, on my first club trip to Japan.

Since that first time, I have joined several such trips to Tokyo, latterly even, as group leader. I have become quite familiar with the place, or at least, with some of its main landmarks and principal districts. The more familiar I have become, the greater the effort it requires to remember, let alone to find, that hallucinatory city I first encountered. A city not of connected spaces, of things understood in relation and proportion to one another, but a city made of fragmentary dreams and visions, each occupying a separate bubble-universe of its own, appearing, brief and brilliant, before fading back into the haze of astonishment and fatigue.

I suppose it would have been natural to speculate about taking time one day, to try to find the location of the Arrow

Garden. But I didn't. There wasn't much time to spare on those expeditions and I soon came to understand that in this fast-moving city, whole neighbourhoods could vanish and transform in a matter of days.

No, I decided, no more fantasy, no more dim dreams and half-light imaginings. A real place, real people, real food and drink I could touch and taste. Bows and arrows that, under the flat neon lights of the school gymnasia in which we were able to practise, played no tricks at all, but only reflected with sober faithfulness my attention or inattention to the craft of shooting.

On that first trip, our hosts from the local archery club had not only arranged our accommodation, but scheduled our days down to the last detail of comfort and entertainment. An ambitious itinerary of bars, restaurants, meetings with persons of note and visits to tourist sites saw us climbing out of taxis one sultry afternoon at the entrance to the Nakamise-dori. This street is both the processional approach to the great Sensoji Buddhist temple and a market for every item of tourist tat, sacred and profane, that could conceivably be offered. The formal entrance to this wondrous alley is the famous and quite hallucinatory Kaminari-mon, the 'Thunder Gate', itself one of the great tourist sights of the city. Painted bright vermilion red under a huge sweeping roof, the Kaminari-mon houses images of Raijin and Fujin, the gods of Thunder and Wind respectively, a spectacle which left me somehow not quite in the right frame of mind to run the gauntlet of 'assault by retail' that fills the next quarter of a mile.

Weaving our way through the crowds, as our minders worked hard to keep the group together and not lose any stragglers to the siren charms of the market booths, I began to understand those coloured flags and fluorescent lollipops that Japanese tour guides hold aloft to rally their troops in foreign cities. At last, passing under the enormous red paper lantern that hangs in the Hozomon, the 'Treasure House Gate', we found ourselves in the calmer and more open spaces of the temple's forecourt. Here, our little group huddled closer, drawn steadily toward the centre of the courtyard, where incense smoke was tinting the surrounding air with its blue-grey colour and heavy scent.

A vase, perhaps five or six feet across, of polished black-green bronze stood under a small square canopy supported on four thin pillars. Beneath it, the thick-rimmed bowl reeked and smoked, being filled from side to side with a deep bed of smouldering charcoal and incense. As they approached it, temple visitors would stop, while tourists stared and briefly waft the purifying smoke onto their clothes with hands, mobile phones, or occasionally, fans.

Following our guide, who was encouraging us at every point to enter into the spirit of things, we too approached the glowing coals, hot even in the roasting heat of the afternoon and diffidently wagged our hands with varying degrees of enthusiasm, to encourage the smoke to favour us.

If you asked me to say at what precise point in the sequence of that afternoon's events it happened, I could not swear it was then, but I cannot think how it could have been otherwise. It just seemed a moment outside of time. Another of those moments in that 'first encounter' city, a city I shall never be able to visit again, whose inhabitants I can never again meet. A city isolated in memory from the flow of time. Paradoxical. Eternal. Vanished.

*   *   *

Spring, although the cherry blossom is all but over. They are on another excursion to pass the time. She has promised to show them…

'The ducks! Can we see the ducks?'

Down a side street, there is a bridge over the small river that runs behind the shops and houses. Its banks have been concreted over, but near the bridge a little island of fine sand has grown, some green reeds have taken root and every year a pair or two of ducks nest there. An old woman, her wide-brimmed hat firmly tied down with a scarf, is waiting, a brown paper bag in her brown hand. The children run up and greet her. She is by now an old acquaintance on these walks. She doles out little handfuls of millet for them to throw over the low parapet. When it is all gone, they stand on tiptoe, eagerly discussing the family gossip of the ducks.

'They are growing fast, Mie-san!'

Mie looks over at the ducks and nods. Last week's clutch of ducklings, she notes, are indeed bigger balls of fluff that already almost begin to look like real birds.

'The children I mean!'

The old woman chuckles softly. She is used to Mie's distracted ways.

'Ah! Yes!'

Mie smiles, embarrassed at overlooking the obvious. And it is true. They will be content to observe the doings of ducks for a year or two more yet, but after that?

There is a thick, languid smell in the air. An old smell, a smell from the time beyond. It is partly the river, partly the little noodle restaurant, and partly, as one returns from the river bridge toward the street of shops that still follows the river's curve, the incense and stationery store across the way.

She has brought them here often, since Emi first showed her the way back through streets unfamiliar with rebuilding. Streets that seemed to her like impostors, falsely bearing the names of old friends. In fact, all that remains the same here is the little river, the echoing curve of the street and the incense business. Even that occupies entirely rebuilt premises, although on the same site as before. Oh, and one other thing: the small shrine to Jizo Bosatsu, tucked in between two apartment block entrances, a little way down the alley that runs between the incense store and its neighbour.

And when she stands and looks down that alley, forested with stray bicycles and little clusters of pot-plants, she knows she has her back to the Arrow Garden. If she were only to screw her eyes tight shut, turn around and open them, surely she would be facing the heavy, dark blue noren curtains with their big white three-feather mon and she would only have to slip inside to resume her old, interrupted life?

Instead, she finds an unfamiliar window, full of the dull glow of rolls of expensive brocades, with discreet little handwritten cards promising personal service and skilful attention. The kind of brocades that respectable women her age still sometimes have made up into kimono for the grand family occasions of grand families. It occurs to her that with her brother's steady rise in public life, she perhaps ought to go in and open an account there, just in case. The children are getting fretful. Perhaps it would be a distraction for them. She gathers them to her, pushes open the door and leads them into the fragrant gloom.

The door had set a chime tinkling, but for a long while there is no sign of movement. The children stare about, fascinated by this new space, dark, quiet and smelling of silk and cedarwood. Mie also cannot help glancing around the room, looking for signs of the past, but of course, the building is post-war, even if it has been decorated in a dark, old-fashioned style.

After a long while, someone is heard, calling a repeated, tremulous apology, and an elderly lady appears, wrapped in an almost cylindrical kimono of a shimmering, pale, celadon green, a simple obi in darker malachite green brocade around her high and entirely nominal waist.

She smiles at the children, eagerly asks their names and ages, offers them small, old-fashioned sweets from a Chinese jar.

They instantly adore her. Eventually, she apologises and returns her attention to Mie. She seems to understand Mie's situation instantly and reassures her that they will be ready for her at a moment's notice. Cards are exchanged and the business concluded with stiff, low bows. The children are reluctant to bid farewell to their new 'grandma', who accompanies them to the street door with smiles and more sweets.

Back in the open air, Mie and the seamstress exchange final bows and she finds on glancing aside, that the children are making their own low bows with unusually perfect etiquette. The old lady laughs and claps her hands together delightedly before returning the compliment. Mie smiles to herself as she leads her borrowed ducklings away. Perhaps present and past can speak to one another.

They stroll slowly and contentedly along, but they have scarcely passed three more shops when Mie senses a sudden alertness in the little girl. The boy continues chattering a moment or two, but then he too notices the ticking noises and the rhythmic swinging of the electricity and telephone cables that drape this way and that across the street. Instinctively, she grabs their hands to pull them into the centre of the road, but the little boy stumbles and falls. She stops to scoop him up and finds that it is his sister who, gently tugging on her skirt, calmly leads Mie into the middle of the road, looking left and right to be sure the one approaching car has stopped. Mie glances nervously upward as the earth begins to sway in earnest and with difficulty, they stagger toward the more open space of the junction with the bridge. Looking back, they see the old woman looking anxiously out into the street, supporting herself on the side of her shop door.

With sulky reluctance, the tremor fades. Stillness returns to the street for a second or two, before doors and windows open and neighbours call questions and reassurances to one another. But then, a dull thump, and a few seconds later Mie can see a plume of black smoke boiling up from a building on the other side of the river. An alarm begins to sound and there are shouts. Somebody comes running across the bridge and stands looking anxiously down the street.

'The fire brigade should come this way any minute! Watch out when they come round this corner!'

Mie steps back a pace and sets down the little boy, whose weight is making her shoulders ache. The children watch attentively but silently, perhaps catching something of Mie's rising panic. Her one great terror: fire and the smell of smoke. It seems the earthquake has fractured the pipe from the noodle-restaurant's kerosene heating-fuel tank and it somehow became ignited. The smoke is beginning to drift across the river towards them, rolling lazily up over the buildings, over the haberdasher's that was once the Arrow Garden and into the road. A thick acrid, kerosene-fuelled smoke, just like...

She pulls the reluctant children urgently through the small but growing crowd of onlookers, back up the street, past the incense store and down the little alley almost at a trot, only to pull them up sharply in front of Jizo-sama. She drops to her knees, shaking and begins to pray. The little boy is crying, the girl stands silent, an arm on Mie's shoulder, then she too drops to her knees. The boy, still snivelling, follows his sister. He reaches in, searching for Auntie's hand, finds it and squeezes hard. His hand is cold and wet. With a convulsion of horror, Mie remembers the cold vagueness of a ghostly hand. Remembers running, on a wild impulse, into the night of another world.

With a skirl of sirens and a small lightning-storm of flashing lights, the fire engine rushes past the end of the alley, squealing and growling around the corner and across the narrow bridge. A minute later, the smoke, which had been flying high and ragged above the rooftops, begins to diminish. Mie makes a last obeisance and gets shakily to her feet, brushing grit and incense-stick ash from her skirt. She pulls a tissue from her handbag and dries the little boy's red face, talking reassuringly to them both.

'It's alright now, the firemen are putting it out! We must go home and tell your mother we are all safe — we had an adventure, eh?'

They look at her solemnly. They understand very well that the incident has been more than a mere earthquake and fire. They have witnessed another kind of convulsion: a grown-up, seriously frightened.

It is a subdued little group that wanders on down the alley, across a grid of small streets and into the shiny bustle of the metro station. The children grip Auntie's hands, as if to reassure her, as much as themselves. Although they do not know it, the shadow of distant war has touched them. Should she tell someone? Unburden herself of this thing she has carried, this taint of smoke still clinging to her clothes? Will it be to these two, she will confess, when they are old enough? She looks down at their sleepy faces, swaying against her arms as the train lurches and squeals through the once more quiet earth.

Handing them over to the parents takes longer than usual. They want to tell the tale of their adventures, in which sweets, a newly adopted honorary grandma and a fire-engine, loom much larger than any mere earthquake. Their mother of course has many anxious questions which are very much not about sweets, grandmothers or even fire-engines. She offers Mie tea, but Mie is anxious to get home and makes her excuses. The mother lingers on the doorstep, for once fulsome in her thanks, as the children cling to her skirts and wave.

Reaching home, Mie slowly and deliberately strips off her smart clothes, every last stitch and places them, with her expensive shoes, in a tightly sealed plastic bag. She takes a long shower and washes her hair again and again, until her arms ache. Then she dries herself, slips on a yukata and puts the bag out for the rubbish collection, before finally returning indoors to wash her hands.

*　*　*

I was standing, watching people around the brazier, trying to distinguish locals from visitors, tourists from worshippers and wondering at the uniform of muted casual clothing that hid these distinctions. As my gaze swept past the smoke, everyone and everything behind it, blurred and shimmered in the fumes and heat-haze rising from the coals.

I must have been standing quite close to the brazier and therefore, in the middle of my companions, but I don't remember them being there. I remember only becoming aware that a woman, smartly dressed in a dark blue business suit, was looking steadily at me through the shimmer of incense and heat. Her hair was iron grey, cut in a short bob, her throat concealed by an elegant ruffle of silk. She looked, I thought afterwards, like a million other smart older women in that city, a little unusual only in the slightly more than average formality of her dress, as if she had just stepped out from some important board-room meeting. I looked back at her, unable to see her with any clarity as her image faded and brightened, alternately blurred and sharpened by the boiling air above the coals. But I do remember the vivid moment of shock: she had returned my stare, as if she too, were reading mysteries through the smoke. Our eyes locked for a brief second, a second in which I felt myself suspended in infinite space.

I did not know then what an unusual contravention of unspoken social mores that frank, serious stare was. Before I could speak or move, she gave a quick, sharp bow of acknowledgement and turned away. But in that very movement I saw, or thought I saw, just for a second, as if in slow-motion, someone quite different: a high-cheeked profile. A white keiko-gi, black muneate and black hakama. Long, shimmering black hair tied loosely back.

Already she was stepping backward, away from the brazier, her figure dissolving in the haze as she began to walk briskly toward the Hozo-mon, away from the temple. I moved quickly aside, peering around the plume of heat and through the crowds. A woman who might have been her paused briefly beneath one of the giant votive rice-straw sandals hung on the back of the gatehouse. Bizarrely, she seemed to be barefoot. A moment later, she stooped, slipped on some low-heeled shoes and hurried on through the gate into the seething crowds of the Nakamise-dori. I ran forward, craning my neck, shouldering through the moving forest of people. There was no sign of such a woman. I halted, a perplexed rock in the stream of humanity. Once more, she was no more than a memory. And yet I was utterly convinced, for no other reason than a certain intense, focused concentration in those imperfectly seen eyes, that I had been, once more, for a brief moment, in the presence of Tanaka Mie.

I turned and made my way back towards the temple. As I passed the brazier, a feeling rushed over me like a scorching wind, that I had just bid a final and irrevocable farewell. To someone I had never really met. To a future I never really had. To a part of myself.

And then I was dodging and stumbling through the slow moving crowds to rejoin my colleagues on the steps of the main hall. The huge bulk of the temple, a distant haze of red, gold and black, loomed above me until it became a darkness, deep and broad, from which the glimmer of gold leaf and the rich colours of rank upon rank of massed flowers slowly emerged. Somewhere in the incense-heavy gloom, golden faces glowed softly amid the shadows.

My group was nowhere to be seen, but I was no longer looking for them. Searching for air and space, I descended the temple steps and wandered out into the surrounding gardens.

It was there that I met her. The bodhisattva, the Kannon herself. A plain stone statue, the figure seated in meditation. There is a wonderful thing that sculptors of the Buddhist world do. The Kannon does not stare, like Christian saints, into your sinful soul, nor upward to imagined heavens. Attentive, she listens to the cries of the world. Her gaze is downcast, but not unseeing. Inward, but not unaware. Seeing no-one, she sees everyone. Seeing nothing, she sees all. She looks, with steadfast compassion, into the heart of the moment and from it, forwards and backwards, into everything that is, was, or ever might have been. Hers is a gaze I can return, faithfully, calmly and without distress, even though I know I am seen.

It was not my father who had battered my gaze to the ground, that day he shouted at me. No one had. I had been that way long before. Indeed, I think it was his own unwillingness to accept that he too had this reluctance, that made him so angry with me. This was not some aberration. This was who and what I was. The problem was not my unwillingness to stare and be stared at. It was the shame. Shame that was thrust upon me by others, shame which I created out of my own anxiety. I was no bodhisattva, but in the gaze of the Kannon I saw that there are other ways of paying attention, other ways of seeing, other ways of meeting. Ways that could be mine if I would only take hold of them.

I had become so used to looking sidelong at the target, with only half my attention, that even in memory it appeared to me only on the edge of vision. After that day at Asakusa, it moved slowly back to the centre of my attention. Today, it is no longer the eye of my father's wrath. It is the gaze of compassion, of acceptance. It is bow, arrow, hand, arm and self that fade. The target seems to grow and grow until it fills the whole of awareness. It remains only to place an arrow in the dark centre of the moment.

* * *

The tourist leaflet, thrust into her hand as she crosses the bridge, is peremptory. The Asakusa Temple, the Senso-ji and its Kaminari Mon, the Thunder Gate, must be seen. The temple is dedicated to the Kannon, the Bodhisattva who embodies merciful compassion and who works to release those snared in the circle of suffering, trapped on the wheel of rebirth.

Is that what she needs? Compassion? Forgiveness? She has always blamed herself for living. The force of this realisation brings her to a halt in the middle of the Azuma-bashi. Buffeted by the tide of people, she has to lean for a moment against the stone parapet, staring unsteadily down at the flow of the wide Sumida River. Is that what she needs? Forgiveness? How alone she is, a stone in the stream of these hurrying crowds. There is no one she can talk to about this. Even the ever sympathetic Emi referred her to a higher authority. Emi now signs herself Emi Anderson and is a US citizen. They keep in touch, but it is not the same.

She pushes her way through the crowds to the head of the Nakamise-dori and is just passing under the shadow of the giant paper lantern in the Hojo-mon gate, when the scent of incense makes her stop short. A woman behind her mutters something and barges past. Mie has forgotten the brazier. She had been thinking of a cool, moss-covered basin, a copper ladle, cold, crystal clear mountain water. But this of course, is a big Buddhist temple in a big city not a Shinto shrine. No time for queues, no time for lustrations for the hundreds of people milling around her. She is brought to a stand as she catches sight of the wafts of grey smoke writhing out from under the small bronze canopy.

It had been necessary to attend a meeting with publishers and editors in some anonymous hired offices near the Azuma-bashi. She had held herself together, but talking in such detail about her parents' work seems these days to bring the past closer and closer, to unearth more and more unwanted images and emotions. She had tried not to close her eyes too often, tried to breathe and focus sharply on each moment of the present. The meeting, the last in a long project, had broken up with the usual chatter: of thanks, of farewells, expressions of respect, agreements to meet again. Out into the corridor and down in the lift, more necessary chat with enthusiastic scholars and admirers of 'The Work'. At last, she is released into the anonymous crowd. Perhaps prompted by the bustle of the city street, the past floods in, relentlessly filling the space in her mind, now emptied of business concerns.

There had been nightmares last night. And for many nights previously. She has been repressing, denying to herself that they are in fact, not dreams, but memories. Old familiar visions she now realises, but kept behind lock and key for all these years.

A street scene devoid of almost all colour in the grey light of day. Receding into the distance, a row of old fashioned, black, curvaceous cars. Stationary. Parked at odd angles, as if a whole queue of impatient drivers had been just starting to overtake each other when a policeman had raised a white gloved hand and shouted 'Stop!' Except there is nothing white here. A rock garden of ugly black forms, heaped up or scattered across the street, that resolves itself under her horrified, reluctant stare, into piles of bodies, flesh transformed to charcoal. Some of the car doors are open, the occupants leaning stiffly out of them, faceless, featureless. An indescribable, nauseous stench in the overwhelming heat. No relief from this landscape of hell, for block after burned down block, trying constantly not to tread on things one does not want to feel, see or even recognise.

She shakes her head. Tries to sweep the night's dreams from her vision. They blend tauntingly into the brazier smoke and the milling crowds in front of the great red temple.

Paralysed. Unable to move forward or back. Willing herself to approach, to pass the censer, but she cannot move forward. Trapped in the Burning House.

For the last few years, she has been poring over calendars,

calculating obsessively on scraps of paper. But she feels it coming anyway. The time when she will be doubled in the world. Can that happen? Or will she die? Or is the Ghost World truly another world, different from this one?

She must thank someone. Apologise to someone. Is that it? Whatever the case, she must lay her confusion before someone, or drag it with her to the grave, a stinking, smoking burden. She must somehow let go. She had laid it before Emi, but Emi had turned it back on her, like the mirror she had once polished on the altar of the village shrine. She had laid it before young Hiroshi, but he had become obsessed with maps and details. Perhaps the Goddess, with her calm golden gaze, can gently prize her fingers off the hell-toys of the past and release her back into the present? Before it is too late?

It must be tried. Once, she had walked out of a burning city and away to the cool compassion of the mountains. To a new life. It must be done. She must find again that bitter determination that drove her forward. How to recapture that intensity?

Before she is aware she is doing it, she is kicking off her shoes. She leans against the nearby temple office building and, oblivious to shame, rips off her stockings. Panting and scowling in defiance of any who might look, she stands, barefoot, feeling the heat of the flagstones, the rawness of contact. She forces one unwilling foot forward, then the other. Toward the fire-bowl under the bronze canopy and the eternal smoke. The constant conflagration of future into past.

She creeps closer and closer to the brazier. Lets the smoke curl around her with all the enthusiasm of someone overcoming a fear of snakes. She coughs. By an angry effort of will, she forces herself to stand and stare into the coals, the curling smoke and the heat shimmer rising from the bronze bowl.

A face on the other side, staring back, as fixedly as herself. A man. Foreign. Not a tourist, his clothes – odd. She blinks. A practice uniform. White gi, black hakama. He is staring fixedly back at her. As if he knows…

The world suddenly feels like a huge, infinitely fragile burden in her hands. She must not speak. He is there, but she must not reach out again. That face, so briefly seen. Those eyes, a foreign shape, but somehow, she knows, looking into them, that she is looking at herself, in another form. Another life, parallel, over-lapping. Perhaps reincarnation does not have to be sequential. Perhaps one can be present in more than one life, perhaps many. Perhaps all souls are just knots tied in the same stuff. She has shaped him, made him, imagined him. She has done what she has done. She has done what felt right at the turn of the wheel.

The burnt child has feared the fire too long. No more. It is not Bodhisattvas or forgiveness she needs. She bows, turns and feeling the hot texture of the paved courtyard sing beneath her feet, strides briskly away. Beneath one of the huge rice-straw sandals that hang at the entrance to the Nakamise-dori, she pauses to slip her shoes back on before merging into the flow of the crowd.

*   *   *

9 Yudaoshi

Relaxing and stepping back.

'She died.'

It took me a few seconds to recognise the stricken looking man on my doorstep.

'Last month,' he said. 'I had to come.'

'Hiroshi!'

He didn't look older exactly, but he looked like a person who had been through something more than a mere twelve-hour flight. I ushered him in, sat him down and made coffee. For a while he said nothing, just stared at the floor in front of him.

'So … your aunt?'

'Hm.'

A sudden memory assailed me of a young woman, lying on the sofa in this very room. It seemed too strange to talk about. Indecent somehow. Hiroshi looked almost equally lost and out of place.

Desperate to reach into his silence, I said the only thing I could think of:

'You once said she used to give you strange presents.'

For a second, it looked like Hiroshi might be going to cry. He kept his head down and grunted, as if I had made some social gaffe. I guessed he wasn't ready yet.

I opened a bottle of wine and called the local Indian restaurant for some food. By the time it arrived, I found myself doing something else I almost never do: finishing one bottle of wine and starting another. A lot of it was going into Hiroshi. Towards the end of the second bottle, I was beginning to wonder if he would say anything at all. He had gone very pink and kept staring around at my room, at my stuff and then at me. I took a risk and looked back. His look hit me like a blow. But he began, at last, to talk.

'Yes … unusual things. The first thing was … yes, one year she gave us a lot of Christmas decorations! For our birthdays! In summer! She must have bought them the winter before. All this stuff made of gold and silver plastic. You could always get that sort of thing in a few stores. Because of the Americans. After the war, you know. But that year, was it in the late 70s sometime. I don't remember. It was becoming popular. Then they started using that metallic plastic stuff to make them. It had a different look than the old glass and metal, more shiny, you know? She got really excited about it. She kept saying, 'They have things like this in the ghost-world! I saw them! In the ghost shops! And now we have them here, too!'

I sat there toying with the last of the sag aloo, listening to Hiroshi talk, while saying as little as I could.

'Then another year she gave us reflective vests. We didn't even have bikes! I think our parents were pleased. They thought we could wear them to school on dark mornings. We just used them to play at being firemen or traffic cops all summer until they fell apart.

As she got older, it got worse. It became a family joke. We would say: 'Oh dear, what's Auntie Mie going to come up with next?' It wasn't just the presents. She used to say very strange things. When new stuff came out in the shops, like computers or colour TVs, or digital watches, she would stop and make us look, and she would say, in a very serious voice: 'That's what they have in the Ghost World, you know! I've seen these things before!' Our parents would get quite cross. They thought she was scaring us. We were just … confused. Whenever we tried to ask her what she meant, she would become reserved and change the subject.'

Hiroshi paused and stared at his empty glass. I refilled it. He started slightly, as if he had been miles away, took a polite sip and carried on:

'Apparently, they argued about politics, but Father always got angry if he heard of anyone saying disrespectful things about her. He honoured her as his elder sister, I suppose. He would sometimes say that he was only alive today because she somehow survived the bombing raids in the city, got a job and sent little bits of money to the relatives who were looking after him in the country. They were quite old and could not really cope, and it was a time of great hardship, starvation even.'

He paused, staring at the table.

'I'm ashamed to say that we kids ... we would sometimes imitate her. We would point at things in shop windows or in the street, anything that was new, things that had just come out. We would say: 'Oh look, they have that in the Ghost World!' She got really cross with us when we did that. One time my sister pointed at some watches being demonstrated in a shop, they were some of the first ever digital ones, with numbers that lit up, not the modern kind, so they looked blank at first, but when you pressed the button they lit up red. My sister was wondering about all the blank watches and she said 'Look, Auntie Mie, Ghost World watches!' That time she really exploded. Yelled at us in the store. We both felt very ashamed afterwards for teasing her. 'That's not the kind they have in the Ghost World!' she said. 'How would you know, you silly girl! You've never been there! The ones in the Ghost World are grey, with grey numbers!' My sister burst into tears. I remember being amazed at how sure Auntie Mie was, as if the Ghost World was somewhere you could visit, like India or America. After that we never talked to her about the Ghost World again. If she mentioned it, we would just bow and say, 'Yes, Auntie Mie!' Not even a few years later when the liquid crystal displays came out, with the grey numbers.'

We both sat for a moment, contemplating the mystery of liquid crystal displays.

'When our childhood ended, the Ghost World seemed to disappear. I began to wonder if she had actually been having some sort of breakdown when we were kids, but holding it together in her own odd way. Then one day, out of the blue, she phoned me and asked – *ordered* – me to visit her. She looked very tired. She let me in, let me make tea while she went and lay down on the sofa. I sat next to her like it was some kind of psychoanalysis. I felt very embarrassed.

'I have been having dreams.' That was how she began. And then, for the first time since I was a child, she began to talk about the Ghost World. The room was warm, but I began to shiver as I listened. She told me how during the war, she had escaped the fire-bombing raid that should have killed her, by grabbing the hand of a ghost that used to haunt the old dojo where she studied archery and following him into his world for a day and a night. At first, I became alarmed about her mental condition. But as I listened, I began to feel she was describing a real place. A park with ghostly people in it, a dark tower with lantern-ghosts swinging at its top. Another tower, so tall it seemed to catch the starlight. A ghostly city with its shop windows glittering with strange things. Streets full of strange cars. People who spoke English. It sounded so uncanny. But then she gave me this…'

He put a hand inside his jacket and drew out a small envelope. From inside he carefully slid out a fragile sheet of thin paper, folded several times. He smoothed it out gently on his knee, then handed it to me. I stared in astonishment at the fine, spidery traces that showed, with embarrassing exactness, the indecisive route home I had taken on that fateful night.

'That did it for me,' Hiroshi said, jabbing a finger at the map. 'The afterlife might well have room for mysterious towers and perhaps even shops, cars, houses, and flats. But a place you can draw a map of?' He allowed himself a dry smile. 'This town had to be real somehow, however mysterious. I began to feel very strongly that if I could find the park, the towers, I could find this flat and find – you.'

'Why?'

'I think it was the strangeness of it that appealed to me. A ghost who might really exist as a person. It became … a compulsion.'

'Some detective work!'

'Actually, I was not very good. I think you caught me looking up at your flat that time. Also, I spent two weeks trying to get a job in that big engineering company before I discovered you'd moved across the road. But after that it was easy. When I walked into that little place with a couple of big contracts from people back home, they were very pleased.'

'Yes, I think you made them seem more successful than they really were.'

'At first, I just wanted to talk, to hear your side of the story. But I was embarrassed to just tell you my crazy story. I still thought it might just be all some illusion. I thought if I could get you talking, I might be able to make some connection.'

'Sorry about that!'

'Yes, I should have understood about British reserve.'

'I think it was rather more than that.'

'Yes. Yes, I think I understand that now.'

There was a pause.

'But then I began to be worried. Your life, your habits, did not seem to be what I had imagined. After a time, I could not help asking a direct question. When you said you had never practised archery, I was really shocked. I knew I had the right place – the map was quite accurate. You seemed to have lived here for a while, and it did not appear that you were about to move. It had to be you, so, someone had to make you into an archer. Apparently, I arrived just in time.'

'Lucky you were a qualified teacher!'

'Aah, hmm. About that.'

'Eh?'

'I was not – am not – a qualified teacher. In fact, I have never shot much at all except in high school for a couple of years. I got most of it from a book – my old high school manual as it happens. It was all I could think of at short notice.'

He let out a terse, dry and somewhat embarrassed laugh.

'Anyway, it seems to have worked!'

It was true. I had managed to convince at least two proper sensei that I was a serious pupil. And now I was indeed a dedicated and enthusiastic archer, still practising at every opportunity. What can you say when confronted with a story like that? '

So, why did you suddenly drop it all and rush back home?'

'I got word that Auntie was very ill. It was felt she was not likely to live long. They had sent her home from hospital, as there was nothing more they could do and she was being looked after at home by a nurse and some relatives. When I arrived, she was propped up in bed in a darkened room, really weak. It was hard to see her that way. It was as if her spirit had become very faint, very distant. My memories of her were of such a strong person. The others were getting bored with visiting her and having nothing to say, but I was happy to spend hours watching her sleep, or talking a little about old times. She started to talk about the Ghost World again. She was wondering whether that was where she would have to go when she died.

'The more I sat in the dark room, listening to her whispering voice, the more a terrible feeling came over me. Now I knew that the Ghost World was not a ghost world at all, but was real, it began to feel as if it was I who was becoming less and less real. As she faded, so it felt like I was fading with her, like an old photograph in the sunlight.

'That was when I thought of the picture. She had given it to me when I was a kid. It had always kind of inspired me. When she gave it to me, she said that a ghost had shown it to her in a dream, before it was even taken. And because of that, she knew she had a future and should not be afraid. At the time, I just took it in my stride as one of her crazy stories. But now I was thinking that once she was dead, that would be the only real thing I would have left to remember her by, to prove that she had ever been real. That I was real. And then I remembered that I had lost it. I racked my brains, thinking where it could be. Then I thought of your phone call.

My sister had called the other relatives in because it seemed Auntie would not last the night. After they arrived, I went outside for a cigarette and called you. When I went back in, something important seemed to have changed. There was a different atmosphere in the room. The following day, she started to recover.' He smiled ruefully. 'Maybe I just had a panic attack. I don't normally have those. Talking to you helped somehow. A lot.'

'You know she was here, right then?' I gestured toward the sofa. 'She was there when you made that call. I showed her the picture.' He looked across at the empty upholstery for a long, silent moment.

'I know,' he whispered. 'Just hearing you say that somehow terrifies me.'

There was a faint sheen of sweat on his brow.

'I really think I would find regular ghosts much easier to deal with.'

I stood up and went to the drawer in my desk. The old notebook was still there. I pulled it out and came back to the table, laying it front of Hiroshi. He flicked through it nervously, grunting occasionally with amusement at his old work notes. He riffled through it several times before finding the picture. 'So strange.' he said. 'This is the person you met. The person you remember.' He looked up at me, 'I never met that person.'

* * *

It has been a bad day for the Site Manager. Fighting the damp summer heat has made everybody exhausted and edgy. There are no overt displays of bad temper, or even irritation, but everyone is doing their job with a special kind of tense, sweaty-faced punctiliousness. He feels like he is treading on eggshells every time he has to give an order. He spends a lot of time asking people what they think.

Considering the shop was only built in the 60s, the site has been a nightmare. Visiting head office to get some paperwork signed, shortly after they had started tearing down the shop itself, an urgent call had come in from his deputy. They had found something that wasn't on the plans, a big concrete slab with iron bolts set into it. God knows what for, perhaps a wartime anti-aircraft gun, or some old district loudspeaker tower. Whatever it was, it would have to be broken up and fast.

He had cleared his diary and spent the rest of the morning on the phone trying to find a specialist firm who would do the job the next day without breaking the bank as well as the slab. Apparently, it would be too much even for the compressed air drill they had for the excavator, and hiring something bigger would mean hiring a bigger excavator and then the budget would go to hell, and… Another bad day.

But it got worse. Having booked the expensive concrete breaking specialists and their fancy diamond drills and nitrogen injectors, he had arrived early on site the next day and asked to be shown the offending slab. There was still a lot of debris to be cleared from the demolition of the shop, so he told the excavator guy to finish tidying up and went off to the site-office cabin to stare gloomily at the schedule chart. A few minutes later he heard the excavator engine drop to an idle. His deputy came in, pulling off his hard hat and mopping his very red face furiously with one end of an already sodden tenugui scarf. He wouldn't explain, just kept apologising and bowing and insisting that the boss should come and look.

He was quite proud of himself afterwards, telling the story

to his wife over a salad and some cold beer. If he hadn't been feeling so shitty about the whole contract, he might have called it his finest hour. He didn't get mad, he didn't shout at anybody, he didn't even frown. He had just grunted and nodded and gone back into the office to open a can of chilled coffee. There had been nothing there. Bare, black earth.

Of course, there was a hefty cancellation fee to be paid. And the deputy had tendered his resignation. He couldn't afford to accept it. This was no time to have to go looking for key staff.

For a while after that the site threw up no more than the usual hassles. The rush was on to prepare the area under the old shop for new foundations. They found an old charred tree-stump to one side of where the entrance had been, but they had managed to dig down by hand and eventually pull it out with a chain round the excavator arm, even though technically it probably exceeded the weight limit and nearly tipped the whole machine over on its front. Even then, it had taken them the best part of a day.

They had left the jumble of little outhouses and lean-to store rooms at the rear of the site until last, working back towards an old fashioned wall, topped by a rather extravagant roof, that stood along the river bank. The bank would need pilings and a new concrete retaining wall, so the old wall would have to come down. Viewed from the river bridge, it had looked like a traditional mud and tile wall, with a plaster render to protect it from the weather. It was seamed with cracks, older than anything else on the site but, surprisingly, still standing complete in spite of earthquakes and war. He should have guessed there would be a reason for that.

The young labourer scrapes away some of the muddy sand with a ringing shovel, then bangs the tip of it two or three times on the stepped, sloping mass of solid brick that runs along the foot of the wall, several courses high, for its whole length. The foreman loses his presence of mind sufficiently to find himself saying, 'Why did nobody …?' before throwing his hands out sideways, then letting them drop, the sentence unfinished. Why had *he* not waded along the riverbank, looked more closely at that cracked and flaking render? In the uncomfortable silence, he removes his hard hat and mops his face with the end of his scarf.

One of the labourers steps forward, an older man. He raises his arms high above his head, then spreads them out in an odd, asymmetrically expansive movement. 'Archery, Boss!'

'What?'

'This place used to be an archery range before the war. It's the target shelter. They would pile damp sand up like this…' The man goes down on one knee and makes sweeping movements of his left hand, sketching in the air the angle of the former slope of sand, above the stepped bricks, 'to make the bank to set the targets up on.' The Boss regards him with a look which, if it actually had any expression in it at all, would be one of outraged resentment. *You knew this … all along?* he thinks. *You utter bastard!* He stands, looking. Silent.

The bricks are talking to him. Old, stained, perhaps by iron deposits in the river sand. Meiji era, pre-war. Unusual, outside of factories, railway stations and government buildings, especially for something traditional like this. A skilled job, too. Someone left gaps every few meters, slots for the wooden posts of the wall, but also to allow movement in earthquakes. Must have been expensive to design and put up. Some little deal perhaps, done on the side, to reinforce the difficult, subsidence-prone riverbank. Which perhaps also means… His heart sinks. He wipes his brow again. He is about to issue an order, but thinks better of it. Instead, he reaches out for the shovel in the young labourer's hand. It is passed to him diffidently, the young man's face, puzzled. He hefts it, steps forward and in two or three skilful strokes, cuts away earth from the foot of the bricks. As he feared. A deep concrete foundation. He straightens up, stands staring once more in silence. He gently kicks the brickwork with a disconsolate boot. It feels very, very solid. This is not going to be a pushover. Literally.

He sees his budget and his schedule both going up in flames. He sees a very awkward meeting at headquarters. He stumps off without a word to the site office, to see about the hire of a bigger excavator, with a bigger compressed air drill.

Three days later, they are almost ready to start on the wall, when the old lady wanders in.

* * *

As the first light of dawn did its cliché glimmering outside the windows, Hiroshi at last declared himself, with a self-deprecating little smile, unable to keep his eyes open much longer. 'Of course!' I said, apologising. He looked at me for a second, with an odd, almost shy expression. I said I would take the sofa bed and he should have the bed in my room. The sofa bed however, refused to co-operate, jamming halfway through its deployment. He looked on at my struggles with a patient, weary smile. I sat back on my haunches, baffled and tried to work out what was wrong with it. 'Don't worry,' I said, dropping on all fours and crawling under the half-raised portion of the frame. 'You go on and get some sleep, I'll sort this out.'

'Leave it,' he said quietly, looking steadily down at me. 'We can share.' He turned and walked through toward the bedroom. I heard him detour into the bathroom on the way, to splash some water on his face.

I am good at 'reading' mechanisms. It goes with the job. *This hinges there, this swings that way and therefore...* But the chain of logic gave out at a broken weld. The pull of sleep was overwhelming. I struggled back to my feet and, following Hiroshi's example, had a quick splash in the bathroom sink before heading for the bedroom.

The only light came from the street lamps outside and a bedside digital clock. Hiroshi lay on the far side of the bed. He had pulled off his shirt and trousers leaving an oddly old-fashioned vest and a pair of expensive looking white boxers doing duty as pajamas. He seemed to be fast asleep.

I peeled off my own outer layers and settled awkwardly onto the remaining space, trying not to disturb his repose. I lay on my back and stared up at the ceiling, noticing for the first time how unpleasantly grey and cracked the plaster above my head was. I began to feel a little chilly without the covers. I wondered if Hiroshi would be feeling chilly. I got up and pulled a spare cover out of the bottom of the wardrobe and laid it softly over him. He did not stir. I lay carefully down again, gingerly arranging the other half of the cover over myself. I closed my eyes.

A sudden precise, gentle pressure of his warm, dry hand on mine did not, just for a second, strike me as remarkable. Then it suddenly brought me back to full awareness of myself and of my surroundings. 'Gareth? ... I don't think I will catch that flight,' he was saying quietly. 'I think, instead, I should like to stay here.' There was a pause, while I wondered what on earth this meant. 'Always.' he said softly, giving my hand a slight extra squeeze and then releasing it. Rolling over, his back toward me, he arranged his limbs comfortably, gave a sigh and a few seconds later was breathing deeply, the gentle pressure of an accidental heel against my calf, the only contact between us. Looking across at his slumbering outline in the dim light, I was suddenly overwhelmed by something I had no words for.

Blinking, I turned my gaze back to the ceiling and lay stunned, a helpless witness to the final, inevitable and inexorable collapse and airy dissolution of a vast, dim, grey and entirely imaginary edifice. How had I managed, for so very, very long, to so utterly and wilfully mis-read the mechanism of myself?

'We ought to look for a nicer flat,' I thought and fell asleep.

* * *

It has taken her all her determination to get here. She feels the ground against her back, hard and real and thinks, 'Because of me, a whole world has come into being'. Emi and the hundreds of people she must by now have helped to find each other. The families they made. The children – now surely, even the grand-children. A million lights reflecting each other's presence, a jewelled web of coincidences. Younger Brother, his politics affecting the whole nation, even, from time to time, nations far overseas. And Hiroshi, his quiet, self-effacing son, so different in his manner of living. Hiroshi, who has, she now realises, even as he left childhood behind, still spent a lot of time with her, under the excuse of 'helping out'. She had always assumed it would be the girl.

It is dizzying. Extraordinary. A whole world of people, the present shape of whose lives is made possible only by the strange shape of her own. A shadow darkens her thoughts. What if – it cannot surely be so long now – what if as she dies, that world also fades away? Can that happen? Can it even be otherwise? Is she, in fact, lying unconscious even now, in the charring ruins of the Arrow Garden? Or of her parents' house? Dreaming, as life ebbs away, a 'dream of a single night'?

The story of the Man and his Ox, the one Father had drawn the little picture of for her in the margin of his book. In his deep, half-whispering voice, the voice of one who tells a story to a sleepy child, she hears it again. How the man – or the boy was it? – finds the stable empty. The farming family's precious draught animal, an ox, has escaped and run away. Disaster! The boy sets off to try and find him. For a long time, he searches without success, but then he comes across a hoof print in the mud. Encouraged by this sign, he presses on and soon comes across not only more hoof prints, but an even more reassuring sign: a fresh pile of dung. Now the hunt is really on and soon the boy catches sight of the ox grazing and swishing his tail in the undergrowth ahead. But catching him will not be easy, he is skittish and enjoying his holiday too much. The boy stalks him carefully and at last succeeds in slipping a rope through the ring in the ox's nose. Now the ox knows the game is up, and the boy can begin to lead him home. But it is a long way and the boy is tired. He talks to the ox, encourages him, establishes a bond. Soon he is happily riding along borne on the strong shoulders of the now tractable beast. Arrived home, the tired ox is content to re-enter his stable, and the door is firmly shut behind him. Order is restored.

The next day is market day. The boy walks to the town with his father, hands in empty pockets, whistling cheerfully. To look at him, nothing has changed. But everything has changed; he has a new confidence. Back home, he knows, is a securely stabled ox. Everything is as it was before, but something big has changed.

The story ends, leaving her somehow, oddly contented. She sits silent. Instead of bundling her off to bed, her father hitches up his sleeves, rubs a little ink on his inkstone, picks up the brush, smooths down the empty margin of the book he had been reading and begins to draw.

The moths by the lamp. The warmth of his body. The smell of the bronze-brown silk haori. With a cry that is almost like pain, she knows who she is.

Be here now. In this moment. The moment that is always burning away. The same moment out of which everything grows, forward and backward. Forever.

In this moment, there is room for everyone, all those people, the past she cannot now take with her into the future. Younger Brother as the serious, thoughtful little boy he used to be, not the deal-cutting politician. Her parents as she used to know them, simple, kind, not troublesome radicals, or morally agile survivors. And the man who had surrendered fatherhood to another, but who had remained her faithful guardian and teacher, even after death.

Apologise! For abandoning all those people, all those corpses, all those existences, to steal a future for herself?

Perhaps you don't have to die and be reincarnated to find yourself stuck on the wheel of rebirth. Perhaps it can happen in a single lifetime, too. This, then, is the question. Has she used that re-birth, that second existence, well?

A dream city, an imaginary city, a city of the future. The kind of future her parents dreamed of? Certainly not the one they got.

A puff of wind and the tree releases a million petals. The Walt Whitman poem Emi sent her from America: 'I contain multitudes'. All one has to do, to release the future into existence, is to let go of the present. The past will always be there.

That moment between there and not there. That moment that one is always working carefully towards, or following on from. That moment that is forever passing away, is never present and yet still comes. The moment that brings the past to a point and releases the future into existence. That moment between moments, that is gone even as it is named: *Now*.

They are sliding something under her, gently lifting and adjusting limbs that seem to be less and less her own. Men and women in bright-coloured clothing with reflective patches. Workers of the Ghost World, come to dismantle hers and carry away the pieces.

The ground drops away from beneath her. She turns her head with some difficulty to the side. There, glimpsed in a gap between work-suits and paramedic uniforms, in the shadow under the old roof, are those not the shafts of a pair of arrows, wedged into the lumpy, moss-covered pile of muddy sand and fallen bricks? Or is it just the stems of dried-out weeds?

The white interior of the ambulance slides around her, but her eyes are closed. The vehicle rolls slowly over the uneven ground of the building site and onto the street. A brief blip of its sirens and it is gone, swallowed by the crowds and traffic of the city.

A man in blue overalls with reflective patches wipes his

glistening head with the blue and white cotton scarf draped around his neck. He settles his white hard-hat back into place, climbs into the big excavator and fires up the engine. It jerks forward a little. The banksman glances earnestly around, then raises his fluorescent orange plastic wand to indicate 'All clear'.

The engine rises to its task. The mechanical arm reaches languidly out toward the sagging, but still elegant target shelter. For a moment, it rests its cupped steel hand gently on the threadbare shoulder of the old roof.

*   *   *

I knew immediately. A different light. Different motes hanging in different air. No swirl of wrinkles left on the sheet beside me. No empty glass or cup. No clothes in laundry, or on hangers. Absence so thorough and complete, it seemed more likely that he had never been here at all.

Grief takes strange forms. Mine was to doubt, some days, that the past had even happened. That the years had been good to us. That the new flat had indeed been nicer. That until his illness and even after that, Hiroshi had been the key that unlocked a world in which I could live a real life. His casual, polite ability to talk to anyone, his gentle but insistent attention to whatever they said in return, seemed to effortlessly generate friendships in which I too could share. When, in time, we opened our own part-time dojo in a rented hall, these proved to be the qualities of an excellent teacher.

Waking that first morning after flying home from the funeral ceremonies in his hometown, it finally registered with me that he was gone. No more administration of estate. No more correspondence or condolences to acknowledge. A new phase of life. The reality on the other side of a shot, in which the drawing and aiming are only memories.

Grief, but quite unlike my old despair. His photo and the one of the young woman shooting, stands on its own shelf, on which rests nothing but a few symbolic offerings and, from time to time, my gaze. When I look at it, I have the feeling that one gets in the final posture of shooting, when each step has been good and the arrow in the target reflects that.

*   *   *

The windows of the office cabin glow dimly in the dark of the cleared and deserted site. The bare black earth makes the darkness outside seem unusually thick amid the light-haze of the city. Inside, the Manager is working late. A small desk-lamp and a screen cast the only light over beige walls, safety posters, a clock, a calendar and the long schedule charts. He has been staying late a good deal recently, juggling figures, revising and adjusting those charts. His wife has complained, as she always does, but in a flat, stylised manner, without much hope of effect.

He sighs and runs his fingers through greying, stubbly hair. Leaning forward in the worn swivel chair, he rests his elbows on the desk and gently massages his eyes with slow, circular movements of the palms of his hands. The day's figures jump and dance in his inner vision, then break up and fade into dull swirling colours.

He snaps off the lamp, closes the spreadsheet and sits for a moment in the dark. Feeling for his jacket on the chair-back, he slips it on and pulls out his keys from deep in the familiar pocket. The screen of his phone, a gift from his wife, shows him to the door with a glow-worm light. He steps out into the dark, breathing balmy night air and savouring the tang of freshly dug earth. The keys clash against the metal door; he tugs it a couple of times to be sure, then turns off the phone and waits for his eyes to become accustomed to the hazy glow that bounces down from the low clouds over the city. A few lights on the opposite bank glimmer on the dark surface of the exposed river.

It had all worked out in the end. The site engineer, after much grumbling, had signed off on leaving the concrete foundation in place. The riverbank would have needed reinforcing anyway. They had got all but the last meter or two of the old target shelter wall down and carted off site, but time was running out on the excavator hire and there were still the foundation trenches for the main building to be finished before the machine could go. He could not afford to extend it any more, so they had agreed among themselves to break up the last little section of the old wall and take it out by hand. He had swung the sledgehammer himself for a while, just to show willing. The old mortar had been stubborn and hard and his shoulders ached. They had got it down to a last small stump of bricks, but it was starting to get dark, so he had thanked everyone for their efforts and sent them home.

He stands looking at the shadows of the dark plot. Every job, every patch of ground was like this. Each with its stubborn story that must be told. With his charts and spreadsheets, he had to make all the loose ends meet, all the different characters in the play appear and disappear at the right moments. And so often, as with this place, unforeseen events would occur and un-expected characters appear on the scene, with their own ideas about how things were going to go.

In the gloom, he could just about see the traditional small votive figure crouched in the corner, looking across the site. Tomorrow morning, the concrete truck would back in through the silver gates of the metal street hoarding and they would pour the foundations, tying together with concrete the tops of the steel pilings already sticking up like roots from the bottom of the trenches. A new building, a small residential block, new lives, a new spirit. He sometimes wonders, with a kind of amazement, what lives, what stories will unfold in the buildings he helps into existence.

He turns and starts to walk slowly toward the gates, negotiating cautiously the dark, shadowy trenches that seam the ground. It would not do to fall in and break a leg. In fact, he should not really be here on his own like this. It is not Best Practice. It had been useful to work late, but to tell the truth, he always liked to spend an evening like this, communing for a moment with the cleared space, before the real build begins. Feeling the point of transition as one sense of place gives way to another, different one. Breathing in the smell, so rare in the city, of raw, naked earth.

When you expose the bare earth, on a site like this, he thinks, here in this city of so many souls, you expose something powerful. What has this ground borne? What existences has it supported? What insupportable things has it carried? What lives have burned and died away? What ashes of human life is it made of? It is dizzying to think about. This is what makes him pause in the dark, at this point on the Gantt chart, when the ground is naked and ready, when the dismantling of the old is done and the idea, the dream of the new, hangs like a ghost in the air above his head. Amid all his responsibilities, for time, for money, for safety, for quality, he never feels so needed as at this hour, this time, when the dark earth of the city must spend a single night, naked under the stars.

When he had been quite young, too young really, to understand, his grandfather, a literary man, had taken him to the Kabuki theatre. Grandfather had made no secret that he thought Kabuki was beneath him and they should really be going to see a Noh classic with an uplifting Buddhist moral. He was only taking his grandchild to see such frivolous things as a great concession to the degraded tastes of modern youth. It must have been among the first performances to be put on after the war. He remembers nothing of the stories, except this: at one point, there had been a loud roar of 'Shibaraku!' – 'Just a moment!' and a character with huge red and white kimono sleeves, wild hair and a big sword, had suddenly stamped onto the stage and struck a dramatic pose, which he held, in utter silence, while the other characters and the audience too, froze. And he had understood. Felt the moment freeze solid around him. The moment between 'before' and 'after'. That instant when everything changes, but which you can never see, unless, perhaps, you stop time, like they did in the play and stare at it. In the dark, silent building plot, the noise and rush of the night city is held at arms length, as it is from the stage of a theatre. He stands, waiting for the unexpected character to step out of the shadows:

'Shibaraku!'

* * *

It was two in the morning when I padded quietly into the bowling green, a new moon gleaming like an archer's bow through the treetops. Despite my careful preparations, I was as nervous and worried as if I were going for my first dan grading. For one thing, what I was proposing to do was illegal, probably since medieval times. For another, I had just heard they were planning to dig up the old asphalt and that the space was going to be re-landscaped, turned into a proper garden with a lawn and seats. I feared it would be full of contractors' equipment, maybe even cordoned off.

It had been years since I had last visited the bowling green, but it had been visiting me, at night, for months. At first it was just the dark square, always night-time, the laurel shadows piled behind it. But then I began to see shadows within shadows. Human figures standing on the dark plane of the empty ground. A silent invitation in their presence.

As I came down the steps from the promenade, my worst fears seemed to be confirmed – the entrance did indeed have a barrier across it. I squeezed through, but was immediately forced to a stop. The whole space within the walls and hedges was a deep pool of darkness. It took a few seconds for my eyes to adjust, but from the smell of damp soil I guessed that the old asphalt surface had already gone. I bent down and felt the moist earth. How long since it had last felt the touch of air? As my eyes adjusted, it became clear that the whole ground had been cleared and raked over, ready for lawns and paths to be laid out. I stood, looking this way and that into the shadows, checking the familiar outline of the sunken square.

Seeing that the space was clear, I tiptoed around the edge of the raked ground, as if following the arrow-collection path and set up a target. Returning to the notional shooting line, I saw that the kasumi-mato glimmered like a small ringed moon in the dark, everything else around it receding in the deep shadows. I took off the jacket I had put on over my practice uniform against the night chill. With an apology to the god of grass-seed, I scattered a handful of salt on the ground, consecrating this notional dojo. It was time to begin.

Taking up the starting position, I make a deep bow towards the target and begin the actions of the Hassetsu: the stages of movement, alignment and adjustment that slowly build the quality of the shot, until the moment the arrow sinks down into place, its silky bamboo shaft level with the archer's cheek.

As I reach full draw, the world drops away, leaving a lone archer with the moon for a bow and eternity for a target, hanging without self in the empty expanse of the universe.

In the eternal moment, the intentionless action: the purity of a dewdrop gently swelling, before suddenly falling from the tip of a leaf.

Two shots: hai-ya and oto-ya, clockwise and anti-clockwise, yin and yang, balancing the universe. The slow descent of the bow-tip. When all is complete, the final retiring obeisance.

I step back and kneel in the seiza position, laying the bow down by my side. Alone in the void, I call to mind the figures of my dreams.

I did not bother hunting for the arrows.

I am an archer.

I know how to let go.

*　*　*

A night bird? He had been just about to step gingerly onto some metal planks thrown across the top of one of the foundation trenches, when he had felt the whirr of it brush against the leg of his full-cut builder's pants. He turns, involuntarily following a flicker of movement to the last ragged lump of the target wall. A second flicker – and this time he distinctly hears something smack into the brickwork. He glances back toward the metal hoarding along the street frontage. Nothing. No-one there. An unbroken horizontal between the shadowy, planed-off earth and the pale glimmer of silver corrugated metal.

He turns back to the river frontage. Something lies on the ground in front of the bricks. He walks over and looks down, puzzling. An archery range, his colleague had said. He shivers, glancing across at the corner where the little kami figure watches over the site.

Professional instinct kicks in. In days gone by, the master builder was also a priest. Nowadays, the architects have taken away much of his prestige. But not his priesthood. This midwifing of the past into the future is his and only his. Evidently, this ground, this place, still clings to old attachments. It is his responsibility to see it across the moment of change; to prise the fingers of the past gently off the hem of the future. Grunting at his own stiffness, he reaches down and gently picks up two light, insubstantial sticks. Barred feathers gleam in the half light. Carrying them over to the trench, he kneels carefully on the edge, lowers them down as far as he can reach without overbalancing, then lets them drop the last few inches into the dark. A foundation offering. A tribute, to whatever the spirit of this place once was. Tomorrow, the concrete truck will back in through the corrugated metal gates and they will become the hidden soul of this new community.

He stands up, brushing his knees. With the edge of his boot, he scrapes up some dirt and carefully kicks it into the trench, until there is nothing to attract a curious eye. Then he claps hands softly, twice, calling whoever might be listening to attention. He prays, briefly but intensely, for the welfare of all who will occupy this building, all who will look out upon this street, this riverbank, from windows yet unmade. All who will be born, live and die on this patch of black earth.

He pulls shut the metal gates of the site as quietly as possible, making sure the keypad lock engages. For a moment he stands, savouring the stillness of the suburban night. In nearby apartments, the more restless inhabitants hear the soft clunk of a car door, the brief whine of its electric motor and the hiss of tyres fading down the street.

終 わ り

Postscript

This book has been written by a student of Kyudo who has, in at least fifteen years of intermittent shooting never punctured a single target, other than by accidentally treading on it. Any reader whose interest in the art is sparked by this tale would therefore be wise not to treat it as a manual.

The form described herein follows the practice of the modern branch of the Heki-ryu known as 'Insai Sekka-ha'. Though broadly similar, the different lineages or 'ryu' vary in details of method and terminology. Any reader expert in Kyudo is begged to forgive any mistakes and to allow for artistic licence. The descriptions of each stage of the 'Hassetsu' used as chapter headings, are the invention of the author, although I have tried to reflect the spirit of the best teachers and their texts.

The 'Arrow Garden' dojo is fictitious, located in an imaginary district of a non-existent suburban ward of Tokyo. The site of its supernatural manifestations however, is entirely real, and can be visited in Bristol's Brandon Hill Park. Now a pleasant enclosed garden with a grass lawn, visitors may perhaps still feel the secluded and slightly mysterious atmosphere of former times. Please note however, that archery of any kind is explicitly prohibited in Bristol parks!

While the London dojo in the story is also fictional, there are several real ones there and elsewhere in the UK.

The appropriateness of setting stories in other people's cultures is much debated these days. The 'Great Pacific War' as experienced by both the Japanese and their neigbours is still a sensitive topic, and probably always will be. I have not worked as a historian, but as a writer, keen to depict a range of characters and their different responses to a terrible situation.

My approach to research has been simply to listen -both to

living voices and to those preserved in written record- and to try to reflect that experience with respect. In this I am indebted to several contemporary eyewitness accounts available online in translation. In the realm of books in English, I would single out Hiroko Sherwin's absorbing family saga *Eight Million Gods and Demons* for giving an absorbing picture of everyday life during the Great Pacific War, and her scholarly study *Japan's WWII Legacy, Interviews with Japanese Veterans.* In non-fiction John Dower's *Embracing Defeat, Japan in the Aftermath of World War II* provided a helpful chronological framework.

Buddhist ideas and imagery appear throughout the story, as essential to even a partial understanding of Japanese culture. Like many in the West however, I am attracted to Buddhist accounts of the universe as composed not of discrete objects, but of interdependent processes in constant flow and motion. As a storyteller I find it adds a necessary complexity to ideas of cause and effect -a thing just as important in a novel as in real life.

Shinto, 'the Way of the Kami' is of equal if not greater significance. I am grateful to those Japanese acquaintances who introduced me directly to Shinto ritual and practice, enabling me to see and feel for myself the texture of an everyday living faith.

Japanese manga, anime and films are more widely noticed in western culture today than formerly, but are still too often dismissed in the West as trivial exotica. The Confucian value of 'harmony' is important in the moral structure of Japanese culture. This can sometimes, I hear, stifle the discussion of 'difficult' social and political issues. The media of graphic story-telling, having such deep roots in Japan, seems to serve there as a safe space in which controversial ideas and issues of social justice can be ventilated. This gives them, even some that superficially seem trivial, a remarkable power. Far from trivial is Isao Takahata's animated re-telling of the short story by Akiyuki Nosaka, *Grave of the Fireflies*, in which the dislocation and horror of war is seen through the incidental lives of two very ordinary children. I have watched that film once, and may never have the courage to watch it again. I would like to express my profound respect for all those, Japanese or otherwise, who make us look clearly at the consequences of cruelty and violence, and reflect.

Acknowledgements

While it may feel like a solitary craft, writing a book is never the work of one alone. Grateful acknowledgements are therefore due to a number of people:

My late mother Anne, sharer and encourager of my interest in literature, and a perceptive reader and constructive critic of early drafts. Her great skills as a dressmaker, as observed by my young self, also contributed to my construction of the character of Emi.

My sisters, Heather and Abigail for cheering me on and for being exemplars of creativity and resourcefulness, and our late father Joe for showing us how we could make or do anything if we set ourselves to learn the necessary skills.

Kyudo sensei and friend Tim Macmillan, whose invitation to accompany him on a spectacular extended trip around northern Honshu in 2011, confirmed and deepened my lifelong appreciation for aspects of Japanese culture. Perhaps the most useful among the many extraordinary experiences of that adventure was the opportunity to meet people and listen to the rhythms, cadences and concerns of everyday speech. To Tim's extraordinary 'time-slicing' photography I also owe the image of an arrow frozen in flight, the seed from which this story grew.

Maria Peterson Sensei of Redwood Kyudojo for enthusiastically welcoming a 'Kyudo novel' and for giving valued input on some technicalities of archery.

Anna Reynolds, a writer to whom I was introduced by the Cornerstones Literary Consultancy. Her detailed and useful critique confirmed that the bits I was worried about needed worrying about and the bits I felt were good, really were OK.

Diane Simmons, a friend whose successes in flash fiction opened my eyes to the value of competitions for an aspiring writer.

The indefatigable Caroline Ambrose and her collaborators on the Bath Novel Award, an international contest for unpublished writers in English. A determined advocate for all her finalists, Caroline greatly encouraged me to persevere in developing the book.

Fellow Japanophile and BNA finalist, Clarissa Goenewan, who exemplifies the friendly and supportive attitude that seems to surround this competition. Also, former BNA reader and another Japan-focused novelist, Stephanie Scott, for warm support and generously sharing her own experiences of the process of publication.

The Arvon Foundation for a 'work in progress' week at Totleigh Barton. The diverse, talented and mutually supportive group of writers from genres and cultures very different from my own, I met there. Our tutors Kamila Shamsie and Gillian Slovo for five days of helpful input, but most of all for their 'stern auntie' stares whenever I expressed self-doubt.

My tremendously impressive agent, Jenny Savill, determined and resourceful in getting this book into the hands of a publisher, a skilled and insightful editor, and absolutely the most appropriately connected person to be promoting a book like this.

Sensitivity reader Kay Akiko Leary whose insightful notes prompted significant improvements to the plot as well as helping me dodge cultural faux-pas. Also for her very kind and positive unsolicited review of the book, which was very important to me.

Longtime friend Grace Macmillan for her kind encouragement and unfailing patience with my impulse to chat about matters Japanese and literary. Most of all, for generously allowing me to curate and use her beautiful bamboo yumi.

Brother-in-law Mike Kingsley-Heath for many glimpses into the job of building site manager. A tip of the hard-hat to the unknown crew on a site near Ueno station in 2011 who demonstrated how it's done in Japan.

My friend since schooldays Paul Woodley, for being warmly supportive of the project and bringing his lifetime of experience as a journalist to bear on proof-checking early drafts.

Rebecca f John, not only for being my publisher, but also for her rigorous, effective and patiently supportive work as editor.

And finally my wife Hilary, whose voracious consumption of novels has presented me with many opportunities for a furtive 'catch up' on how the rest of the world writes. But mainly for being my steadfast friend and companion without whom everything would be much more difficult.

Brought up to value thinking and making equally, Andrew J King's first degree was in English Literature and Fine Art.

After ten years in graphic and product design, he gained an MA in Visual Culture at Bath Spa University, and began a second career encouraging art and design students to rediscover writing as a tool of creative thought and expression.

A lifelong interest in aspects of Japanese culture led to an extended trip in 2011 in the aftermath of the tsunami, assisting and observing participants in spectacular Shinto rituals of horseback archery.

The Arrow Garden is his first novel. Early drafts were longlisted for the Bridport Prize and The Bath Novel Award, before winning the BNA outright in 2020.

Andrew lives in Bath, England. When not writing he is to be found riding strange bicycles or, very occasionally, practicing traditional Japanese archery.